TORCHES & TROUBLE

GORD HUME

ST. PETERSBURG
— PRESS —

GORD HUME

TORCHES & TROUBLE

A Samantha and the Sheriff Adventure

ST. PETERSBURG PRESS

ST. PETERSBURG
PRESS

First Edition Copyright © 2023
Burnstown Publishing House
Burnstown, Ontario, Canada

Paperback ISBN: 978-1-77257-373-2
eBook ISBN: 978-1-77257-374-9

Second Edition Copyright ©2024
Published by St. Petersburg Press
St. Petersburg, FL
www.stpetersburgpress.com

Composition by St. Petersburg Press and Isa Crosta
Cover and Interior design by W.D. Clements
The cover art is a compilation of works created by various artists who are generous to license for free usage. Images and characters used are found on vectorcharacters.com, freepik.com, all-free-download.com, www.vecteezy.com. and stock.adobe.com

Paperback ISBN: 978-1-940300-94-8

ᴘRELUDE

A secret location in rural central Florida:

THE OILY BLACK smoke from a hundred torches spewed into the darkening sky.

There were 87 pick-up trucks in the dusty field, mostly black and all with tinted windows, oversize tires and high running boards.

There were seventeen Harley hogs, many throatily roaring.

There were four sedans of various hues.

And there was one light green family van. It looked embarrassed to be there.

Nearly two hundred people swayed and sweated in the humid evening heat. The smoke and the breeze at least kept away most of the mosquitoes; it was only the most intrepid insect that would brave the sweat-stained and very pungent odors emitted by most of the men and a few of the women.

Many of the men wore wife-beater shirts. A lot of excess flesh hung out of the armpit holes. Man-boobs jiggled fleshily. Eventually most of the mosquitoes decided it wasn't worth the offense to their own olfactory systems to dive-bomb these otherwise tempting targets. They left in a swarm of smoked disgust.

The crowd's demographic profile was overwhelmingly forty-plus, white and male. Sweaty bandanas in red, white and blue wrapped foreheads, necks, biceps and boobs. Cowboy hats were pushed back on to the napes of red necks. A few coonskin caps hung their tails down sweaty shoulders. A Viking helmet paraded through the crowd.

A lot of alligators had been sacrificed to make the dusty boots that were the footwear of choice for many of the women and most of the men.

There was a lot of facial hair, much of it on the men.

The rifle racks on the trucks competed with portable ice chests of beer for the most avid attention. Confederate flags were being waved, along with American decals and flags on jackets, trucks and mugs.

Tattoos of all kinds, and in all kinds of places, celebrated the land of the free and the home of the brave. It would take a particularly brave person to pursue the path of the many eagles that were shown diving into crevices on the human body, places that real eagles with any sense of modesty or good taste would be exceedingly unlikely to visit.

Bumper stickers proclaimed a wide variety of slogans, but all had similar themes: take back America; kick out 'furriners'; buy American; gun rights; no taxation; make the US great again.

There were also much darker memes and slogans: "blood and soil"; Amaner; doubled lightning bolts; a number of un-flattering phrases about the mainstream media, Jews, blacks and several other ethnic groups. The international banking system came in for a particularly pithy portrayal.

It was a grand conglomeration of hate.

One of the black trucks had a picture of a former US president on its side window. Several men made a point of stroking the picture with their right hand.

The crowd was growing restless when one of the organizers, a big man with a big gut stretching his once-white flag-emblazoned T-shirt, stomped onto the stage.

"HEY!" It took a few more shouts into the microphone on the temporary wood plank stage, and the firing of a rifle into the sultry air, before the buzz of the crowd diminished enough for the speaker to be heard.

"We just got a call! He'll be here in 15 minutes!"

A rabid cheer went up. Fresh beer cans were popped. Cell phones were readied for video recording. Three guys peed in the bushes.

The torches burned raggedly. The sky drew darker. The air grew more fetid.

CHAPTER 1

"HE COULD TEACH a post-graduate course in stupid."
Sheriff LeRoy Perkins grinned at the description of the man, now nestled in the cells of the county jail, who had tried to rob a bank, except he had dropped his gun on the bank's faux marble floor, couldn't untie the bag the teller was supposed to fill with cash, and finally ran outside only to find a parking enforcement officer ticketing his car. She turned out to be a lot smarter and tougher than he was: She clouted him with a bag of quarters and sat on him until the police arrived.

Dumb criminals: they helped keep his department in business.

He looked around the table at his top management team, assembled for their daily briefing. "Anything else?"

Captain Willie Williams raised a massive right paw. The veteran officer was a big, solid man. Large. He was a top officer in Perkins' command, now supervising major crimes, homicide and the intelligence unit.

"We've got a couple of reports recently of some activity by a new, well, we're not sure…protest group? White supremacists? Nut bars?"

Williams was an African-American officer who had come up through the ranks the hard way, when it was really tough for people of color to get promoted. Perkins had elevated him to Captain a year ago. He had only grown closer to the man since then, and more appreciative of his policing skills.

"We're just getting wisps of information so far, but I wanted to alert you. Our Intel people will do some more probing on the internet. Some rumor that a bunch of those right-wing radicals had a big pow-wow the other night." He shrugged. "We're looking into it."

"OK. Stay on it. Nothing else? Thanks, everybody."

The nine women and men gathered their notes and hurried out. Williams remained seated.

Perkins looked at him expectantly. "More to the story?"

"Shit yeah. Bunch of these characters had a big rally in some field off Highway 13 east of here. Lots of torches. Pretty big crowd. Shot their guns off, drank a lot of beer. We think they had some speaker come in to rev 'em up, but we don't know who." He sighed heavily. "After the Capital riot in Washington, we're seeing a real surge in domestic terrorist groups. Let's face it, law enforcement and Intelligence looked bad on that. It energized a lot more of these yahoos."

He reached over to the dregs in the box of donuts that typically joined the management meeting. Perkins held his breath. He'd been savoring the thought of the last apple fritter. Williams waved his hand over the chocolate, the maple glazed and the cruller before unerringly settling on the fritter.

The evidence disappeared in three big bites, leaving a satisfied Captain and a disconsolate Sheriff.

"Let's elevate this in our Intel work," Perkins ordered as he rose. "I think these people are dangerous and we need to get ahead of any trouble."

Williams nodded, dipped into the box one more time for the cruller, and strode out of the board room.

Perkins was left alone, dismayed over the intelligence and the donut debacle.

CHAPTER 2

THE BANK MANAGER was a pinch-faced woman in her late 30s who had the sour look of someone who had just swallowed a bite of apple and then found half a worm in the fruit.

Samantha Summers put on a warm smile as she looked across the desk at her. "All I am asking is to transfer the residue of my account from New York into my bank here in Florida so I can close that NYC account."

"It is a different bank. We don't do that."

"But my former bank in New York doesn't have any branches here in Port Manatee."

"Don't make your problems my problems."

Steam began to escape from Samantha's ears. The reddish-gold hair that caressed her neck couldn't contain the flushed color and her rising temper.

"That is hardly helpful!"

"I have explained that you need written authorization from your New York bank manager, Form 188-B, Form 189-C, your passport, proof of residency here, Form 191-D(3) letter of intent, notarized of course, and your last two years tax records. And a notarized statement from your husband." She glanced down at some of the records Samantha had given her. "Your ex-husband, I see," she said flatly. The disapproval in her voice was loud.

"This is all about a lousy 728 dollars," Samantha snapped. She looked at her most recent statement. "And 55 cents." She glared across the desk. "It is the last joint bank account he and I shared. It got forgotten in the divorce settlement. I'm just trying to close the books on him. Forever." She tried a last stab at charm. "Help a girl out here, won't you?"

"The transfer of interstate commerce and banking is regulated by the federal government. If you are not satisfied with my explanation, I suggest you take it up with the federal government," Mrs. Pinchbottom concluded primly.

Chapter 3

Chapter 3

"So THAT'S WHEN I might have gotten just a little peeved," Samantha admitted to Sheriff Perkins during her interrogation. "Just a tad, mind you."

"Uh huh." He sighed loudly. "I'm not surprised, you being a little part Irish and red-haired and from New York and kind of...uh...spirited," he concluded lamely.

"I mean, her attitude was just so...so...pompous! Unhelpful! Dismissive! Nasty! A loathsome little woman!"

"Sure, I can see that."

"Anyway, I guess that's when the ugly little mostly-dead nasty stupid flowerpot fell off her desk. An orchid. She overwatered it. Killed it, really. Can she be charged with murdering a plant?"

"Uh, no. I don't believe that case would be viewed with great distinction by the courts."

"Huh. Lousy system." Samantha percolated a little more. The Sheriff waited patiently for more of her confession. "Everybody knows you just put one ice cube in the orchid's pot each week to water it. Stupid little bitch she was. A real pinch-bottom."

Perkins twitched. "A who?"

"Pinchbottom. Tight ass. Anal. Mean." Samantha thought for a moment. "It is also her name." She chuckled for the first time. "Best likeness of a name I've ever heard of."

She let out a big sigh. "I think that's about it for my crime spree. Oh yeah, the complimentary calendar from the bank that she gave me...it sort of fell apart in her office. Poor printing quality control, no doubt. I left it there so the bank wouldn't think I was taking a calendar and then not doing business there ever again. Which I won't."

"The officer's report said the calendar was shredded and pages were thrown all around the office."

"Oh, gee, I'm not sure that's correct. Maybe a few little pieces fluttered to the floor...no biggie."

The Sheriff cleared his throat. "Uh huh. Anything else you'd like me to know about this incident before I drag you off for punishment?"

"Incident? Oh, really now, I don't think this was an incident. More an expression of different philosophies between two professional women when it comes to financial services. I am simply a respected bank customer who was dealt with rudely by some junior management person," she concluded indignantly.

Perkins moaned softly.

"Oh. Maybe one other little thing…hardly worth mentioning really…but the window in her office door was obviously installed incorrectly, because it happened to fall out after I shut the door on my way out."

Perkins tensed. This case just got deeper and darker. "Shut it?"

"Well, firmly. You know, in case the door didn't fit properly. I didn't want to be rude and leave it ajar."

"Slammed it like Xena the Warrior Princess proclaiming the wrath of Thor, from what the report said," the Sheriff said darkly.

"Oh, pish. Just faulty construction. Nothing to do with me." She thought a bit more. "So yeah, that's it."

Perkins grimaced but continued bravely. "How did the fire alarm get pulled?"

"Oh, that. I was just being careful and really concerned about the safety of the other customers. I was pretty sure I saw some smoke coming out of the bitch's office. Although looking back on it, it might just have been the wisps of sulfur burning in her hell-hole," she added tartly. "But saving other bank customers from a fiery death or eternal damnation is what any good citizen would do." She paused. "You'll probably be recommending me for a medal."

"Uh huh. You'll want to wait for that to happen." She glowered at him. "That fire alarm kind of disrupted their entire business day."

"Really? Good, because they surely disrupted mine!" She reached for the glass of water sitting beside her and drank a bit. "She is a horrid little woman. Probably got promoted from teller because she screwed up so much at the counter. They probably figured that she could do less harm in management. Well, I'll show her not to treat me like that!" She put the glass down. Firmly. The wood on the table barely cracked.

"Absolutely nothing else happened?" Perkins demanded after a long pause.

"No." She thought again and then sighed. "Well, I mean, the thing in the parking lot really doesn't count. If the stupid bank had curbs in their parking lot, cars couldn't accidentally drive into their flower beds, now, could they? I certainly can't be blamed for their faulty landscape design."

Now it was Perkins sighing. "OK. I think I've got the picture. But that's it? Truly?"

She nodded. "My full confession."

"Yeah." Disbelief dripped from his tongue. "So how did the pen get buried in the ceiling tile?"

"Oh. Well, that's sort of a funny story. Along with their stupid cheap calendar, Pinchbottom thought she could buy me off with a pen. One of those horrid cheap ballpoint bank pens that never writes well. I was demonstrating to her the aerodynamic properties of a poorly balanced pen and how that could impact high-quality cursive writing. Did you know that kids today can't even write in longhand? It's not taught in schools anymore. Tragic. Cheap pens must be part of the reason. Anyway, somehow the pen never came down. Obviously an act of God. I'm completely off the hook."

A huge sigh of despair from the Sheriff. "That isn't quite how Mrs. Pinch...I can't even say her name...described it, but it's kind of her-word-your-word on this pen thing." He sighed again. He had never in his career had such a cooperative nonresponsive interviewee. How could she have an answer for everything when the destruction was so rampant?

"We'll likely confiscate the money in that account to pay for the damages."

Samantha shrugged her indifference.

"I'll try to avoid having the bank press charges against you. Bad publicity for them." The silence stretched. "Except you have to promise to be a good girl from now on."

Another long silence. They both knew that was an unrealistic expectation.

She looked down at her naked body, then over at his. "This is a really good way to conduct a police interview," she giggled as she rolled on top of him. "But," she warned her lover, eyes narrowing and voice steely, "I'd better be the only one you interrogate like this."

Then there was no more talking.

CHAPTER 4

THE GUT ON the pit-master looked as if he'd just swallowed a ten-pound watermelon. It was big, it was hard, it was round, and it stuck out from his body for many inches. Many.

In some cultures, it might have inspired awe. Even reverence. In today's American culture it was just a reflection of a lifetime of pulled pork sandwiches on white bread, beer, and a complete indifference to any form of exercise.

Jud was his name. His greasy gray hair stuck out from under his dirty John Deere baseball cap. It had been permanently stained by a thousand smoky fires and ten thousand fat-laced pork butts and racks of ribs.

The hickory smoke curled deliciously from the home-made smoker. The big metal cylinder had once been part of a train locomotive. Now the rotating spit and shelves produced 120 pounds a day of smoked brisket, pork shoulder, home-made spicy sausage and turkey, in addition to the star of the show—slabs of baby-back pork ribs.

A small wooden shack served as kitchen and cash register. Nobody except the pit-master, his wife, his oldest son and one trusted employee ever entered the back of the shack. Nobody else but his wife knew the recipe for his secret blend of fourteen different herbs and spices that he used as the rub on the meat before it entered slow-smoked paradise. The son might get the secret once he'd proven himself as a true southern barbecuer.

Customers sat on a variety of reclaimed things: half-tires from old semis made into swings; a children's merry-go-round that no longer went around that had been liberated from a schoolyard that had closed; some unmatched bar stools; and several cheap aluminum lawn chairs that looked as if they would collapse when the next big butt hit the fraying yellow nylon webbing.

There were several tables made of old wooden slabs from an ancient barn that had collapsed. The benches around the tables were made of very attractive and expensive teak lumber that had fallen off a delivery truck that was being driven by one of Jud's cousins.

The place was jammed. Drooling customers waited impatiently for their orders. There was always a risk in arriving late because once the food for that day was gone, it was all over. Many tears had been shed by frustrated and hungry visitors.

At the far table under a spreading live oak tree, four men sat alone. Their lunch orders were identical—a full slab of ribs each, and sides of deep-fried okra, mac and cheese, and collard greens. Empty beer cans littered the table.

None of them displayed the glorious belly that the pit-master had, but dedicated culinary excesses had created a second tier of gutdom that was still impressive. All four were examples of what cruel manufacturers of boys clothing had once labelled the "Husky" size.

Watching them inhale their lunch was a frightening sight. Their conversation was even more terrifying.

"Good rally th'otha night," Jed proclaimed as he chawed all the meat off a rib bone.

Grunts of agreement. Talkin' was one thing, but eatin' ribs was a higher priority. Especially ribs from The Ugly Porker. The pit-master had displayed an unexpected sense of humor in the name of his restaurant.

Finally, the last bites of mac 'n cheese, okra, and greens were finished. The last bone was sucked. Greasy, sauce-stained hands were wiped on paper towels or the sides of their Wranglers. The last beers were popped. A few belches reached the adjacent table, as did the loud farts that encouraged the two couples in preppie northern clothes delicately eating the smoked turkey to move to another table.

"Speaker was good. Got'em fired up, din't he?"

"Yup. Who knew a skinny little preacher boy like him would holler that fire 'n brimstone stuff 'bout anarchy? He's on COYOTE News ever' so often. Talks about finally takin' back our govment."

There was a moment of reverence for the news channel that was the only one they believed presented truth and reality on its programs.

"Reminded me of my granpappy's stories about the KKK ridin' out to do their bidness. Good times." A deep, moist burp erupted. There was a brief moment of silence in its honor.

"Gotta give the boys somethin' to do purty soon, some action or other. They gettin' restless."

Nods of agreement. Final swallows of the cold beer. Farts, far from the final ones to be emitted that afternoon, burst forth. There was laughter and back-slapping as the four left the little oasis 18 miles from the city, and a million miles from liberal urban attitudes.

"I got an idea. Lemme ponder it a bit. It'd make a big splash in town if we can pull it off," said Jed, the de facto leader. "Lemme make a call." More nods. Trucks were climbed into. Windows were rolled down. Cigarettes got lit. The black pick-ups soon hi-tailed it out of the dirt parking lot, spitting a bit of gravel from the unpaved driveway.

In the far corner of the yard several people watched quietly.

Pit-master Jud never blinked at what went on in his yard. He just checked the fire in the smoker and then sliced the last of the day's turkey.

CHAPTER 5

"I CALL THIS MEETING of the Sams Club to order!"

Instead of a gavel, Kim Sharpe uncorked a bottle of nicely chilled New Zealand Sauvignon Blanc. The gentle pop as the cork came out brought the other members of the private club to their full attention.

Dr. Samira Al-Saadi was a renowned orthopedic surgeon at the huge Florida VA hospital. She had taken care of Kim's leg since she had been wounded in the Middle East. She had built three prosthetics for Kim's left foot since then.

Samantha had met the two lovely women after she arrived as a burned-out, angry and betrayed ex-wife of a Wall Street hedge fund executive. The divorce had been acrimonious and messy, but her lawyer had fought for, and got her, a substantial settlement. She had bought a penthouse condo at Sapphire Blue shortly after discovering the quiet Gulf Coast city, and had started to rebuild her life.

Kim had started the gathering of her two best friends. She now proclaimed that she was the real Sams Club star because she was 'Sexy And Modest.'

The three had shared much wine, laughter, tears, fears and several adventures together. They had bonded tightly. They trusted one another completely.

Samira reached over for the charcuterie platter Samantha had put out. She slipped a piece of the salami to Rosie, who was lying beside her. Rosie was the Sheriff's dog but had quickly adopted Samantha once the torrid affair between the lanky law enforcement chief and the sizzling NYC red head had commenced.

Rosie also liked Kim and Samira a lot. She was an unofficial member of their exclusive club, although she usually didn't add much to the conversation. Tonight it was Samira who was proving to be the softest touch about sharing those delightful little snacks, so the good doctor was rewarded with Rosie's undying affection—as long as the food kept coming.

Conversation wandered between the latest royal circus erupting inside Buckingham Palace with its new king, the most recent fashion lines from Paris and Milan, plans for a group mani-pedi at the spa, and how good the butt of the latest Hollywood heart-throb looked when he'd stripped down in his latest blockbuster.

"Tight," sighed Samira appreciatively. "Really tight."

Rosie nudged her leg. She was rewarded with a little piece of Edam cheese. Rosie felt that, as she was really the hostess, it was important to have her guests keep the snacks moving.

There was a thoughtful pause as the three ladies mentally saluted the tight butt.

Kim finally shook her head and sighed. "Anyway, city hall is getting all frothed up about security. These QAnon crazies and the people on the left and right fringes are all becoming security concerns."

Kim had been elected to the Port Manatee City Council the previous year. She had quickly become one of the leading voices in the city for modernizing and improving city hall's operations, and accelerating the city's social and economic development strategies. Samantha had run her campaign; it had turned out to be a remarkably poisonous political battle.

City Manager Roy Crawford was supportive of Kim's efforts at rejuvenating the city. As Kim laughed, "That is good, since we are sleeping together."

The two had begun a passionate affair before Kim even knew she was running for public office. Wisely, they had made an open declaration of their personal situation and had established a 'Chinese Wall' between them when it came to city business. It was something they both considered important; neither had ever violated the confidentiality agreement. As a result, there had never been any public controversy about their relationship.

"Threats? Here in our quiet little city?" Samantha asked incredulously.

"Nobody really knows," Kim shrugged, "but the security people are concerned about some people serving in all levels of government. There are some real fanatics, some right-wing nuts out there. Freakin' freaky." She shivered slightly.

CHAPTER 6

"LET ME BE very clear," the Southeast Regional Director of the Federal Bureau of Investigation, James Robertson, slowly began. "Domestic terrorism is the single greatest threat to the safety and security of the United States of America today."

More than a hundred senior law enforcement officers and political officials were seated in the conference room. There was an audible gasp as the implications of his opening statement sunk in.

"As a nation, we have to come to terms with this rising threat," he continued. "Our borders are reasonably secure from foreign terrorists. But more and more, we are seeing, hearing and experiencing threats to federal, state and municipal officials, infrastructure, and governance structures. They are coming from home-grown terrorists. We are discovering plots to pull off everything from kidnapping the Governor of Michigan to attacking municipal infrastructure. And we still have the rabid election deniers. Many of these groups promote anarchy and civil war. They want to destroy our system of government and our quality of life."

He swallowed some tepid coffee and cleared his throat. "And we can never forget January 6, 2021."

Dead silence. The attack on the Congress was a shameful page in American history.

He paused as a map of the United States came up on the giant screen. A brown color soon filled most state outlines. Florida's borders were stained the darkest brown.

"The states in darker brown are the most vulnerable to an attack or insurrection or demonstration that has the potential to become violent. Right now, our assessment is 27 states are at the highest level, 19 at medium, and 4 at little risk. The D of C is obviously in a category all by itself. You will note that Florida is in the highest-risk category."

Another deep breath from those in the audience. Notes were being scribbled. There was complete attention to the FBI Regional Director.

"This is not based on rumor or gossip. This is hard information from our agents, often from Confidential Informants, or CIs, or Human Intelligence. We call that Humint. Our national intelligence agencies have a significant capability for monitoring electronic communications." He sighed. "What we are discovering, and overhearing, is dramatic and worrisome."

He paused again, swallowed the last of his coffee, and stared at the audience. "I also must warn you that many of these organizations are smart, they are vicious, and they are unlike other radical threats that you have faced before. They use the Internet and smart phone apps for communications with other radicals. They use social media effectively. They have private communication back channels. Many are lurking on-line. We have been tracking threats and have even heard talk about assassination of certain public officials. There is always a risk of more mass shootings. A few of these people are calling for a 'Second Civil War.'"

There was another gasp from the audience Robertson paused to let the implications sink in before continuing.

"They are good at attracting fringe people, many of whom are lonely or isolated. Many recruits are anti-government just because they don't like government period, or they have been inflamed by some rabid politician or activist or even a clergyman. They might have had an ugly experience with some order of government. Many of them become fanatical followers or believers in some crazy story or theory, but it is one that they fervently believe is true or will happen. Certain media inflame those beliefs. These people are not bound by reality. Let me repeat that. They do not have the same constraints on their thinking and belief system as you and me. It is going to be very hard for you to wrap your heads around this kind of thinking and these threats to your communities. But believe me, you must start understanding right now how serious these risks are. Your communities are under severe threat. And it is urgent."

With that he sat down. Nobody knew whether to applaud or not. The vibe in the room was peculiar; awkward and uncomfortable.

Finally, Sheriff Perkins moved to the mic at the podium on the head table.

"Thank you, Director," he said nodding in Robertson's direction. He then turned to face the audience. "Perhaps now you understand why I asked Director Robertson to come here today as the keynote speaker for this seminar. The three most serious menaces facing our towns and cities today are domestic terrorism, white supremacists, and the lone-wolf radical with hatred in their heart and a gun in their hand." He paused so his words would be absorbed by the audience. "Now we're going to break into smaller groups and get into detailed planning. My staff will show you to the break-out rooms."

Terrorism had come to them and to their cities in fast and shocking ways.

CHAPTER 7

THE DINING ROOM at La Casa Adrianna was quietly lit. There were candles placed strategically around the room. The soft light flattered the guests and showed off the beautifully inlaid mahogany wood panels and trim.

The long-time hostess for the exclusive restaurant showed Samantha and the Sheriff to a crisply-linened table. Heavy silverware and Waterford crystal glasses quietly emphasized the heritage and commitment to excellence of the dining room and its veteran staff.

"Ah, Signorina Summers, how lovely to see you once again," said Rosita as she seated them. "And Sheriff Perkins, I hope you enjoy your first meal with us." She nodded politely and slipped away, motioning for a young waiter to serve ice water.

"This is really nice," Perkins said as he peered around. Then he jerked. "Hey. How did she know me? I haven't been here before."

Samantha laughed softly. "Rosita knows everyone of a certain position in town. She has been the hostess here for years. She is beloved for her discretion. She once had an ex-husband and wife come in for dinner at the same time. They had just gone through a long, screaming divorce. Somehow she kept them on opposite sides of the room and nobody got killed in here that night."

Perkins smiled. "Should we tell her that..."

"She'll know."

A moment later Rosita escorted James Robertson to the third seat at the table. "Director Robertson has arrived," she said softly as she seated him. Perkins remained standing for a moment, shocked that the hostess would recognize the little-known FBI Director from Atlanta.

"Hi. I'm James Robertson," he said immediately as he sat down and looked at Samantha. "You are sensational. Glorious. Stunning. You look nothing like Perkins has described to me."

Samantha shook his outstretched hand and then held it more tightly. "And just how did he describe me?" she asked, a dangerous note in her voice.

"I don't recall exactly, but it was something about a wrinkly, middle-aged crone he was trying to rescue from the depths of perdition...something like that."

Perkins' jaw was on the table as Samantha's steely gaze turned on him.

"Really? How lovely." Icicles crackled above her words.

"No. Uh, I mean, un-unh. I...I...nnnn...never..." he flailed. His face reddened. Beads of sweat appeared on his furrowed brow.

Only then did he realize that Samantha and Robertson were doubled over in laughter.

"I told you it would work!" said the FBI Chief through his chortles.

"Did you see the look on his face?" Samantha was dabbing away tears of laughter as she looked at the stunned look on Perkins' face. "Ah, poor baby." She reached over to pat his cheek as Robertson was still laughing into his napkin.

Perkins' eyes stopped popping out and he slowly regained his composure. "This...this was all...a set-up?"

"Oh yeah. And you fell for it hook, line and sinker, pal. I've never seen anybody go sheet white and then beet red before. What a hoot!"

With that he waved Rosita over. "How have you been, my darling? It is too long since I've been back to dine with you."

The plump fifty-year-old woman in a stylish black dress casually put her hand on Robertson's shoulder. "It is a privilege to have you back with us, James. And I have two bottles of the 2005 Chateauneuf-du-Pape breathing for you. That was such a wonderful season for grapes in the Rhone district. I will have Raoul get them for you."

The sommelier promptly came over to decant the first bottle. He poured a taste into Robertson's glass. The FBI chief swirled, tasted, swallowed and smiled. "Oh yes. Superb."

Raoul carefully poured Samantha a glass, then Perkins, and then topped up Robertson's glass. He withdrew, and Robertson immediately offered a toast: "To finally meeting the gorgeous woman who conquered this dusty, ugly bum of a sheriff."

Samantha laughed as she clinked glasses. Perkins glowered at the FBI man, but finally touched the other two glasses. "Pretty mean of you both," he muttered darkly.

That brought new peals of laughter.

"You are just fabulous," Robertson said focusing on the beautiful redhead. Samantha smiled. She was wearing her favorite LBD, the one that clung to what Perkins always called 'the cutest butt in the Southeast.' Samantha had secret hopes of it eventually being proclaimed 'the cutest butt in the United States,' which is why she was doing squat thrusts and a half-hour on the elliptical machine three times a week.

Well, she at least wanted the Continental United States title. She'd heard reports that there were some cute butts in Hawaii. Probably a combination of swimming in the ocean and hula dancing—all that hip-swiveling. That was hardly fair to mainlanders. Oh well. And in Alaska? Maybe from being chased by grizzlies; yeah, that would work up some tight butt muscles. Damn. This was a tough competition.

The dress was cut above her knees and showed off her elegant calves and ankles as she walked proudly in her black heels. She'd bought it after the sales lady at her favorite boutique said, "Honey, with legs like yours, show 'em off."

She knew that Perkins loved to drop back a couple of steps just so he could watch her walk. Sometimes she threw a little extra oomph into her wiggle, just so he could enjoy the view.

Of course, she liked to watch him walk too, with his strong shoulders and narrow waist. Tight butt, too. Maybe not Hollywood-icon tight, but real nice.

Samantha and Robertson were quickly bonding as the sautéed shrimp in a diabolo sauce, the perfectly cooked rib-eye steaks accompanied by caramelized onions, sautéed mushrooms and grilled asparagus, and a lovely dessert of fresh blueberries over a rich, tart lemon curd were presented in a leisurely fashion by the crack service staff. Rosita kept an eagle eye on the table.

It was only over coffee that the table talk turned more serious.

"How was your seminar?" asked Samantha.

"This big ugly was really good," Perkins replied. "But I'm not sure how many of the people attending truly believed his message. Particularly the municipal officials. It is hard for them to imagine some mob attacking city hall or damaging their community. These municipal leaders are the builders of neighborhoods, not the destroyers of public dreams and civic places. I get that is a big mountain for them to climb and to truly understand." He stared into the distance. "But I worry that our towns and cities are really vulnerable."

"I think that's right," agreed James Robertson. "I'm always worried about local infrastructure being unguarded—electricity grids, generating plants, bridges, sewer systems, water treatment plants and all those other things that keep cities operating. Nobody ever thinks of them as being vulnerable to an attack, but it is a huge problem that nobody wants to confront. Just look at what Putin did to so many communities during his stupid war in Ukraine."

Coffee over and liqueurs declined, the dinner eventually came to an end. Robertson offered his arm as they exited the dining room. Samantha hooked her left hand over his right elbow.

"You are ravishing. Thank you for taking on the onerous job of keeping this big lunk on the straight and narrow for a change. It's a relief not having to rescue him from cheap bars and cheaper floozies."

"Floozies, huh?" Samantha's eyes narrowed. She turned to look over her shoulder at Perkins, who was innocently walking behind them admiring the way Samantha's bewitching behind twitched as she walked in her black spike heels. Golly he liked that perfect little derriere that—

"What?"

"Floozies? Really?"

"What?"

"We will talk later."

"What!?"

Robertson and the stunning redhead glanced at one another and grinned. For a tough and skilled sheriff, Robertson thought, Perkins was an easy mark when it came to his girlfriend.

They all slid into the car driven by a special agent and headed for Sapphire Blue to drop off Samantha and the Sheriff.

Chapter 8

"WHATCHA MEAN?" DEMANDED Jethro as he listened to Jed talk about taking back the government—whatever that meant. Take it back? Who would want the damn thing?

He spat chewin' t'backy juice onto the ground, narrowly missing his left pant cuff.

"We gotta right tuh how we're governed. Constitution says so. If governments don't respect us, then we gotta right to boot 'em out. Thass why we got thuh right to own AR-15s."

It was a unique interpretation of the constitution, 200 years of Supreme Court decisions and many scholarly treatises about the Founding Fathers and their intentions. Several constitutional experts would have choked upon the conclusions that Jed made, but it played well to the boys sitting around on the tail gates of their trucks. More than one cold brew had already been swallowed.

"Looky, we IS the govment. It only exists tuh serve our needs. We pay taxes, we get to decide. Boston Tea Party all over again. Time fer us to take back our city."

Jethro listened intently. He wasn't going to get short-listed for MENSA membership any time soon, but he was a loyal follower. He was 6' 4", 245, and strong as a bull. He and Jed had hooked up on the high school football team 20 years earlier. Jed was the running back, Jethro the left tackle. That team had set some rushing records, a couple of which still stand.

The friendship had remained solid through two divorces, one bankruptcy, one vicious quarrel over a busty blonde in a very short denim skirt at a C&W bar one Friday night, and a bunch of fights against other guys who attacked one or the other. Rarely were people drunk enough to challenge Jethro, but Jed certainly had that big mouth and quick temper that could get him in trouble or at least bounced out of bars.

The pretty blonde had gone home with the guitar player.

Jethro looked up to Jed. He had his back in the barroom brawls. And Jed protected Jethro from those who would prey on the intellectually weak.

Jeb was also listening. He was the smartest one in this group. He knew that because he was too smart to let on how smart he was. Still, being the smartest one in this group of J-Men was like being the thinnest person at an Overeater's Anonymous meeting; it wasn't necessarily a great achievement.

He pulled on a Bud. Jed was orating again.

"We gotta right to take over. We gotta scare them politicians. And all them left-wing media types we got 'roun' here. Prissy little people they are. They need a good ass-kickin'."

Jeb grinned. "Yeah, I'm with you on that, Jed. The local paper barely covers the high school football team anymore. My kid's out there catchin' passes and he gets nothin'. How's he gonna get a scholarship to Miami or Florida if he don't get no press coverage?"

'Uh huh. Yur right, Jeb. Lemme think now. The boys want some action. Us J-Men need to lead this resistance movement."

"No shooting, Jed. You know you're still in trouble over firing off that S&W of yours outside Julie's last month. That big sheriff slammed you down pretty good."

Jed flushed, remembering the night when he'd indulged in a beer or two at the popular honky-tonk bar. The sheriff had been one of the arresting officers and it had not gone well for Jed. His left shoulder still hurt, and his favorite revolver was still in custody.

His blood alcohol reading of .18 would suggest that more than two lite beers had been consumed; at least that's what the DA's office was saying. His lawyer was struggling to figure out a defense strategy. Still, it would be smarter not to get arrested again.

"Yeah. Yur right." Silence as the group thought that through. "But," Jed said suddenly, "we got every right tuh parade downtown. Thass just peaceful protest. Righta free assembly. Free speech. We can kick some political ass while we're there. Ain't nobody can do nothin' to us. God bless our founding fathers."

The constitutional scholars hovering above went paler in shock.

CHAPTER 9

THE VIOLENCE CAUGHT everybody by surprise.

The convoy of pick-up trucks roared into downtown Friday night. 15 or 20; witness reports were a little shaky.

They threw two Molotov cocktails at the front of the Port Manatee Observer. The flames did some damage to the exterior. A couple of windows got smashed. Then it all escalated. Two trucks did ueys on the front lawn before racing off, leaving mangled turf and flowerbeds. Garbage cans on Main Street got knocked over, leaving filth and debris everywhere. A few shots were fired into the dark night sky. Rocks and bricks were heaved at store windows, smashing them. Several thugs were waving torches and a couple of the burning tikis got tossed. Three small fires were started.

By that time pedestrians, shoppers and those out for the evening had scattered, ducking behind whatever protection they could find or running into the few businesses that were open. 911 calls exploded.

The convoy veered into the front driveway of city hall. Three more gasoline bombs were thrown. Their explosions started two fires on the outside walls. The flames licked up, leaving ugly scars on the coral stucco walls. A few more rocks shattered office windows on the first floor. A can of pig manure was dumped on the front sidewalk. More shots were fired into the night sky.

With sirens wailing and emergency vehicles pouring into the downtown, the trucks honked derisively, swerved over lawns, and then disappeared as their dying torches sputtered.

The fires were extinguished. Business owners came to pick up the pieces and assess damage. Dazed pedestrians stood up again, brushing off dirt and fear. Roy Crawford and Kim Sharpe drove to city hall to help with the clean-up. Maintenance was called in to wash down the sidewalk. The manure stank.

Police vehicles fanned out to search for the culprits, but identifying the trucks involved in the insurrection was futile.

CCTV footage later revealed that license plates had been covered with mud or black tape.

In a county where nearly 50% of vehicles were black pickups, proof of who was there was unlikely to stand up in court.

Perkins puzzled over the whole scenario. He thought about it as he tossed and turned in bed after returning from his visit to the downtown. He finally gave up at 5am, got ready for another long hard day, walked Rosie, fed her, played with her, and got to the office at 6:25am.

He wasn't the first senior officer to be there.

Captain Williams was there, with a fresh pot of coffee and some interesting intelligence.

CHAPTER 10

"BEST WE CAN figure," Williams began, "it was a political rally that got mixed with some angry stuff about our local media and local government and who knows what else. Our assessment is that this was the first white supremacist demonstration in our county."

"Source?" snapped the Inspector who had been on duty the night before and was running on two hours' sleep and a lot of adrenaline and stale coffee.

"We have a CI who has sort of infiltrated this group of wacky right-wingers. We think they're called the J-Men because a bunch of them have names that start with J. You all know Jed Boone—he's been arrested for a buncha drinking offenses, firing his gun inside city limits, at least two DUIs and probably should have been charged with others. His sidekick is a big piece of beef named Jethro Mathers. You don't want to go one-on-one with him."

Grunts around the table.

"We suspect they were together in the lead truck," Williams continued. "We know where they live. We just don't know why they pulled this. And proving their identity is impossible because most of them wore ski masks or bandanas."

"Why them? Why now?"

"Fair question. A'ja."

Lt. Stokes had recently been promoted to head the Intelligence Unit. She was a graduate of the University of Georgia. Williams and Perkins had been impressed by her smarts and savvy.

"My guess is it was driven by the political climate in America these days. It is rough out there, we all know that. The lockdowns from COVID, the economy, inflation, politicians not working together but instead fighting little personal political battles...election deniers...it is a messy climate. There are people wanting to manipulate others with misinformation and conspiracy theories. The lies on social media are just...

staggering. Some of these radical leaders are coalescing to form bigger groups and recruit local muscle. The trials and jail sentences from the January 6 riots angered some. Others are just preying on public fear." She looked down at her cold cup of tea. "There is a growing number of threats against local city council members and school board trustees, even volunteers who work at voting stations. Our election and political systems are being attacked. And part of their playbook is violence. That all creates a volatile situation. Some of these people dehumanize the political structure. Vandalism and fear are just tools. And there is a generation of political leaders who have traded their ethics for short-term political gain." She looked down again at the empty cup and then looked around the room. "I think we've just had the opening skirmish with this new, radical white-supremacist group that is now in our city."

A restless silence settled over the conference table as they all absorbed the assessment. Perkins spun his pen around and finally looked up. "OK. This is why we had that conference with James Robertson a couple of weeks ago. I think A'ja is right. This kind of demonstration is happening more often. It looks as if now we're in the middle of it. Think about this, folks. Our community is under attack. It is going to change how we do our police work."

Solemn nods around the table.

"That's it. Gather all the body cams and any media video we can get. Work with the DA's office and see who we can identify and what charges can be laid. OK, thanks," Perkins concluded.

The officers rose. Perkins remained, facing Williams and Stokes.

"Is this really what we've got here? A white supremacist group?"

"I think it is. I've been getting odd pieces of intelligence for the past few months. That Washington riot really energized some of these local groups. My fear is they are going to try something big here in Port Manatee. I wonder if there's some honcho above these local clowns, directing them somehow. Jed and his pals are not very bright. It is all toxic. It is attacking our political system, and our belief in democracy, and that scares me. Never mind what goes on in Washington, I think we have our own little nest of vipers to worry about."

CHAPTER 11

THE WIVES WERE pissed. And when The Wives were angry, the earth trembled and strong men hid in dark caves.

The husbands and lovers of The Wives—who were not necessarily the same person—were generally not strong men. They once had been industry titans but then had sold their companies or retired. Now they just wanted to play golf, do some drinking around the pool, spend their money on fun and games, and talk sports, politics and business with their pals. They didn't want problems.

Several of the women had themselves been successful, and all had prodded and pushed their spouses and kids to be all that they could be. Now that their men didn't have an office to go to, the power base in their households had shifted dramatically. It was all pretty much dominatrix now.

It was a fascinating study of family structures. Some anthropology professor would have a most interesting paper to write.

The men fluttered around their beloveds—not necessarily their wives—as the women ranted from their throne room in the SW corner of the huge swimming pool concourse that was set in the middle of the rough triangle formed by the three six-story condos that made up the Sapphire Blue enclave.

The Wives took over several tables, chaise lounges, umbrellas and other paraphernalia each day. They began with noon-hour pick-me-ups and proceeded through afternoon cocktails, late afternoon drinks and then cocktail hour specialties. Wine with dinner was a given. Good wines.

A few innocent new residents and guest visitors had occasionally tried to sit in their throne room. The stains from their bodily fluids were still visible on the concrete deck.

"HOW DARE THEY RIOT IN OUR CITY!" exclaimed Rebecca. She was the de facto leader of the tough little cabal that ran the social and political structures at the high-end condo complex.

Nowadays she pretty much always spoke in capital letters.

"Riot? You sure, honey?"

Wife #4 was a recent recruit. She was still in the outer circle of the outer circle but was being considered for promotion to the inner circle of the outer circle. It was a complicated order of majesty for The Wives.

In fact, what to call the events of the night before was creating a lot of angst in senior police and media circles in town.

Channel 10 had opted for a 'demonstration.'

Channel 7, always more aggressive and generally not as burdened with concerns about sensationalism, had gone with 'riot.' The word was emblazoned over a dingy picture of a Cambodian uprising from some years before. Flames were rising from the edge of the visuals.

The news pages of The Observer had used 'fracas.' Their editorial page, sometimes more thoughtful, chose 'tumult.'

The Wives had no such constraints. "Rioting and fire-bombing in our downtown! For God's sake. Who are these people? How dare they!"

"STRING 'EM UP!" was Rebecca's answer. Actually, it was her go-to answer for many societal ills. Rebecca was brassy, loud, and all 188 pounds of her physique projected her ideas with considerable enthusiasm. She did not tolerate opposing viewpoints very elegantly.

The husbands continued their pouring of cocktails and soothing of brows. It was almost a full-time job for two of them.

"I just don't get it," complained Stephanie. "Why here? Why now?"

Wife #7 nodded agreement. She was a candidate for the exalted outer ring of the inner circle. A decision would be made soon. She didn't want to jeopardize her chances by voicing an opinion of her own.

"Hey, Kim! C'mon over!" June Rose hollered as Kim and Samantha arrived at the pool. They looked at one another briefly. They had wanted some quiet time to talk about the melee downtown, but it was hard to ignore a summons from The Wives.

"Good afternoon, ladies. Gentlemen." Kim nodded at the men scattered behind and around the throne room. Most of them looked startled to be acknowledged.

"Now just what in the hell is goin' on downtown?" began JR.

"I spent the morning at city hall," Kim replied. "The Mayor has called a special city council meeting for 7pm tomorrow. Our

City Manager will have a report then. I guess the Sheriff will be there as well."

Samantha gave a slight nod of confirmation. She had spoken with Perkins just a few moments before.

"It looks as if it was some alt-right group or something like that. There was a lot of damage to property. No one was seriously hurt. Nobody recalls anything like this here before. I worry it might be the start of more civil unrest."

The Wives saluted her with their drinks, and Kim and Samantha escaped to a far corner of the concourse. They talked quietly about the situation and what options the city council had.

Talk at the Wives table was less constrained and more action oriented. Tarring-and-feathering and running them out of town on a rail were both popular choices.

Chapter 12

THE CITY COUNCIL meeting room was jammed with angry citizens. The riot downtown had shaken the mid-sized city to its core. There was confusion about the who and the why, and there was anger about the what and the how.

Mayor Sonja Rodriguez pounded her gavel exactly at 7pm. The cable TV telecast started. The buzz in the audience softened but didn't go away.

"We are here tonight in special session to get the facts about the situation downtown," she began.

"The big riot!" rang out from the public gallery. A little applause from the crowd.

Rodriguez pounded her gavel. "It was not a riot! It was a...a...a ruckus. Listen! We are here to get reports from the City Manager and the Sheriff. You are welcome to be here and listen, but there will be no more outbursts from the audience."

Grumbling but obedience from the mostly older crowd.

"Mr. Crawford?"

The handsome, brown-skinned man rose from his desk in the center of the horseshoe that made up the council chambers. Impeccably dressed in a tan suit with a crisp white shirt and striped club tie, he exuded confidence. That stilled the crowd.

"Madam Mayor, Council members, ladies and gentlemen. It is a sad time for us that we have to have this special meeting. I think we all regret the circumstances. It is a rarity in Port Manatee to have this kind of situation. No one at city hall can recall anything like it."

He paused to glance at his notes. "Our preliminary view is that this demonstration"—the Channel 10 reporter flashed a smirking, triumphant sneer at her inferior Channel 7 colleague—"was obviously a surprise. There was no parade permit sought or obtained. The good news is that there were no serious injuries, but there was considerable property damage to several businesses and here at city hall. All of us are working to calm the news reports and to reassure business owners, residents and visitors."

"Why? And who?" broke in Councillor March.

"Good questions. I'd like to invite Sheriff Perkins to join me."

Perkins was in full dress regalia. During his years in authority, he had learned the power of a uniform, especially one with medals and service ribbons. He walked to the podium. "Mayor, Councillors." He paused briefly. "The answer to the Councillor's questions is both simple and complex. Who? We believe that area residents are the leaders. We have identified possible participants."

There was an audible gasp from the council and the crowd. The riot itself was bad enough; to have it championed by neighbors was shocking.

"The why is more difficult. You may be aware that recently I hosted a conference for politicians and law enforcement with FBI Regional Director Robertson as the guest speaker. He warned us at that time that home-grown domestic terrorism was now the greatest threat facing the United States. Florida is very high on the list of states that are particularly vulnerable. The reality is that there is a growing number of quasi-military groups who threaten our system of governing and our way of life. They have become increasingly violent, as you all witnessed on January 6. I must report that increasingly, local officials are being targeted. My department's intelligence assessment is that the melee the other evening was just the first skirmish in a self-proclaimed war against America. And Port Manatee."

Stunned silence in the room. The wagging tongues in the gallery hanging out of gaping, dentured mouths were now stilled. Kim had advance knowledge of the seriousness of the event, but even she was taken aback at the import of Perkins' words.

Mayor Rodriguez finally shook her head and looked hard at Perkins. "Are you saying that we can expect an escalating campaign or something?"

"Yes, ma'am. Our best estimate is that there will be further incidents. Experience has shown that there is a higher and higher risk of greater violence or other acts of civil disobedience." He paused as the audience absorbed his words. "These situations tend to build over time until they are sparked by more lies, fear or preying on the public. Then there can be a major confrontation of some kind. That could include an attack downtown or on some infrastructure owned by the municipality. We just don't know."

The mayor swallowed hard. "Well. That is…disconcerting. What, uh, can we do?"

Perkins nodded. "Mr. Crawford and I have created a special Task Force to coordinate intelligence-gathering and simplify command-and-control if and when action is needed. I have assigned one of my most experienced and trusted officers, Captain Willie Williams, to head it up. Captain."

Williams was sitting in the back of the gallery. He rose slowly to attention. He was also in full uniform. His broad chest was half-covered with medals and citations. He exuded strength and confidence. He nodded at the mayor and council, and then sat down.

Roy Crawford picked up the narrative. "Madam Mayor, the city's participation will be headed by City Clerk Kathy James. I have also asked Councillor Sharpe to serve on it. As you know, she is a decorated Army veteran with experience in terrorist activity. We will keep the mayor and council informed, although obviously that will usually be done in confidential session because of security concerns."

A few more questions from the councillors. It had been a night of extreme shock and awe for them and the audience. They were all glad to see the gavel come down on a situation that had moved from scary to threatening.

CHAPTER 13

"WHOOOEEE!"
Jed's shouts of glee echoed around The Ugly Porker's outdoor dining area. He was reading the recent edition of the Port Manatee Observer. This was not part of his usual daily routine. In fact, it was the first time in, oh, twenty years that he had read a newspaper.

Jeb, Jedediah, Jethro, Jack and Jimmy clustered around the wooden table to peer at the newspaper. It was already a bit grease-stained from simply lying on a table which had only been scrubbed by wind and rain; even mother nature couldn't eradicate the residue of a thousand dinners of greasy ribs.

The pictures and stories in the paper were very clear: the demonstration had been a big success that scared the city and its city council.

The callers to The TALK 1410 Boomer Bronsky morning open line program had been pontificating in their usual fashion. Several callers thought the J-Men were true patriots trying to take back the city from corrupt local politicians. Several other callers called the demonstrators thugs, liars, cowards and much worse—several times Boomer had to use the 5-second delay to bleep certain words and phrases, grinning as he did so. Controversy always meant bigger ratings. Bleeping callers enraged other callers, and made wonderfully provocative promo announcements to further entice listeners.

Jed was experiencing the rush of fame that sudden media exposure can bring. It was the first time that his exploits had gotten media attention since his high school football days.

He liked it.

"Lookee there! Thass me!" Jethro pointed a thick finger at the front-page picture of the lead truck rolling down Main Street. The last time he'd been pictured in the paper was the high school AA football championship. The photographer had caught him perfectly when he'd pancake-blocked an opposing defensive end as Jed sprinted past him for the winning touchdown.

His mother still had the clipping in her scrapbook. It sat there in lonely splendor. Sadly, the scrapbook was notably barren of any other achievements.

The pit-master brought over a huge platter of sliced brisket, pulled pork, white bread and baked beans. "Looks like you boys shook 'em up purty good," he said as he passed around the bowls and plates. A waitress arrived with a roll of paper towels, plastic cutlery and another tray of cold beer.

"We did. We surely did," Jed agreed anxiously. "Scared that woman mayor an' her weak little councillors, sure 'nuff." He popped another beer and made a sandwich of white bread and brisket, then slathered on the sweet 'n spicy barbecue sauce. "Shook 'em good." He punched Jedediah in the arm. "Whole town's talkin' 'bout us."

Grins around the table as the boys scarfed down the smoky barbecue. Drips of the red-stained sauce were soon prominent on lips, chins and T-shirt fronts.

"Sheriff's too nervous to do anything," crowed Jack. "We pretty much run this town now!"

"Uh, we might want to hold off on that for a bit," Jeb warned quietly as he finished his beans. "Let's not get too cocky."

"Oh, shit, Jeb, let it go. We won. Let's enjoy that. We'll go back, do somethin' even bigger next time. The J-Men are on a roll!" Jed shouted as he waved half a brisket sandwich in the air.

The boys whooped at that and ignored Jeb. He shrugged and popped another cold beer.

Chapter 14

PERKINS LAY WITH his head on Samantha's lap. He was exhausted after four straight sixteen-hour days as his department worked on the aftermath of the demonstration.

It was Friday night. At 4 o'clock he'd finally ordered the investigators and intelligence operators to go home and enjoy a weekend with their families. At 6 he and Rosie had arrived at Samantha's for the weekend.

Rosie had been fed, watered, walked and had her tummy rubbed. She was now on her evening tour of the kitchen, eternally confident that someday she would find some left-over tidbits on the clean floor. Steak was a prized commodity.

Perkins had changed into khaki cargo shorts, a loose white T-shirt that was so faded you couldn't make out the slogan on the front, bare feet and an exhausted look.

Samantha was wearing white shorts, a tight black T-shirt, bare feet and an anticipatory look. She was expecting some torrid lovemaking tonight.

He was sipping his third IPA. She was sipping her third glass of Petit Chablis.

Her left hand gently stroked his forehead.

"Well, at least you've identified the main players in this group," she said. He grunted. "They sound like a high school reunion gone bad. A bunch of ex-jocks getting together for some boozing and trouble."

He grunted again. His eyes drifted shut.

"It is surprising that nobody can figure out some reason for the whole thing," Samantha continued, her fingers soothing his head. "I'm not sure what they really accomplished, other than breaking windows and setting garbage cans on fire. Mind you, it sure got the town talking."

"Yeah, it did," Perkins replied tiredly. "Scared some people. Made a lot of them nervous about what's coming next. That's what we can't figure out, that's the—hey!"

He jerked his right foot and rose to find Rosie pushing her cold, wet nose into his instep. Samantha laughed as he twitched. Rosie came around the end of the couch to nestle against Samantha, who promptly patted her and scratched her in that place between her eyes that Rosie really liked to have scratched.

Perkins rolled over with a groan and sat up. "I'm tired. I just want to sleep for a week," he muttered as they got Rosie settled in her doggie bed in the kitchen, turned out the lights and shut the bedroom door.

When Samantha returned from her closet, Perkins had rolled onto his left side and was fast asleep.

She sighed.

CHAPTER 15

"THE LEADER OF this rat pack seems to be Jed Boone," Captain Williams reported Monday morning to the Sheriff's senior management team. "He's a local boy. High school football hero who got a scholarship to a mid-level college in 'Bama but never made it past number two running back on the depth charts. He got one of the drum majorettes pregnant in his junior year. Her daddy's 12-guage apparently played a prominent role in his proposal."

A few snickers around the table. Some aspects of human life just don't change much as the generations pass.

"Had two kids. Got divorced within four years. It wasn't an amicable split. He left town rather hurriedly before his father-in-law and his trusty shotgun could arrive to help conduct negotiations. He returned here. Got into his daddy's feed and seed business. That's where Jethro works, by the way. Apparently he throws around those fifty pound bags of grain like they're Frisbees." Williams shook his head. He was a big strong man, but a day of slinging those heavy bags would exhaust anyone.

"Jed is running the business now. His daddy's pretty much retired but still owns most of the shares. The business is starting to slip. Jed has lost some customers." He checked his notes. "The old man was not exactly an enlightened gentleman of the old South, nor was his pappy. His boy absorbed those beliefs. Then he got caught up in all the Trump rhetoric and has gone even harder-right in recent years."

Williams swallowed some coffee and looked at his notes as the next mug's shot appeared.

"This is John Edgar Brown. He goes by Jeb. because nobody wants to be John Brown, right, and who names their kid Edgar? Jeb is probably the smartest one in this armpit of humanity. He got a business degree at Auburn, got into the housing development industry in the Carolinas and was doing well until the 08-09 mortgage slaughter. Then the banks and the

IRS came after him. By the time they were done, he owed $378,000 plus penalties and interest. It broke him and he got hugely resentful about government. Any government. He's now building houses one by one and is trying to regain financial stability. Family left him. He's angry and bitter."

Jethro was the next slide. "You know all about him so I won't take more time. Just be warned that he's big, he's strong and he's completely under Jed's control. If you get into an altercation with him, bring the tranquilizer darts we use for angry rhinos."

Laughter from the assembled officers. Williams shook his head. "I've warned you."

A picture of a pale, unsmiling man with a face like a constipated ferret appeared next. "Jedidiah Jenner. He is an assistant preacher at that big fundamentalist church out on County Road 13. You know, the one that seats a couple, three thousand. Apparently, their services include snakes on the altar and live bands and people fainting when they are touched by…something. They take in big money. Their preaching gets political at times. Jedidiah is somewhere between being a recruiter for the congregation and a kinky altar priest. We have had a couple of complaints about him and young boys, but nobody in the church will press charges or even file a formal accusation. We have an open file on this creep."

Head-shaking around the table. Notes were made.

"Jack O'Hara. He is just flat-out weird, even compared to these other paragons of virtue. Sometimes dresses like a Confederate army officer. Waves that big Rebel flag around. Wears this long white moustache that is stained with his chawin' t'baccy spit. His formal attire includes an officer's cavalry sword from the war of Northern Aggression. Inherited moola when his parents were killed in a drunk-driving accident. Big insurance settlement. No family. No siblings. Lives in a big-ol' five-bedroom house on Meadow Lane. Weird dude."

Williams shook his head. He punched the next PP slide.

"Jacob Pew. He is a survivalist. Has a big cache of guns. His house has solar panels and its own generator. He has a thing that makes drinking water out of your urine." He winced. "Story is that he's got an underground survival room or cave or something, stocked with two years of nuked food and canned goods. He figures the revolution is coming and he intends to survive it. He hates the government. He thinks they are spying on him. He is dangerous in a cornered-rat sort of way. He is a very good shot with his rifles. He is not really part of the inner circle of this J-Men group, but he's definitely there for any action against the political establishment. He is a big constitutionalist." He paused. "He doesn't trust anyone in any government. Or any politicians." He paused again. "He likes to shoot."

"The last member of their crack management team—" The phrase drew sardonic grins around the table "—would be Jim Crandall. He's an Army infantry vet who had a tour in Afghanistan. Got wounded. Knows guns, knows on-the-ground tactics. He came back from the war pretty sour about the leaders of our nation and their inability to make smart decisions. He is bitter and he is still angry about how our nation forgot about Afghanistan and everybody who fought there. He's holed up with a woman named Beulah Tremaine. She's a bit older than he is. She owns a house down a gravel road off County Line 22 where she has a big farm of beans, watermelon and corn. It's been in her family for decades. We're not sure what her connection with Jim is. Be warned, though, if we ever got into a fire-fight with this group, he would be a real danger."

The big Captain stopped, shut down the PP and looked at Perkins. "Those are the key players in this alt-right group, but there's a bunch more like 'em out there. They aren't big enough or powerful enough to take on large federal agencies or buildings. City hall is a much more palatable bite for them."

"Was the riot just to get publicity, maybe attract some members?"

Lt. A'ja Stokes handled that one. "That would be part of it. As Captain Williams noted, the leadership of this J-Men group is quite loose and rather ill-formed. No one is clearly in charge. Their political tent is also loose—they've got people from several different protest groups or philosophical genres. It is a rather rollicking group right now that seems to like eating barbecue at The Ugly Porker and shouting about right-wing politics. They get stoked by rabid political commentary, hard right media coverage, and obscure blogs from a lot of crazies."

She sipped her tea. "Their riot would have been noticed by other para-military groups across the country. They all use dark-web communication tools. They stay informed about actions by other, similar groups. The risk for us, of course, is that these may become more focused and more action-driven. It's something like a drug addiction—you start to want more highs and higher highs. That can only be achieved by increasingly violent action and greater media attention."

"What could set them off?"

"Any number of things. A political star who arrives on the national scene and whose rhetoric fires them up. Some action by the government, most likely the federal government, perhaps to pass a new law they don't like. They tend to be strict interpreters of the Constitution. Or at least their version of it. Anything that they would perceive as a threat to the second amendment would inflame them. Election deniers, obviously."

She paused, glanced at her notes, and continued. "Or it could just be media hype of a particular situation—say, immigrants flooding the southern border, or allegations of voter fraud. That would get them panting and angry. The irony is, as much as they distrust the media and scream about 'fake news,' they do watch certain TV channels or listen to certain radio stations to get reinforcement of their own political rhetoric. But they only watch or listen to media that support their beliefs."

She paused. "Candidly, if they get hyped-up sufficiently, we are concerned that something in Port Manatee may be their target. We have no idea what that might be."

It was a bleak assessment. Perkins thought it was probably right on. The meeting ended quietly shortly after Stokes' final comments.

Chapter 16

"AND THAT IS why we are in such trouble in Washington," said the COYOTE News Network host smoothly. His two guests nodded obediently. They had learned that if they wanted to be invited back on the TV talk show, then they had better be supportive of the host's viewpoints.

"You're absolutely right," said Pastor Jedidiah Jenner. It was his third appearance on national television. He was still excited by it. "What we are seeing is the erosion of conservative Christian values by the liberal chattering class. My congregation is outraged at the lack of moral fibre in the Congress right now!"

Sophia Roberts was a veteran commentator. She had her own blog but made a very nice living by being outrageous on television news talk panels. She had dyed her hair blonde some years ago when she recognized that being blonde was pretty much a prerequisite for TV time on COYOTE.

She had learned all the tricks—what style of jacket to wear, what colors showed up best on camera, how much cleavage to display on which host's program, when to wear short skirts or *really* short skirts, and how much to flirt on camera. It all helped to titillate the audience, which was mostly male. Older male. The appearances and commentary built her own brand and drove clicks to her Tik Tok account.

"Michael is so smart to bring up this issue of the rise of these independent militias across the country that are seeking to liberate our nation from the clutches of these leftist dictators. Just look at the brave men and women who marched in that city in Florida last week. They understood that it's not just the left-wing wimps in Congress! Our city halls have also been infected!"

She twinkled at the camera and held her gaze steady without blinking. She had taught herself that trick, because directors nowadays like to keep a close-up of the faces of the panelists on screen throughout the discussion.

Michael Major preened. This was only his third month hosting the coveted 10pm time slot. He needed to drive ratings to keep that slot. That meant being outrageous and controversial.

He liked having Sophia on—whenever she crossed her legs, he figured it bumped the size of his audience, and the blood pressure of several thousand male viewers.

The little pastor from Florida seemed to give off a creepy vibe, but if he sucked up to the host and was shocking every so often, that was good enough.

"Yes, we are constantly being bombarded by the forces of evil in our country. And that evil starts with the people who don't support our places of worship like Pastor Jenner's fine church on the Gulf Coast of Florida. Those godless souls on the left are threatening our American way of life!"

'Godless souls on the left' he thought as he looked deep into the eye of the camera. Now that was a good phrase. His producer had given it to him earlier.

"And that is my point exactly," Sophia responded swiftly. She didn't want to lose her own momentum. "Increasingly we are finding that people are forming their own groups to protect their families and our way of life! We must root out this ill-conceived liberal thinking and bring family values back to our cities and schools."

'Ha,' she thought to herself as she smiled sweetly into the lens, 'suck on that you ignorant twit of a host. Just because you're boinking the Executive Producer and your hair looks as if Vidal Sassoon himself just trimmed it, don't think you can out-right me.'

Pastor Jedidiah was left in the dust by the two experienced TV personalities. His sallow complexion and his shifty eyes were not a good television look. Fortunately, his views were so extreme that nobody looked at him all that closely. The show's director didn't give him much actual camera time; instead, the control booth would throw up colorful charts and words onto the screen so that his face didn't offend the squeamish. Still, Jedidiah thought, it was network TV. His congregation would be awed. So might a couple of the new altar boys.

"And that's our time for tonight. My thanks to my guest experts, Sophia Roberts and Jedidiah Jeffer. I'm Michael Major, and this has been The Major's Report!"

Pounding music up, dramatic logo on screen, cut to commercial.

Nobody cared that he'd screwed up the name of one of his guests. These things happen to little twerps from Florida. Sophia he had to keep happy—and he had dreams of making her very happy some night after a bottle of expensive champagne in a hotel suite that he could charge to the network as part of his guest relations budget.

That is a news network talk-show program's reality today: So many high hopes. So many low thoughts. So many shattered dreams.

CHAPTER 17

"**H**OW DO YOU get middle-aged men to buy investments from you?"

"A little cleavage, flash some thigh and swing your butt."

"What about older men?"

"A little cleavage, flash some thigh, swing your butt."

Pause. Then thoughtfully, "So, men are men?"

"Pretty much."

Kim looked at Samantha and they both giggled at the overheard conversation between the two middle-aged women at the table beside them. It was a warm, sunny day and the two were enjoying a rare day off. They were relaxing under an umbrella at poolside. Rosé was being sipped.

"How about a walk now that the afternoon sun is going down?"

"Great," Samantha replied and drained her glass. They threw on cover-ups, adjusted their big floppy hats, slipped into flip-flops, and headed out to the golden sandy beach.

The Gulf was bluey-green that afternoon. The waves were gentle. The tide was coming in. Pelicans were beginning to hover over the shallow water and dive for their dinner. Seagulls screeched at one another as they circled the beach looking for scraps. The two women stopped to ooh and awe over the antics of three sleek gray dolphins leaping and diving in the Gulf.

The afternoon sunworshippers were starting to leave the beach. Families packed up their tents, umbrellas, kid's toys, beach balls, shovels, pails and coolers. Many of them loaded the debris into a four-fat-wheeled wagon and began to tug it over the soft sand. Grunts and soft curses were the accompanying music to their exertions.

Two middle-aged men, one having made the unfortunate choice of a red Speedo, stomped along the waterline. One of them was gesturing and speaking loudly as they approached Kim and Samantha.

"My divorce finally goes through, but the crazy bitch won't leave me alone. I finally call her back, her maid answers—yeah, she's hired a freakin' maid—and I say, 'Where is she.' And the maid says, 'She's in bed with arthritis.' And I say, 'Well get that Greek bastard outta there and put her on the phone because...'"

The conversation drifted into the early evening sky as the foursome crossed paths. Samantha's eyes were big as she turned to Kim. "Wouldn't you like to write a book about Florida beach conversations?"

"You are so funny. Nobody would believe them!"

The friends laughed and strode along. Occasional waves bumped against their ankles. The temperature had cooled delightfully. The sun was beginning its inexorable departure as they turned back to their condo.

"How's the new task force on security coming?" Samantha asked.

Kim paused. "It is really complicated. Much more so than I'd anticipated. I had no idea our municipal infrastructure is so vast and so complex. Hundreds of miles of roads and sewers and water pipes. Eleven bridges, two lift bridges. Four libraries. The convention center. Our transit system. City Hall. A bunch of other buildings we own for our crews and maintenance and storing trucks and supplies. The water treatment plant. The sewage system. All the city's parks. Recreation fields and the two rec complexes. Parking lots. The electricity grid. It just goes on and on. It is impossible to protect everything all the time. Cities are so vulnerable to attack. Most municipal infrastructure is unguarded. It's scary."

Samantha slowed her pace as she thought about the implications of Kim's analysis. "Golly. I never understood that. Roy and Perk must be frantic about how to protect the city."

"Yeah. It's a problem. And then you add in the college and the hospitals and the downtown..." She shook her head in dismay.

Ahead of them, a group of teenagers were getting ready to pack up their beach items. The girls were clustered together, giggling as the boys circled them and pushed each other, obviously trying to impress their favorites. The girls wore brief bikinis; the guys had multi-colored trunks that went past their knees.

"Ah, to be young and lithe and have no cellulite."

"Shut up."

Suddenly two of the boys picked up a couple of bags of potato chips that were still partially filled. Obviously intending to impress the girls, they tore open the bags and flung the chips in the air. Instantly a couple of dozen gulls swarmed the boys and the flying chips. The two guys ran screaming into the ocean to escape the clawing, pecking attack, waving their arms frantically as their friends scattered on the beach in their own desperate flight.

Kim and Samantha stopped dead in their tracks. They were just outside the radius of the gulls' focus. The screeching was deafening. More gulls arrived to get in on the feast. It was chaos on the beach.

"Well, that was smart."

Samantha shook her head. Teenage boys.

Chapter 18

"THE BODY'S BEEN in the woods for two or three days. It isn't pretty."

Perkins nodded. He'd seen his share of dead bodies during his career in law enforcement. None of them were pretty.

He signed into the official log, nodded to the young deputy securing the perimeter, and followed the narrow path into the patch of scraggly timber and overgrowth. The ground was soggy from recent rains.

Two detectives were crouched over the body. The Medical Examiner was taking off her gloves and booties as Perkins arrived on-scene.

"Hey, doc. Whatta we got?"

"Sheriff. Always a pleasure to see you. Just not at crime scenes all the time." Perkins nodded agreement. The ME took a breath and looked down. "Female. Maybe Latina. Early 20s."

"ID?"

"Yeah. No. No wallet or ID. No obvious distinguishing marks. The critters and birds that have been picking at her corpse have made it more difficult. Damn crows always go for the eyes."

Perkins nodded as he swallowed hard at that image. Bodies in the woods were never easy.

"I'm ready to send the body for the autopsy unless your guys need more. The wagon's here."

Perkins nodded again. He'd seen the ME's van on the side of the road. He walked closer to the crime scene. "Jamal. Fred."

"Sheriff."

"What's your prelim?"

The two detectives stood up, one knee cracking alarmingly. "She was shot somewhere else, and the body dumped here. Obviously they figured the animals would get most of her and nobody would find her for months. They didn't figure on teenage love. Two kids looking for a quiet little area for a make-out session stumbled across the body. The girl is still crying. The boy is shaken but able to explain what they were doing here. They're not involved. We're letting them go home."

"ME tells me you got no ID."

"No wallet that we could find around here. Nothing in her pockets. The shooter probably stripped everything before tossing the corpse."

"Huh. Typical." Perkins thought some more. "OK, wrap it up whenever you're ready. ME's done. Meat wagon is out on the road."

The detectives nodded. It was the city's fifth murder of the year.

CHAPTER 19

THE MURDER CASE was soon mired like the mud at the murder site. No leads. Detectives Cornice and McMurray sat at their desks in the detectives' bull pen. Ten detectives shared eight desks.

A pot of what once was coffee sat on top of a gray filing cabinet. Nobody had the courage to start cleaning it out after the residue of a thousand potfuls had been singed into the glass. A snarky visiting FDA agent, perhaps unhappily suffering from hemorrhoids, might have declared the coffee pot to be a source of some lethal toxin and a biohazard and shut down the bullpen.

As a result, the detectives either brought in their own coffee or sneaked down to the administration's little kitchenette that Mary kept spotless. Woe to any detective who didn't wash out that coffee pot or mop up a spill; weeks of midnight assignments and a sudden delay in getting overtime paid and office supplies delivered would mysteriously overcome the culprit.

McMurray propped his aching right leg on top of a garbage can. The lanky detective was due for a total knee replacement. He just didn't know who, when, where or how to pay for it. The department's health insurance had denied coverage, claiming it was pre-existing from his high school football days. His collection of empty beer bottles would help fund the surgery, but not quite enough. Obviously he needed to drink more.

"We got nothin'."

Cornice shook his head in frustration. "No useful physical evidence at the scene. No witnesses. No idea where the killing took place. The kids who found the body are useless. No other witnesses have come forward."

"Shit."

"Yeah."

The two veteran detectives looked at different walls in the bullpen. There was no solace on display and no helpful information posted on either grimy corkboard. The boards were covered with old WANTED posters, information bulletins, Police Association newsletters, memos from the Sheriff, and a picture of a very buff sergeant showing off his ridged six pack. It had been posted there by two female detectives in response to a picture of a Hollywood influencer wearing what some people might think was a bikini, and others might call just a few wisps of some cloth that had been randomly blown in by the wind and just happened to cling to certain parts of the young lady. The pinup had been stuck on the board by a young detective. The brief cultural war had ended in a draw; nobody cared anymore. No sexual harassment claims had been filed by either side.

"The autopsy confirmed death by gunshot. Fired at close range. .45. No shell casings because we don't know where the shooting occurred. No report of a missing person that matches. Her skirt was pretty short. Her blouse was torn. Wonder if she was doing some hooking on the side?"

"Let's hit the street. Maybe we can pick up a rumor about the vic or the shooting."

Cornice shrugged agreement and grabbed his car keys. They had agreed that he would do the driving until McMurray's knee was fixed. The leg movement from accelerator to brake sometimes shot stabs of pain down his leg; it slowed his reaction time. They hadn't informed Captain Williams of that.

Cornice's unmarked police car was a mid-sized sedan. Gray. Deliberately chosen not to stand out or be remembered. They didn't want to use an official B&W department vehicle when they were trolling the tough east side of Manatee. It would be hard enough to get any information out of the people who populated the cheap bars, pawn shops, tattoo holes, back alleys and street corners where people did business in that neighborhood.

Two ladies of the evening were working the afternoon shift at Richmond and Park in the heart of the east side. One was brown, the other white. One was female, the other was better dressed but the gender was less certain. They waved at the cops as their pimp sat in a purple Escalade a block away, watching the street. The pimp didn't wave.

The car hit another pothole as they drove south. The city had not recently invested in modern infrastructure in this neighborhood. Fast-food wrappers blew across the pavement like tumbleweed on the open prairie. Garbage cans overflowed. Two kids on skateboards zoomed across the intersection.

Cornice braked sharply and swore softly as one of the kids gave him the one-finger salute.

So much for a low-key entrance. It was obvious they could have come down in the Sheriff's truck with lights flashing and a brass band playing and not drawn much more scrutiny.

"Hey!" McMurray pointed at a man furtively entering the opening to a back alley. Cornice slammed the car over the sidewalk and blocked the entrance. They both got out and loosened their service weapons as they advanced into the dark alley. Cat piss, dead things and rotten garbage were the predominant odors.

"Freddie!" McMurray paused for a second. "Vest Man! Get your ass out here."

Nothing for a moment, then a small, very thin man slowly came towards them. "Mac? That you?"

"Yeah, man. This is my partner, Jamal. How yuh doin'?"

"Been tough, man. Tough. Street ain't the same. Coupla gangs tryin' to move in. Makes it hard for legit businessmen like me to survive."

McMurray and Cornice kept a straight face. Freddie was known for fencing interesting things like IPADs and TVs, jewelry of a lesser valuation and assorted other merchandise that happened to accidently fall off delivery trucks. Or packages that were 'misaddressed.' Or left unattended on porches.

"Yeah. Look, we go no beef with you. You an' me, we done a little business in the past. Right? I treated you good? I turned my back on that little problem you were gonna have over the vanload of flatscreens, right? Kept you outta the whole thing."

Freddie nodded. He wiped his face with a handkerchief that had not seen a washing machine in some time. He shifted his feet. Just having these two cops talking to him would get around the neighborhood's grapevine. Coupla people might want to know what it was all about.

"Thing is, Freddie, we're looking for somebody popped a young girl. Latina. Nothin' tuh do with you, I know that. I told Jamal, here, Freddie's one of the good guys. A stand-up guy. Somebody you can do business with."

Cornice nodded, breathing through his mouth.

"OK. Good. Now. You hear anything, you let me know. Right away. You got it?"

Freddie nodded. He licked his dry lips. His small rat-like face stared down at the filthy cracked concrete.

"I mean it, Freddie. Now. You need a coupla bucks? I know things're tough down here."

Freddie looked up. "Yeah, man, tough. Yeah, little scratch be good."

McMurray dipped into his pocket and pulled out two twenties. He held them up as Freddie's eyes lit up. "Wait. You understand? Young Latina girl. Shot. We need info. Soon."

Freddie nodded, his eyes locked on the twenties. "Yeah. Got it."

McMurray gave him a long stare and then handed over the cash. The bills disappeared into Freddie's vest. He always wore a vest. He nodded and slunk back into the darkness of the alley.

The two detectives finally inhaled as they returned to the street.

"My dry cleaner'll be real happy about my clothes, Mac. Why don't you leave me on guard duty by the car next time you talk to Freddie?"

His partner snorted as they clambered in. They rolled down the windows.

"Freddie's connected to the street," McMurray mumbled as he lit one of the three cigarettes a day that he allowed himself. He was currently working on March 19, 2057, but this one was important just to help get rid of the *eau d'alley*. No arbiter would count this one against his daily quota.

For once, Cornice didn't bitch about the smoke.

He started the car and they continued to patrol the east side.

"Remind me to claim the forty," McMurray said. Cornice nodded. Before Perkins took over as Sheriff, trying to claim cash spent for informers and street info had been a difficult and somewhat humiliating process for officers. It involved filling out forms which were often challenged by bureaucrats who didn't understand the street. Perkins had quickly implemented a simple honor system with the reimbursement approved by the officer's superior. There had been no examples of abuse under the new method.

Jamal slid the car to a stop at a corner where two hookers in high platform shoes stood. They wore very short miniskirts and gauzy blouses that revealed far more than they concealed.

"Hey, baby. Whatcha need?"

"Hi, Jeannie. How ya doin?"

"J'mal? That you baby? Hey, I'm better now you here. This's my new partner, Adele. Adele, say hi to detective cutey and his partner, old fart."

Cornice burst out laughing as McMurray coughed.

"Hey, cutey. Hi, old fart."

Cornice laughed again. McMurray glowered at the ladies.

"Listen, Jeannie. We need your help. You ever run into a young Latina girl, early 20s, brown hair, pretty? Maybe she worked the street down around here?"

Jeannie shook her black hair that had magenta streaks in it. She shifted her hips and pursed her lips. "Nah, nothin. Not one of mine."

Cornice sighed in frustration. He started the car and went to shift gears when Adele suddenly raised her hand. "Claudia. I think."

"What?"

"I sorta remember her. Worked the street for a few weeks, then disappeared. Seemed like a nice kid. There were a coupla mean guys running her. Saw 'em whack her more'n once."

"Who was running her?"

Adele paused. She looked around nervously. "Don't know." She checked her surroundings again. "But I hear maybe Tiga Joe." She looked away from the two officers very quickly and shuffled her feet backwards.

"Never heard it from you. Not to worry. And hey, you, uh, ever need a friendly cop for something, you ask for me."

McMurray nodded. "Me too. Good on you both."

The ladies grinned broadly, pleased to have an IOU from the two cops. Someday they'd need to cash it in if the Vice squad got too nasty.

"Adele, where you at if we need to talk again?"

"Right here, sweetie. This my spot. With Jeannie."

"Got it. What about a home address? You know, just in case."

"Don't usually give that out, cutey, but I guess you're OK. The dirty red brick apartment at Glade and North Street. Second floor, back."

"OK. Stay safe, both of you."

Chapter 20

"TIGA JOE IS nothing but trouble," Cornice said to his partner as they sat at their desks in the bullpen. "Got hooked up with some Mexican cartel as a teenager. Ended up shooting to the top of the gang, shooting being the operative word. Mexican cops've got him for at least six murders of former colleagues, but the bodies were dismembered and torched. There were no witnesses. Or at least no witnesses who survived. Hard to prove anything in court without bodies or witnesses. But some of the low-level bangers who got caught for other things squealed to cut a better deal with the DA. ICE suspects he snuck into the country a few years ago. They think he's into drugs and human trafficking."

McMurray nodded as he worked his computer data bases and the FBI's National Crime Information Center (NCIC), which had vast amounts of information about crime and criminals. He focused on the "Gang File" and kept punching his keyboard. Finally he grunted in satisfaction.

"Got 'im. Tiga Joe. Heads a gang that operates in south and central Florida. Miami, Orlando, Tampa. Drugs. Prostitution. Immigration violations up the ying-yang…I guess they're smuggling people from Cuba and other desperate places into Florida. They pimp 'em out on the street or working on farms or sell 'em as sex slaves. Sex slaves! What are we dealing with here? They take most of the money these poor souls earn until they've paid off their 'transportation fee.' That happens about the 12th of never. Good luck paying it off, because they keep adding interest to the debt."

"Dirty people. Dirty business." McMurray shook his head.

"Yeah. Yeah, it is. Wouldn't you like to take them down? Ruthless pack of wolves. And Tiga Joe is without morals from what everybody says. Well, before they get shot, of course. Nasty, vicious man."

Silence in the detectives' bullpen. They were the only two in the office at that moment. They both stared into the walls.

"You figure The Vest Man and the two ladies are safe?"

"Hell, I don't know, Mac. Our drop-in to that street corner was hardly going to be kept a secret. In that neighborhood you gotta figure somebody's going to talk to somebody. On the other hand, Tiga Joe isn't headquartered here so maybe his network isn't as locked into the street." He shrugged.

Fred McMurray spun a cheap ballpoint on his desktop. "It's the drug stuff that started this for us, but it's the human trafficking that keeps me up at night. Who knows what he's doing to women and girls? Makes me sick."

Cornice waited. He knew his partner.

"And the latest murder, of course. Let's see what NCIC says." He two-fingered his keyboard for a while. "Not much else from what we had before. Pretty much a dead-end."

He slumped back in his wobbly desk chair. It creaked alarmingly. So did his wonky knee. "Guess it's time to go for a media release; see what we can stir up."

Chapter 21

"ARE YOUR SOURCES hearing anything?" Perkins demanded. "Because we are getting threats and social media is blowing up about some big explosive event in Port Manatee this weekend."

"Nothing. I asked this morning," Robertson replied. "We'll let you know if we hear anything. There has been a little social media buzz and some dark-net comments about the activity in your County. Some praise of the J-Men. We think it is just talk," the Regional FBI Director concluded.

"Well, I don't know if that's good or bad," muttered Perkins.

"Yeah. Stay safe, Perk."

Robertson hung up. Perkins glanced at Williams and shook his head. They each thought in silence for a moment.

"What if we went out and busted Jed? Charged him with something just to get him off the streets for a night or two?"

Perkins considered the idea. "Not sure, Willie. That might inflame his guys. Besides, what would you charge him with?"

"Being an asshole?"

A pained smile crossed the Sheriff's lips. "Yeah. Then we'd have to arrest Congress next." Williams snorted.

Contingency plans were quietly drawn up. The owners of possible targets were warned. Extra officers were seconded for duty Friday night. Emergency crews were put on alert.

Williams heard nothing from his CI.

A'ja and her team heard nothing but unconfirmed rumors from the street.

Perkins was trying to show calm leadership even while his insides churned. He delivered Rosie to Samantha's for the weekend. He remembered again that he needed to get a key to his house for Samantha so she could pick up Rosie anytime.

Friday morning was the final planning meeting. Perkins and City Manager Roy Crawford were in constant touch throughout the day. The extra patrol cars began to filter out at 6pm, providing a visible presence across the city.

Eight o'clock came. Nothing.

Nerves were jangling inside the Sheriff's department.

Nine. Still nothing.

A'ja Stokes was working all her sources. Social media was buzzing with rumors. Conspiracy theorists were having a field day. Williams tried his CI again. The call wasn't answered. Perkins talked to the FBI again.

Ten pm. All was quiet.

Nothing. Nothing. Nothing. Perkins wanted desperately to be on the street patrolling, but knew he had to stay in command at HQ.

Eleven. Local newscasts offered nothing but speculation and a certain relief that they were still transmitting. There was a palpable sense growing that maybe it had all just been a hoax. Tensions eased amongst Perkins' department heads.

"I guess if we're still good after midnight we'll start to let the extra officers go," Perkins told his Lieutenants. The bill for overtime would be a budget-breaker.

The clock ticked down. He was ready to pull the plug when Stokes looked up from her ever-present iPhone.

"Sheriff? I just got an odd email. It says, 'Enjoy the fireworks.'"

Perkins instinctively glanced at the clock. 11:59pm. Terrific.

"And here's a follow-up. 'Imagine what we could have done.'"

That's when the big booms started.

Chapter 22

"IT'S DELVECCHIO BRIDGE!" screamed one of the officers into his mobile radio as he hit the light bar and siren.

Delvecchio Bridge was a major traffic artery connecting the city. It loomed over a channel of the inland waterway system. It was a vital part of the city's infrastructure.

Emergency vehicles rushed to the site only to discover the bridge intact but a lovely fireworks display going off on the grounds surrounding the new Delvecchio Bridge Towers, the apartment complex that was in the finishing stages of construction.

The site had been vacant for years until unscrupulous developers had connected with a bribable Mayor and two corrupt city councillors. They were all still serving time in state prison.

Councillor Sonja Rodriguez had been elevated to Interim Mayor after the scandal, and then elected to her present position after a vicious race that had been decided by only 5 votes. The new city council had approved a magnificent two-tower development plan in a neighborhood that had been ignored and economically deprived for far too long.

The new developer, Elliott Webster, had designed an elegant complex that included main-floor retail, affordable housing, eight low-rent units for artists, and access to the beach and waterfront. The design also included an innovative children's playground.

Samantha Summers was the designer of that playground. She had been hired by Webster to coordinate with the construction crew about the playground, and to liaise with the neighborhood.

The project was in Kim's ward.

It had been the site of two previous bombings during early construction, but the Sheriff and his deputies had thwarted a third bomb, one that would have crushed the development, just moments before it was set to explode. The perpetrators, a love-struck college student trying to impress a pretty girl, and his dumb cousin, had been arrested.

This time it was radiant fireworks exploding into the night sky. The two apartment towers were outlined in a prism of colors.

Families, predominantly Black and Latino, were standing outside their homes when the first officers responded. Sleepy-eyed kids rubbed their faces and were thrilled by the surprise celebration. Their mothers were a lot grumpier but still eyed the soaring arcs of green, blue, red, yellow and white as they shot into the sky.

By the time most of the emergency vehicles arrived, the show was over. Perkins immediately went to find Mrs. Barkley, who was the alpha-mother in the neighborhood. Her children were clustered around her, wide-eyed at the unexpected evening entertainment.

When she saw the Sheriff, she shooed her kids inside and greeted him.

"We all tellin' our kids this was just a fun surprise." She stared hard at Perkins. "We both know it ain't. What's going on?"

You didn't try to fool Mrs. Barkley. She'd survived too tough and too long to get conned. Her kids didn't even try any more.

"I'm not completely sure, but we think this is a demonstration by the J-Men or some other alt-right group. We think it is related to the fire bombings earlier. We got a warning message at 11:59." He sighed unhappily. "Doesn't look as if anyone was injured or anything damaged." It was scant consolation for this disruption, which was obviously a warning of more serious action to come.

"Huh. Those clowns wanted more publicity. Some kind of threat. And this being a community of color, maybe that's why they went after us." Her eyes narrowed as she thought through the implications. "And, of course, Samantha designed the playground, so this will upset her and piss you off."

Not much got past Mrs. Barkley. She was a church-going lady, but sometimes some language that amplified a key thought slipped out.

"Yeah, that's what I figure. I just made the connection with Samantha. We first thought it was the actual bridge being attacked. I think these guys were just showing off, proving how invincible they are." He kicked at the dirt. "This is escalating.

We're not done with them. And I don't think they're done with this campaign of fear in our city."

Mrs. Barkley nodded calmly. "We'll reactivate our Neighborhood Watch program that we started last year after the bombings. You go out and get these monsters. Imagine if it had been real explosives here tonight!"

She shook her head and stomped into her house. Perkins shuddered at the very idea of explosives being used on this complex, just weeks before the official opening. It would have been tragic for the city and the neighborhood. Tens of millions of dollars in damage. And there would have been fatalities. A lot of fatalities.

He was walking towards the mobile command post when he spotted the mayor and Councillor Kim Sharpe striding towards him. Everybody wanted answers; he didn't have many of those yet.

CHAPTER 23

"THEY WERE DETONATED by remote control," reported Detective Sanchez. "Just like a Fourth of July party beside a lake. You don't have to be very close to start the sequence of the fireworks. It doesn't take a long time to set up if you know what you're doing. And the show...sorry, the incident...didn't last all that long."

"Where did they get the fireworks?"

"Key question, Captain Williams. We have detectives talking to retailers who sell fireworks. Unfortunately, you can also order them on-line. We're checking with big suppliers. We just hope they weren't flown in by drone or something."

The Saturday morning department heads meeting was an 'all hands-on deck' effort by Perkins to follow any clues immediately and not waste any time. The FBI was assisting by scouring the construction location and doing surveillance of known white supremacist on-line sites.

Elliott Webster, the developer of the multi-million-dollar project, was cooperating completely. He was also angry at— well, everybody. He had snarled at the mayor and Kim. He had snapped at the Sheriff. He had growled imprecations at pretty much everybody else.

He had been nothing but polite to Mrs. Barkley, of course, because Elliott Webster was a smart man who liked his body parts just where they were already arranged. He didn't want an ass-kicking from the formidable lady who ran the neighborhood.

Perkins, also being a smart man, had called Samantha early that morning and told her to get that cute butt of hers down to the Delvecchio Bridge project, bring some coffee and donuts for everybody, and calm Webster down. He even played the ultimate card—bring Rosie the Wonder Dog. Even Webster couldn't ignore the joyous slurping and tonguing that Rosie brought to her friends.

Samantha had a special ability to soothe, enchant and win over most men between 14 and 94. Between her spectacular burnished-gold hair, her svelte figure and her natural charm, very few men could resist her.

Somewhat surprisingly, most women liked her as well.

Perkins sort of hated to drag her into this mess, but on the other hand, it was his ass on the line.

She was on-site now. He was heading over there after the meeting finished.

"It does take some training and knowledge to set up and ignite a big fireworks display," noted Lt. Stokes. "We are tracing any connections to the J-Men leadership. We don't know everyone in their gang, but our speculation is that it was likely Jim Crandall, the army vet, who did the job." She paused. "Presuming it is them, of course."

"I still can't figure out why this escalating pattern," said a veteran Lieutenant.

Stokes squirmed a bit. "You won't like this answer, sir," she began slowly, "but the Intel Unit suspects that they are just pushing our faces in the mud. This is some sort of macho, see-how-tough-we-are thing. Anytime they can embarrass law enforcement or government leaders, they win. It is their way of showing, first, how corrupt they believe the system has become and, second, how their concept of personal freedom is winning in American society today. It isn't, but that's how they delude themselves in this battle."

An angry silence met her comments. Perkins let it fester for a minute and then stepped in. "OK, we've been told. This makes it personal for our department. Except remember that it isn't personal for us, it is the Sheriff's department protecting and serving the public." He paused a moment. "It'll be personal when we can string these jokers up by their boots and have a nice, polite conversation about their anti-social attitudes."

Reluctant grins appeared around the conference table as that image developed. The mood changed, which is what Perkins had known he had to do.

"Let's do our jobs. Coordinate intel with A'Ja. Everybody else, speak to your contacts out there. Somebody has got to be talking or bragging or getting drunk and whispering. These J-Men are not the smartest Oreos in the bag. That's it."

With that he poured another cup of coffee and chewed two Tylenol for dessert before heading outside to the site.

Chapter 24

H E STOPPED FOR a moment to watch Samantha in action. She was wearing a pretty ivory sun dress with colorful turquoise and gold swirls on it, low-heeled strappy sandals and a pert little sun hat. She had Webster by one arm. Rosie was frolicking with some neighborhood kids as several mothers watched with approval. Webster's clean-up crew had just finished picking up the debris on the site after the FBI had cleared it.

Media were swarming. The timing of the fireworks last night at midnight meant that none of the local media had footage of the actual event, so they were now desperately trying to get eyewitnesses to re-create the midnight scene. Their filmed interviews offered a widely varied view of the truth of what had really occurred. Of course, truth was not the reporter's primary objective. An exciting recounting of the skies exploding and the threats to the community was much more entertaining for viewers. And for generating high ratings.

Several area residents, and a couple of people who lived fifteen miles away and had in all honesty seen nothing but were media hounds always looking for camera time, were commenting to various media outlets.

His Public Information Officer was answering questions. The PIO was a media-savvy veteran who did her best to keep Perkins off-camera. This was a private arrangement between the two of them.

Perkins joined Samantha and Elliott Webster, who looked considerably calmer than he had been a few hours before when he had been rousted out of bed and summoned to the site.

Rosie saw him and barked hello, but she was happily playing with the kids. Samantha looked up and smiled at him. She admired his lanky figure in the tight tan-colored uniform. She kept a grip on Webster's arm and finished what she was saying. Only then did she drop his arm and turn towards Perkins.

"Hi." Even that was enough to send little frissons of excitement through his body. She smiled as she spoke. He had a sudden urge to grab her, squeeze her, kiss her passionately and then—

"Hey, Perk." Webster's hello broke the lascivious thoughts pouring through Perkins' man-brain.

"Elliott. How ya' doing?"

"Better now, I guess. Samantha has been a big help. She pulled me down from the ceiling." He shook his head and looked around. "At least there's no damage to the buildings." They all paused to admire the soaring twin towers and the elegant new streetscape.

"I just can't figure out why somebody keeps running at us. Everybody loves this project. The neighborhood is fantastic about supporting us. What the hell?"

"Yeah. Well, I just had a meeting with my brain trust. We're getting into this thing deep and fast. I'll keep you informed."

Webster nodded. Rosie had appeared and nudged his leg. He bent down to pat her. Samantha made a quick nod to Perkins over his head. He nodded back. Rosie then bounded over to Perkins for a head-scratch. He obliged. "We're going to do more patrols here, just to be extra careful," he told Webster. "The neighborhood is going to resume its watch programs at night."

"Yeah, that's all nice, but the fact is somebody infiltrated our project, set up a bunch of fireworks, and then detonated them. Sparks could have ignited building materials. Somebody could have been on the site. Something could have misfired or exploded. Or worse, they could have used real explosives." He was getting worked up again. Samantha stepped over to take his arm. "I bet my company's future on this project. It's the biggest thing we've ever built. If it goes under…" His voice trailed off. Samantha squeezed his shoulder.

"We won't let that happen," Perkins said firmly. "No way. Besides, if anything happened to her playground, Samantha would slaughter me."

That drew a laugh from Samantha and a wry smile from Webster. "Yeah, that would happen. For sure." He looked at the Sheriff in a steady gaze. "If that's my guarantee from you, then I guess it's a good one."

With that he turned to check his clean-up crew on the site and the soaring towers. "Man, she's a beauty," he breathed a moment later. Samantha blushed a bit. Then she realized he was talking about his apartment towers.

Perkins grinned at her.

CHAPTER 25

"WHOOOEEE! THAT WAS some kinda fun las' night!"
The beer that Jethro was holding was not his first.
The Ugly Porker was crammed, but the leaders of the J-Men
were at their usual corner of the property. The spreading oak
tree offered dignity and beauty. The assembled J-Men offered
neither.

They were celebrating the previous night's fireworks and
the subsequent failure of law enforcement to do anything to
stop them.

"Yuh did a helluva job," Jed said to Jim Crandall. It had been
a simple job for the Army vet.

Crandall nodded. He swallowed more beer. It wasn't like
patrols in Helmand Province in Afghanistan, but at least it cut
the boredom of life in central Florida—and nobody was shooting back at him.

He clinked cans with Jeb and Jack. He did a security check
around the sprawling barbecue yard. It was a reflex from his
tours of duty that soldiers never quite lost.

He scrutinized the few tourists who had found the place.
Some local families out for Saturday lunch. One brown-haired
man sitting by himself, eating pulled pork. Some ladies in the
corner near them. All the tables were taken. A few anxious
groups waited impatiently in the yard to be seated and served.

Pit-master Jud began to chop up more blackened butt for
the pulled pork sandwiches. The bark was dark and lustrous.
Afficionados fought to get pieces of the crust that had so much
seasoning, smoke and flavor.

Staff scurried around with trays of cold beer and soft drinks.
It all looked secure. Crandall relaxed a bit.

Jacob Pew leaned over to the big former Ranger. The survivalist smirked at the beer-drinking group of J-Men. "Not
exactly the leaders of a revolution, are they?"

Crandall grunted, "Yeah." He wasn't a man of many words.

Jed hollered for another round of Buds. Jeb sat back and punched Jethro in the arm. "Big night, big man, big night. We've got 'em all confused and scared. Even that damn Sheriff is runnin' round, shaky and trembling. Great night for us!"

Jed leaned back in his shaky lawn chair. "Yeah, man. They don't know what we're gonna do next. We pretty much own this town." He laughed coarsely and finished his can. He crushed it and threw it on the lawn. Jethro laughed with him, drank the dregs of his can and then crushed the empty on his forehead. He didn't even blink at the impact.

Boone popped another cold one. "Man," he said admiringly, "that is one good-lookin' piece of ass that Sheriff's got. She was wearin' this little summer dress this morning..." He sighed in appreciation.

It took Crandall a minute. "Hey. Wait. Where'd you see that broad?"

"Jethro 'n me had a little drive-by this morning. Boy, lots of people. Dozens of cops runnin' 'round. It was great! And this fab-lookin' red-head with legs all the way up to her ass! Man, I'd like me a piece of that!" He looked at Jethro and they exchanged coarse smirks.

"Are you telling me you were so stupid as to drive by the site where we did the explosions last night?" Crandall's voice had gotten cold. Quiet came over their little corner of the yard as the J-Men shut up at his tone.

"Aw, nothin' happened. We just had a little look at the scrambling goin' on. It was fun. No biggie."

Jim Crandall paused before he stood slowly and said quietly, "Stupid. You never return to the scene of the...well, whatever last night was. What if the cops were filming all the cars this morning, just in case somebody involved was dumb enough to return? What if somebody recognized you or man-mountain here," he said, pointing at Jethro. "He's sorta hard to miss."

"Oh. Well, yeah, maybe. But nothing happened."

Crandall gave him a flinty stare for a long minute. "Yeah." He got up, left his beer unfinished, and headed for his truck.

The remainder of the J-Men looked at each other. Finally Jed laughed shakily and swallowed some beer. "Touchy, isn't he? Well, more barbecue for us."

The group regrouped. A platter of ribs arrived, with sides and more beer. Conversation was subdued.

CHAPTER 26

PERKINS WOKE SUNDAY morning to Florida sunshine bursting through Samantha's bedroom window. He was alone in the king-sized bed. He groaned a bit as he stretched arms, legs, back. A combination of the two bullet holes in his body, exhaustion and—much to his dismay—just getting older, sometimes made mornings torturous.

He finally rolled over and looked at the clock. Shocked, he looked again. 9:05? That couldn't be right. He usually existed on five or six hours sleep on a good night. Some nights it was two or three as he tossed and turned. But this was what, over ten hours?

He hit the head for a badly needed few minutes, washed his face with cold water, dug the grit out of his left eye, and cleaned up as best he could. He looked into the mirror; it was not a pretty sight. He groaned, did his best to comb his hair, and wandered into the rest of the penthouse condo that Samantha owned at Sapphire Blue. She was sitting quietly on the lanai, sipping coffee and reading the Sunday paper. Rosie was lying beside her.

"Morning."

Samantha looked up. "Well, good morning to you. How are you?"

"Did I really sleep for ten hours?"

"Yes. You were exhausted by the time we got home last night and had dinner. I thought it was more important to let you sleep in. You needed it. Coffee?"

"Lord yes."

She got up to pour him a cup as he sagged into a patio chair. Rosie came over for a good morning hello slurp. He patted her for a moment. Samantha returned and handed him a large mug. He tasted the Blue Mountain blend gratefully. "Ah. Good. Thank you."

She tucked one long, graceful leg under her as she returned to the two-seat patio couch. She eyed him over her own mug.

"You look better. Last night you were a wreck. You slept like a log."

"Yeah. Guess so. I was tired."

"Well, you've been working sixteen-hour days for a week or more. What do you expect? Of course you're exhausted. And I know you don't sleep very well."

He sipped again. The caffeine was beginning to jolt his weary brain back to life.

"I guess I should check in."

"Why? If they really need you, they will call you or text you. What you really need to do is go have a nice hot shower. I'll make brunch. Then you're going to go down to the pool, lie down for a while, have a swim, enjoy the hot tub, and drink a couple of cold beers. Then we're going to give Rosie to Kim to look after for a couple of hours and you are going to bring me back here, sweep me off my feet, slowly undress me and then ravish me." She stared at him. "Anything in there you don't understand, cowboy?"

"Uh, no, ma'am. It all seems pretty clear to me." With that he swallowed the dregs of his coffee and enthusiastically headed for the big shower stall.

Half an hour later he was gorging on fruit salad, country sausages, scrambled eggs, whole grain toast, strawberry preserves bought at the farmer's market, and a final large mug of coffee.

Samantha monitored his calorie intake carefully. "Eat hearty," she told him. "You're going to need your strength later." She licked her lower lip slowly and sensually.

Perkins smiled at his lover. "Yes. Yes I am." He finished his final swallow and peeked at her. "Ah, the order of that agenda you outlined...any chance of moving a couple of items up?"

"No. Now go and walk the baby so she'll be quiet while we're at the pool. I'll clean up here."

Rosie seemed to understand the program and was waiting impatiently at the door. Perkins leashed her and they spent almost an hour walking the condo grounds and the sidewalk outside.

They returned to find Samantha dressed in a green two-piece, a gauzy cover-up and a large sun hat. A big bag of towels, sun block, snacks and other requirements for an afternoon at the pool waited in the kitchen.

"Grab the cooler, will you? Rosie, here's a cookie for you. You be a good girl. We'll be back soon."

Rosie promptly went into her wounded puppy act. She was being abandoned. She would live out the rest of her days alone, dejected, and rejected. She scrunched on the floor and whined.

"Go change," Samantha told Perkins. "I'll handle this."

He went into their bedroom and slipped into his baggy yellow trunks and grabbed an exquisitely worn T-shirt that he loved and which Samantha thought should have been thrown away several years ago. She had remarked tersely, "It is more holey than righteous." Perkins had blithely ignored her fashion advice.

He stuck his feet into size 12 flip-flops and headed back to the kitchen.

Rosie hadn't relinquished her role as a poor puppy being marooned on an island of despair. Samantha had tried cookies, patting and conversation. Perkins tried another tactic. "Stay. Behave yourself."

With that he grabbed the beer cooler with one hand, Samantha with the other, and headed down the corridor to the elevator. Rosie retreated to the shady corner of the lanai to have a nap and get ready for her performance when Mommy and Daddy returned. She was pretty sure she could guilt them into a new bone. Besides, she was tired after the long walk. A nice nap would be pleasant.

Perkins could feel the tension and stress slowly leaving his brain and body. Kim and Roy joined them at their pool-side table. He updated them on the progress of the Delvecchio Bridge investigation. He had snuck in one call to the office while Samantha was using the bathroom. There wasn't much new to report.

The pool was great, the hot tub soothing, the screaming of the kids was at a tolerable decibel level. The Wives were bickering amongst themselves, so they left Samantha's group alone. The afternoon sun was warm without being scorching.

"Can you take Rosie for a walk and some playtime? Perk and I have something we have to do at 4 o'clock," Samantha asked Kim.

"Sure. We'll keep her at my place. Why don't you join us for dinner? 6-ish?"

"Great. What are you ordering?" The idea of Kim cooking dinner was no longer a plausible concept. Samira and Samantha had learned that for all the skills Kim had, and they were many, cooking was not one. It had been a hard lesson. The taste of her kumquat, limburger and sausage casserole still lingered.

"Pizza? One meat lovers, thin crust? One Canadian, extra bacon?" Roy nodded approvingly.

"Perfect."

The four of them assembled the pool detritus and headed up to Samantha's condo. Rosie was delighted to go visiting with Kim, who was always an easy touch for snacks.

Perkins shut the door, turned, and eyed Samantha. "I think you're over-dressed for our meeting." With that he took her hand and pulled her into the master bedroom. The late afternoon sun set everything glowing.

He slowly slipped off her gauzy green cover-up. The rest of her bikini didn't take long to remove. He gently pushed her onto the bed and gazed at her with devotion and admiration. She smiled back.

An hour later, they were both still smiling.

They were a few minutes late getting to Kim's because the shower they shared led to some more fun and games. Nobody said anything as they sat down and reached for the pizza boxes on the dining room table. Perkins drank most of his favorite IPA before sampling his first slice.

"A little dehydrated?" asked Kim with a coy smile. Samantha laughed out loud.

Perkins blushed and went looking for another slice of the pepperoni, mushroom and Canadian bacon pizza. Rosie got a nice little dividend.

CHAPTER 27

"IT WAS THEM. The J-Men. I overheard some of the dumb ones at The Ugly Porker squealing and laughing about the fireworks."

Captain Williams listened and made notes as his CI spoke softly into the phone.

"I'd be careful about this Crandall character. The tough ex-Army guy. I'm betting he did the wiring for the explosives. He stormed out halfway through their boozy lunch. I don't know what that was all about, but knowing Jed and Jethro, I'd bet on them doing something stupid."

Williams made more notes and doodled a couple of question marks over the flow chart that he was trying to develop on the group of weirdoes.

"They were also whooping about some red-headed beauty they saw at the site. I don't know who that might be, but they were excited about her."

Williams' pencil snapped as he suddenly tightened his grip. It could only be Samantha Summers, the Sheriff's girlfriend. Perkins was not going to be happy to hear about that.

"Huh. Yeah, I think I know who that would be. So, these clowns actually did a drive-by the morning after?"

"Yeah."

"Wow. Dumb and dumber. OK, anything else? This is good stuff."

"No. I need some more money."

"No problem. I'll leave it in the usual spot tonight."

The CI hung up. Williams slowly replaced his phone and looked at his notes. He called in A'ja and they reviewed the phone conversation. "Did we shoot the lookie-loos?"

"Yes, sir. We have pictures of most of the cars that drove by."

An hour later, they were sitting in Perkins' office. "We are now certain that the culprits were this J-Men group. My CI overheard them celebrating. Our surveillance team has a picture of Jed's truck driving by the site the next morning. It seems conclusive that they were responsible."

Perkins looked at them. There was a long pause. "OK, do we charge them now? And with what?"

Silence. Finally, Williams shifted in his chair. It creaked in protest. "Well, sir, that's the thing." He licked his lips and swallowed a bit of water. "We aren't really sure that charges are warranted."

Perkins stared at his two officers.

"Oh, we are certain they're responsible. The problem is, for what? We haven't talked to the DA yet, but let's face it, a bunch of people had a little parade down a city street and a garbage can got turned over. A window got smashed. The other night, some fireworks got set off. No permit, agreed. Trespassing on private property, certainly. Malicious damage at best. But do we risk getting laughed out of court with, well, let's face it, pretty minor stuff?"

Perkins impatiently shuffled his pen, stared at the ceiling, drummed his fingers and then glared at the two.

"You suggesting they just walk on all of this? The community will spit on us."

"Yeah. Prob'ly will. But what's worse, get thrown out of a courtroom or give them a little more rope?"

"Sheriff." Lt. Stokes interjected for the first time. "I took some courses at university about these kinds of groups. They tend to escalate their activities. There will most likely be a larger, potentially more violent, confrontation. Our analysis is that they are far from done. If we try to move on these minor charges, there's a risk we just accelerate their plans or drive them underground to plot whatever they can concoct before we can trap and charge their entire leadership. At least this way we have eyes on them, and a CI inside."

Perkins didn't say anything as he absorbed that. "But you're saying they are not done. There will be bigger protests? More violence?"

"Yes, I think that is certain."

"If we don't move now, we endanger the community to some greater hazard in the future?"

A'ja shifted uncomfortably in her chair. "There is that possibility, yes." Assessing risk was easier in the classroom than in real life, she was discovering.

"And if the community ever finds out we didn't stop these clowns early, and something bigger happens, or god forbid somebody gets badly injured, or, help me lord, killed, they'll run us all out of town." He paused and scanned the ceiling again, looking for answers. The ceiling declined to provide any. "So, we're screwed either way?"

A'ja didn't say anything so Williams stepped up. "That's about the size of it, Sheriff. We can increase surveillance. We can monitor social media more closely."

Perkins ran his hand through his hair. God, if this kept up, he wouldn't have any hair left, only ulcers and residual anger. Samantha would dump him then. He'd end up alone and friendless. Rosie would probably vote to live with Samantha because she had great hair and smelled a lot better. Nobody loved him. His life was ruined.

"Well, hell."

Both his officers nodded in sympathy.

Williams finally broke the silence. "One more thing. You should know this. These yahoos apparently saw Samantha at the Delvecchio Bridge Towers the other morning. They spoke, uh, admiringly of her."

Perkins stiffened. He spoke slowly and softly. "Are you saying that she is in danger?"

"We don't believe so. There have been no threats of violence or suggestions of danger towards her. But she did come up in their talk. I thought it was the right thing to do to make sure you were aware of that," Williams said flatly.

"OK." Perkins was visibly trying to get himself under control. "You're right. Thanks. I'll have a word with her." He swallowed hard and pressed his fingers into his desk. "Anything else?"

"Not at this time. We'll keep you informed. And it might be worth talking to the DA about potential charges. Maybe he can come up with something to get them off the street for a while."

Perkins nodded curtly. His mind was already leaping ahead to what was going to be a very uncomfortable conversation with the volatile redhead in his life.

<h1 style="text-align:center">Chapter 28</h1>

"SO, MY NAME came up in their conversation?"

"Apparently, yeah."

"Well, shoot." Samantha was quiet for a moment and then brightened. "Hey, why don't you just do that?"

"What?"

"Shoot them."

Perkins sighed heavily. "I can't do that. The law sort of frowns on that."

"Oh pooh." Samantha waved her hands dismissively. "You can figure out some way to do it."

"Uh, no, honey, I really can't."

"Huh. Well, I'm going to have to find a boyfriend who isn't so squeamish about doing little things like that for me."

Perkins blinked thrice and swallowed hard. "Again, we don't think there is any danger to you. This was beer talk from some right-wing nut cakes. I'm just saying, like always, be alert. Be aware of your surroundings. If you have doubts about somebody or some situation, just get out. And remember your self-defense instructions."

Samantha perked up at that. "I'm glad you made me take those classes. I've gotten pretty good at defending myself. My go-to move is stomp the stiletto on his foot and then a knee to the groin."

Perkins felt his scrotum shrivel at the thought, but he tried hard to be encouraging. "Good. Very good. Remember that. And your car keys are a good weapon. Just be smart out there. Check your back seat before you get in the car. Don't go into unfamiliar places without somebody. Take Rosie if you want, although she's more likely to lick somebody to death."

Hearing her name, Rosie raised her head and woofed congenially.

"I've got to get you that key to my house so you can pick her up if you ever need her. The point is, just be alert. Be defensive out there. Stay aware of your surroundings. Don't take chances."

Samantha studied him. "You really are concerned, aren't you?"

"I genuinely don't think there is any immediate danger to you. My team thinks these are just beer-drinking yappers. But, there have been these two incidents. There is a possibility of others. They might get larger. We don't know. But I wanted you to be aware of these people."

With that he opened a folder and shook out seven photographs of the known J-Men. He went over each one.

"This Jedediah is the preacher. He is slimy…"

Perkins concluded his summation of the grubby group ten minutes later. "Now you've seen them. The ones to really watch out for are Jed and his big pal Jethro." He pointed to their two pictures again.

Samantha kept looking at the rogue's gallery. Finally she looked up. "OK. I've got it. The uglies are imprinted on my brain." Her eyes narrowed. "Say, these are the same clowns who might blow up Delvecchio Bridge and my children's playground, right?"

"Yeah."

"Well, then they had better be looking out for me! Imagine! Hurting my poor kids in that neighborhood! I'll poke their ugly little eyes out!"

Perkins moaned. "No. No, absolutely not. Do not confront them. Listen to me: Do. Not."

Samantha snorted. "Right. Well, if you won't shoot them for me, and really, Perk, have I ever asked you for anything before?"

"Uh…" he stuttered as the long list flashed before his eyes. Unusually for him when personal relationships were involved, his brain intervened before his mouth could speak.

"Of course I haven't," she continued with relish. "Anyway, you'll have to live with that. But I'm going to…to…well, never mind, I'll figure something out."

With that she leaned forward, grabbed her wine glass and drank the final inch of the very nice California white.

Perkins sagged into his chair. What on earth had he unwrapped? How would the city survive two opposing forces like this? And somehow, he was in the middle, and there seemed to be a growing likelihood that he was going to get his ass shot off by one or both sides.

Some days life is just crappy.

CHAPTER 29

THE SHOOTING RANGE faced a hill whose dreams of becoming a mountain had withered a long time ago. The range was on a dingy piece of scrub land ten miles out of town. There was a gate with a card-control lock system so members could come and go when they wanted. There was a small shack that sold soft drinks, ammo and day-memberships when somebody was around to man the booth.

There were targets at 25, 50, 100, 200 and 300 yards. The hill started to rise about half a mile from the shack, so a few of the club members wanting to stretch out their big rifles could use their scopes to pick out rocks and clumps of scraggily vegetation on the lower slopes of the hill. Any wildlife that had once existed in the desolate landscape had long since fled, even the snakes.

Both pistols and long guns were being fired. The range usually wasn't very busy. In fact, the five J-Men had the place to themselves. There was intermittent firing interspersed with a lot of ribald commentary on the shooter, his gun, his aim and his manhood.

A cooler of beer sat in the back of Jethro's truck. It only got opened after the shooting stopped and the guns were put away. They were scrupulous about that.

The boys clustered together in the steamy late afternoon Florida sun.

"So, what's next for us?" Jack O'Hara demanded as he popped a top. He was perspiring in his Confederate army gray jacket and felt hat. He had taken off his sword while shooting.

"Workin' on somethin'," Jed winked. "Somethin' big." He grinned sloppily as he swallowed a cold Miller Lite.

"We sure kicked some ass th'other night!" Jeb whooped. He was still excited after the explosion of the fireworks. "That Sheriff don't know which end is up!"

"You are right, my brother! We are kickin' ass all over town!" Jed was getting more pumped every time he thought about it.

"What about Jimmy Crandall?"

The question sobered the group for a minute. He was now acknowledged as the group's military and tactical expert. Nobody had seen him since he'd stormed out of the lunch at The Ugly Porker three days prior.

"Ah, no big deal," Jed assured those assembled. "I'll go see him, make sure he's OK. Maybe take him to the Bonga Bonga Room."

"Hey, that's a good idea. Let's go now. I hear they've got a new dancer, some brunette with big boobs."

That met with the favor of the group. They finished their beers, tossed the empties in the direction of the overflowing rusted oil drum masquerading as a garbage can, and headed back into town.

Curiously, the flashing neon sign outside the Bonga Bonga Room indicated it was a club for gentlemen. The evidence from looking at the sweating, swearing and horny audience inside indicated that there was, in fact, a considerable absence of gentlemen in attendance.

There was, however, a brunette with big boobs dancing around the pole. She got a lot of tips from the J-Men. Jed became a substantial donor to her retirement fund. He really liked big tits. She really liked big tips. It was a relationship that worked out nicely for both.

CHAPTER 30

DETECTIVE MCMURRAY STAGGERED a bit as he pushed himself up from the low chair. The sheriff happened to be walking by the bullpen.

"Hey, Fred. How you doing?"

"Fine, sir, thank you. Just doodling on the murder."

"Uh huh. What's happening with your knee?"

"Last doc said it should be replaced. Our health insurer denied me for some reason. I'll just tough it out, I guess."

"Yeah. Weren't you in the navy for a hitch?"

"Long time ago. Reserves."

"Ever tried the VA Hospital?"

"Once. The bureaucracy beat me."

"Uh huh." Perkins strode out. In his office a moment later, he called Samira Al-Saadi on her private line. "I've never asked you for a favor, but I've got a detective, a good guy, had a brief time in the Naval Reserve, got knee problems. It's affecting his work. It's getting dangerous for his partner, although neither will admit that. If he doesn't get it fixed, I'm going to have to do something I won't like. Could you see him?"

"Hang on. Hmmm. Just had a cancellation. Wednesday at 7:45am."

"You are the best. Thank you. I owe you one."

"That's what friends do. You owe me nothing. But I am Persian. I will remember," she laughed as she hung up.

Perkins scribbled the details on a piece of paper and returned to the bullpen. He folded the paper and slipped it to McMurray. "Don't be late."

Chapter 31

"C'MON, JIMMY. WE need you."

Jed was hung-over. That was a not-unusual state of affairs. Beulah had commented on that. Several times.

He slurped some of the coffee the waitress at Aunt Betty's Breakfast Bar had just poured. Damn. He gulped some ice water to ease the burning.

Crandall looked at him with distaste. He poked at his bacon, eggs over easy and whole grain toast. The eggs weren't just over easy; with a little CPR they might have regained their original oval shape in the shell.

He gnawed on one slice of the toast, ate the bacon strips with his fingers, and then pushed the plate away. He drank some of his cooled coffee. He looked hard into the blood-shot eyes of the alleged leader of the J-Men. "Why?"

"What?"

"Why do you need me? For what? Just what are you planning for this rather amateur group you've got around you?"

"Aw, Jimmy, that ain't nice. The boys are good. And they all respect you, man. You are, like, our expert on warfare."

Crandall snorted his disdain. "You clowns think this is a war? You don't have a freakin' clue." He swallowed the rest of his coffee and started shuffling his feet, the way people do just before they get up from a booth in a diner.

"Yeah. Maybe. Anyway, I'm thinkin' 'bout a big show. Somethin' to really scare the shit outta this town. Show 'em who's the boss around here."

Crandall paused for a moment. "Yeah?" There was disbelief in his voice.

He'd known Jed Boone for a bunch of years. And there was one trait that had not changed in those nearly twenty-five years: Jed Boone was a liar. He was an expert liar. He was a dedicated liar. He was as experienced and committed a liar as a witness at a Senate confirmation hearing. He was a liar who just might be a first-ballot nominee to make it into the Liar's Hall of Fame.

And Boone would never admit lying. That made it hard for anybody to figure out just what he was actually doing about anything. The trail of bodies who had believed him once, only to be betrayed, had started with kids in public school, girls in high school, then veered into his college days and his shot-gun marriage, then through his business career, and now as the supposed leader of this alt-right group of clods.

Crandall had gotten involved with them just because he was bored out of his gourd. Beulah had kicked him out of her house for the day more than once because he would just sit around, drink beer, watch some cable TV news show, and bitch about the world.

He missed the action he'd experienced in the Army. He'd been promoted a couple of times to Sergeant before he got wounded. He liked his platoon, he liked the shooting, he liked defending his country.

He hated the dumb politicians who'd gotten them into this mess and then bailed. He hated the Taliban and how they fought and how they abused women. He wasn't all that thrilled with the Army hierarchy and chain of command, and that attitude had got him busted down to Corporal on a couple of occasions. But his skills at that hit-and-run style of warfare had been undeniable, even to brain-dead Lieutenants, so he kept getting promoted.

He cared about his platoon and the men under him. He protected them. There was nothing like being shot at by a bunch of bearded fanatics wearing dirty turbans and brandishing AR-15s to bring a group of guys together.

He supposed he was seeking some kind of tribal community when he'd hooked up with these J-idiots. Beulah had said that. She also told him that it would end badly, because she had gone to the same high school as Jed. Even if she'd been a couple of years ahead of him, she knew all about him. And didn't like him at all. The whole lying thing. Pree-var-i-caatoor, she called him. And not in a nice way.

Jim Crandall stared deep into the runny whites and smeared yellows of the eggs on the plate.

"OK. Here's the deal. If I stay in, I'm taking over control of operations. I plan 'em, I execute 'em. The guys do what I say. First time anybody squawks, I'm outta there."

Boone paled, although with his pasty morning complexion it was hard to tell. "But...but...I'm in charge. I started this militia."

"Militia. Right." Crandall shrugged. "You can still call your-self the leader. I don't do the whole political and media bullshit anyway. But I get to oversee the operations. Because frankly you guys don't know what the hell you are doing, and the Sheriff and that big Captain are going to stuff it down your throats one of these days. I don't want to be part of that. So that's the deal. Take it or leave it, I don't really care."

With that he pivoted out of the bench seat and stood up. Boone suddenly grabbed his wrist. "OK, OK. We can do this together. I trust you. It'll be good."

Crandall looked at the hand on his wrist until Jed jerked it away.

He stood there for a long moment, thinking. On the one hand it might be fun to shake up this city and its boring political leaders. On the other hand was the whole lying thing. You couldn't trust a word that came out of Boone's mouth.

Crandall finally looked fiercely at the other man. He was sweating out the cheap bourbon from last night at the Bonga Bonga Club. It was not a pretty sight. Or smell.

"Just remember. I'm now running the ops. You don't com-mit to anything without my say-so. First time you screw me, I'm gone. And I'll hurt you."

Boone paled even more, if that was possible. His hand shook as he gulped some water. He nodded and looked away.

Crandall paused for a moment. "Remember to tip the nice lady," he snickered as he pushed away his breakfast plate. He strode out the door of the diner. Boone remained in the booth, limp.

The nice lady brought the bill for breakfast.

Boone tipped Edith big.

CHAPTER 32

BEULAH TREMAINE WAS lean, tanned and hard. You don't work in the fields in Florida's sun and humidity and have any excess flesh left on your body.

She had inherited the farm from her pappy, who had inherited it from his pappy, whose pappy had started the whole thing. She loved this piece of property which was just inside the city limits of the now-sprawling Port Manatee. More than one developer had tried to beat her out of the land and use it for another cookie-cutter suburban housing development.

She had sent all of them packing. This was her life. She made a decent, honest living by growing her corn and beans and watermelons. She grew and harvested fine-quality produce and had regular customers who went back to her gran-pappy's day.

Jim Crandall was a new addition to her life. It had taken some adjustment on both their parts when they first hooked up. It had come as a surprise to her, and even more so to her closest girlfriends, who had given up in despair at ever getting their tough friend married off—or at least into a satisfying relationship.

They had met on a Saturday night at the Broken Boot, a C&W bar with a mediocre house band, a great bar and a sawdust dance floor. Crandall had been sitting by himself at the bar, watching the action, sipping some Bud. She had spotted him early in the evening. There was an attraction. She didn't know why.

Their eyes had locked a couple of times. He hadn't made a move. At 11pm she finally gave up and marched over to him. "Hey. Cowboy. Stop staring at me and ask me to dance."

With that she'd grabbed his hand and pulled him onto the dance floor. It happened to be a line dance. He turned out to be the worst line-dancer in the history of line dancing. She finally took pity on him and swung him off the floor and back to the bar where they both caught their breath and really looked at one another.

"You're a terrible dancer."

"Yeah. Want a beer?"

"Yeah. Want to come home and screw me silly?"

"Yeah. Oh, I'm Jim, by the way. What's your name?"

It hadn't been her finest social etiquette moment, she had admitted to her two bemused girl friends on Monday. Still, they hadn't spent much time out of her bed for the rest of that weekend except to eat and keep hydrated and feed the dogs.

Monday morning she'd asked him if he wanted to stay at her place for a while.

He'd said, "Well, yeah."

And that had been that. They'd been together for almost a year. They both had their moments, but it was usually OK.

Her girlfriends were thrilled for her and approved of him.

He didn't have any close friends or need anyone's approval.

She had coaxed a few details about his Army career out of him, but like many veterans he didn't talk much about his war. She respected that. Besides, it meant she could talk more about the always fascinating subject of beans and watermelon and renovating the second bathroom. She was an HGTV devotee.

Right now, she was sitting at the scarred wooden kitchen table in the farmhouse that had housed her family for more than a century. Her face was still dusty from the day she'd spent in the fields. She hadn't had time to wash up because she had opened a letter from the city that had been in her mailbox.

She sat there re-reading it. Her taxes were going to go up *how much?*

That's where Jim Crandall found her when he got back.

"The damn city is raising my taxes by 28%! Something about a reassessment and a new valuation of the land. I mean, I'm doing alright, but I can't afford this!"

Crandall reached for the letter that had fluttered to the table. Yup, 28%. Ouch.

He re-read the letter. On city hall letterhead. Signed by the mayor and the city manager.

He peered over at Beulah. She was alternating between wanting to cry and wanting to swear.

Taxes. He thought that taxes in the United States of America were too much. Too high. Too onerous. Every level of government charges a bunch of taxes on everything from airplane tickets to cigarettes to funerals to your house.

Federal. State. City. County. Rural. Sales. Income. Excise. Capital gains. Didn't much matter, the greedy bastards always have their hands out.

He patted Beulah on the shoulder as he went to get her a beer. He pondered the letter again.

Maybe he could do a little something to shake up city hall.

Maybe shake 'em up real good.

Chapter 33

SHERIFF LEROY PERKINS had faced down some dangerous criminals in his distinguished career. He had been shot at several times. He had been wounded twice, once life-threatening. He had fired his service revolver four times while on duty. He had killed one man, the crazy Campanelli brother who was holding Samantha hostage, with a single deadly shot through the wicked desperado's right eye. He had broken up vicious bar fights, and even more vicious domestic disputes.

Not much fazed him, in life or in law enforcement. Nothing scared him.

He was acknowledged as a rough, tough sheriff who operated without fear to protect his citizens and uphold the law.

But sometimes there are situations that test even the most fearless of men.

He stood in the room, paralyzed. He swallowed hard. His throat was dry. His hands shook. He waited in terror for the next move to come.

He looked around. He couldn't see any back-up. He was alone in this desperate situation.

"Oh, for heaven's sake, Perk, it's just a baby! Now hold her!"

And with that curt order, Dr. Samira Al-Saadi thrust the squirming little bundle wrapped in a pretty pink blanket with ribbons on it into his unwilling arms.

"No! She's not a football! Get one arm under her head to support her neck. Get the other one under her bum. Gently. Relax. She's probably more scared of you than you are of her."

"I seriously doubt that," he mumbled as he readjusted his arms. "Seriously."

The tiny little bundle squinted up at him. He peered back. The kid was...well, not entirely unattractive. You know, for a baby. Bit of brown hair. She seemed to have, uh, two eyes and two ears and certainly one mouth. A nose. Nothing too freakazoid. Golly, that mouth was sort of smiling at him.

Very gingerly he moved his arms just a bit to rock her. He pasted a sort of smile on his face. He happened to glance up to see Samantha, Kim, Samira and the baby's mother collapsed in laughter on the couch.

Very nice. His support team. Good to know they always had his back.

He rocked her a little more. An adorable little burpie bubble emerged as she smiled back at him. Huh. This was kind of easy. No big deal. The kid just lay there without being any trouble. How hard could parenting really be?

He raised his arms so he could get closer to the precious little bundle. There was a kind of powdery, sweet, baby smell going on. Another of those cutesy little bubbles emerged. He smiled down at her. Wow, he was getting to be a real pro at this. It just goes to show that a tough Sheriff can handle any situation, no matter how—

And the baby barfed all over him.

Chapter 34

THE REST OF the J-Men could sense the shift in power. Jim Crandall was, for the first time, talking and leading; Jed was, for the first time, silent, sullen and in the background. He had tried to tell the group that he was appointing Crandall to run the Ops side but that he would remain in charge. Nobody was buying it.

If nature abhors a vacuum, in politics it only exists for nanoseconds before someone steps up to grasp whatever power and prestige is available. There are few things more certain in life and politics than the never-ending quest for the top job by most elected officials or wanna-be leaders. They all believe they are qualified to rule; almost all of them are wrong.

Jethro was trying to make sense of it all. His loyalty was to Jed. He'd always considered Jed to be the leader of the pack. He was happy in his own secondary role. But now, suddenly, it was all muddled. He scratched his head and popped another beer.

The rest of the group didn't seem to care. Nobody had considered Jed to be much of a leader at the best of times. Who cared who ordered them to do something as long as the beer flowed, the ribs were sweet and spicy, and they managed to poke a finger in the eye of some government asshole every so often.

None of them really wanted a revolution. They weren't Bolshevists wanting blood running in the streets. They just wanted a small insurrection from time to time, just enough to make the ruling class panic and sweat. And they had to defend the Constitution from the Radical Left, of course, those nuts wanting to expand voting rights and ensure civil liberties and restrict gun rights and crazy stuff like that. That was a given.

That's why they were all a little surprised at Crandall's vehement put-down of the local government in their City of Port Manatee.

"Robbing from us little folks, raisin' the taxes all the time, screwin' family-owned businesses that have supported this city for decades! Are we going to allow this to continue?"

"Nah. Nope. Yea. Uh huh. Unh um. Yo."

It wasn't exactly a rallying cry from the proletariat to storm the castle walls, but Crandall didn't care. He oversaw operations now. It was his group. And he was going to exact revenge on city hall after they'd upset his lady.

He looked around the yard at The Ugly Porker. He didn't see any immediate threats. A table of four women eating brisket. A couple of families. Two van loads of tourists wearing white socks and sandals. Several regulars at their usual tables. Wait. Wasn't that single guy with the brown hair, hadn't he been here during their last meeting? Crandall looked hard at him. The guy was in his early forties. Looked to be in decent shape. He was gnawing on a smoked turkey leg. He was alone at a table for four. He didn't seem to be paying any attention to the cluster of J-Men. Still, a commander had to be alert for infiltrators and spies.

Crandall instinctively lowered his voice. The J-Men leaned a bit closer as they swallowed their beer. "I'm going to design a protest that will shake up city hall," he declared. The boys nodded agreement. "Got to teach them a lesson about respecting us local taxpayers." More nods. More beer. "Stay ready. Stay alert. Watch out for spies."

At this the boys looked at each other and then anxiously scanned the yard. The bowl of fried okra certainly looked suspicious. "Jed, you contact some of our brothers in other districts. Tell them to get ready to join us for a major protest." Jed nodded importantly. "OK, that's it. For now."

Jim leaned back in his chair and picked up his beer. This leading a revolt was hard work. He wasn't going to tell Beulah about it until it was over and the city had capitulated and agreed to lower her taxes. It would be a nice birthday surprise for her.

He checked the yard again. That man with the brown hair certainly seemed to be taking his time chewing that turkey leg.

CHAPTER 35

THE DRIVE-BY WAS short, disturbing and reckless.

The J-Men gathered a bunch of their buddies, lit torches, and sped down Main Street, honking horns and throwing an occasional Molotov cocktail. The local newspaper and Channel 9 were particular targets. And city hall.

The J-Men considered it all a hoot. Their torches left a trail of sparks as they rumbled through the main streets Pedestrians ducked into stores or bars for protection. The liquor store owner locked his door as soon as he heard the racket. He had no idea what was going on, but liquor stores are usually a target of whatever bad was happening on the street.

Music blared from the sound systems in the pick-ups. Most of the participants were wearing camo gear. A few parked cars got bumped or scratched. A couple of garbage cans got burned. One citizen shot a video and recorded license plates.

Wisely, the arriving police did not provoke a confrontation. There were too many guns on too many of the trucks. A shoot-out on a public street would have been a disastrous law enforcement error.

Jethro, who was driving the lead pick-up, honked a few times, flashed his lights and took off. The little convoy quickly followed him. They tore through the night and ended up at Jack O'Hara's house; his Confederate memorabilia was much praised by the convoy members as they celebrated another victory over the local establishment.

A couple of sheriff's patrol cars parked on the highway across from the dusty grounds of Jack's estate. They were there to keep an eye in case of a further excursion.

That wasn't going to happen, as the boys settled down for some cold beer and the pizza that Jed ordered.

Jim Crandall grinned all night. His rehearsal had gone great.

Most of the boys slept in their trucks that night. The two who ventured back on the roads were arrested on DUI charges.

CHAPTER 36

"YES, THE MAYOR and city council in Port Manatee down on the Gulf Coast all look like tiny tyrants and bullying bullies today after their stunning over-reaction to a purely peaceful civil demonstration recently. That Sheriff who thinks he's such a hot-shot and the local authorities obviously went over the top to threaten these innocent participants in a mild protest about civil law and order…well! One must wonder what dark secrets are being hidden in this Florida Peyton Place when law-abiding citizens are harassed by these out-of-control local authorities!"

With his commentary over, host Michael Majors angrily threw a fist at the camera focused tightly on his reddened face. A second later the COYOTE NEWS NETWORK went to a commercial for the problem of anal leakage and how to, um, plug it.

Sophia Roberts checked to make sure they were off-air. She swung her low-back stool towards Majors. "That was really good, Mikey. Peyton Place! Boy, that's a hoot. Haven't thought about that little town of sin and corruption for a long time."

She smirked, but only internally. Who would know that literary reference from the 1950s? She wasn't all that sure that half the COYOTE audience could spell '1950.' She kept that to herself, of course, not wanting to jeopardize the $340,000 a year she was now getting to appear exclusively on COYOTE.

Majors was regaining control after his faked outrage. He wiped the spittle from his mouth and turned to grin at the luscious blonde. "Yeah, I thought it went well. That'll shake 'em up!" He offered a coarse laugh.

"Back in 10!"

They both put on their TV faces and swung to face their cameras. "And five, four, three, two" and the floor director pointed his finger at Majors.

"We are back! And the phone lines and texts are exploding about this corrupt little bastion against freedom on Florida's west coast. I want to thank you, my loyal viewers of The Major's Report, for understanding so quickly the implications for those of us in this country who believe in personal rights and freedoms. A few friends drive down the main street of this sordid little place and the Sheriff threatens to lock up innocent people! Truly shocking! Sophia!"

"It is surprising," she began smoothly, re-crossing her legs as her mini skirt rose another tempting half inch, "that those local authorities apparently panicked and over-reacted so strongly. It is a credit to the demonstrators that they did not provoke confrontations and they handled these ugly threats peacefully. Who knows what kind of police misconduct occurred, who knows how these law-abiding citizens may have been threatened or even had their lives endangered! If a city can't even handle a little parade down Main Street on a Friday night, then you must start wondering who is running this place, and who is covering up for whom?"

"Indeed! You are watching The Major's Report exclusively on the COYOTE news network. We will be right back with a shocking story about corruption in Congress! Who got caught with their fingers in the public purse? WE WILL REVEAL THIS BREAKING NEWS WHEN WE RETURN!"

The indignation shone through the camera as the show went to a station break.

Kim Sharpe and Roy Crawford sat together on her couch, in shock over the lies and obfuscations and spin spewing out of the TV program's commentators.

Crawford finally reacted by rewinding the program. They once again watched the massacre in silence as the vitriol and hate rolled across her 65-inch screen, all in glorious 5G Hi Def.

"How in the holy hell can they get away with that crap?" Kim demanded as she shut off the TV and threw the remote on the floor. "They totally spun the thing upside down! The Mayor and Council weren't even involved!"

"Yeah. I guess that's our 'free press' today. All sensational with very little fact." He thought for a moment. "The mayor will not be very happy. I'll have to show her this." He sipped his drink and put the glass back with a weary stretch. "And Perkins will...well, I don't know what he will do."

"Don't worry about Perk," replied Kim quickly, "worry about how Samantha will explode after she sees this!"

CHAPTER 37

THE POLICE ARTIST'S facial sketch of Claudia that aired on local TV drew several tips. The detectives spent some time sorting through them and discarding most. Finally, they caught a break.

"Her name is Claudia Cabrera," reported a soft Latina voice on the tip line. "She is from a small town in Venezuela. We came here together. Some big men took us to an underground room. I don't know where. We got separated after a few days." The voice broke down in tears. "Claudia was a devout girl. Her family lost everything in a mudslide. Her father was killed. She thought she could come here and work and send money home to help her mother and little sister." More tears. Then the phone clicked dead.

"That sounds legit," McMurray said quietly after they'd listened to the tape twice.

"Yeah." Cornice groaned. "This case is getting bigger and messier by the day. Big men? Underground room? And obviously something happens to the women. They get them on drugs, put 'em on the street, maybe sell the prettiest ones to some pervert? Sex trafficking must be big business."

"Millions of dollars, I'm guessing." McMurray shrugged. "What an ugly, filthy thing to do to another human being."

His partner turned to his laptop and began hammering at the keys. It took him several minutes and more than one muttered curse before he finally sat back and turned to McMurray.

"You were a little light on thinking this business is worth millions," he began. He shook his head in disbelief. "Would 150 billion in profits from human trafficking around the world get your attention?"

"What!"

"150 billion. With a B. And yeah, it doesn't happen just in some little foreign country, it is all over the USA. Florida is one of the worst states." He peered at the small print on his screen. "There are an estimated 40 million people in slavery in the world today. Millions in forced labor. Holy shit. Listen to this. Sexual exploitation is the biggest, most common form of human trafficking. Strip clubs, prostitution, porn, massage parlors, mail order brides. And most are women or children." He read some more. "Oh God. Child soldiers and organ harvesting are two other big reasons for human trafficking."

He slammed down the lid on his computer in disgust. He shook his head angrily.

McMurray finally cleared his throat. "What the hell have we gotten ourselves into?" he whispered.

<CHAPTER 38

"TIGA JOE IS a thug, a madman and is as corrupt as a Congressman's fundraising. He slipped into the country a few years ago after massacring the upper echelon in the Mexican drug gang he had joined. He killed the mayor of a village down there and is suspected in the executions of two other civic officials. The police feared him, so he could act with impunity. Rapes, murders, drugs. It was a reign of terror."

FBI regional chief James Robertson exhaled noisily. "It got so bad in the region that the Army finally got sent in. Tiga Joe then pulled up stakes, fled Mexico and went to Cuba for a while. He got some false documents made down there. He got thrown out of the country and somehow got past Miami's Immigration Center about five years ago. He had set up his organization in Florida a year or two before that, so he just took it over. He's now expanded his drug and trafficking business onto the Gulf Coast, which is how you got involved, Perk."

Sheriff Perkins, Captain Williams, Lieutenant Stokes and Detectives Cornice and McMurray listened on the speaker phone.

"From what my people tell me, he is a man without conscience or any sense of morality. He kills ruthlessly. He traffics women into prostitution, strip clubs, whatever. We are pretty sure that he sells some of the younger, prettier ones to men, and you can only imagine what kind of life that is going to be for them."

"Where is he getting the women?" asked Cornice.

"Mexico. South America. A few from eastern Europe."

"Venezuela is a feeding ground?"

"Sure."

Cornice looked at McMurray. They were both thinking about Claudia.

"How does he get the women into Florida?"

"Well, Captain Williams, that is a bit of a mystery. We are coordinating with the Coast Guard and ICE, but let's face it,

Florida has 1,350 miles of coastline and a bunch of small, private marinas. The simple reality is that you add that to the coasts of the Panhandle, Louisiana, Texas, and you've got yourself a big, big security problem."

It took all the veteran officers of the law a long moment to absorb this depraved and heinous scenario. It was the ugliest situation any of them had faced.

Perkins finally broke the silence. "You'll send us whatever intel your people have?"

"Immediately. We have no pictures of him, just an artist's sketch. There was a rumor that when he first arrived, he wanted to be considered respectable and donated money to some charities around here, but there don't seem to be any records of that. People from outside his gang who have interacted with him don't tend to live long enough to take souvenir snapshots. He's described as about 5'7", 190 pounds, much of it muscle, and thick black hair. Moustache is a maybe; that seems to change."

The officers could hear Robertson shuffling papers and talking to one of his staff. "You tell them."

A woman's voice came over the speaker. "Good morning, Sheriff Perkins. My name is Gwen Boothe. I serve as Director Robertson's Intel Chief."

"Agent Boothe, thank you for assisting us."

"Believe me, if you can find this piece of dog poop on the heel of life, you would be doing a considerable public service." She waited for the harsh snorts to cease. "This is some degree of speculation, but it may assist you in understanding him. Tiga Joe pretends to be descended from Mexican aristocrats, the conquistadors of the 1800s who built much of modern Mexico. He is not. From what Interpol tells us, he is the child of a prostitute from Guadalajara. We don't think the father ever played a role in his life, if in fact the father even knew of his existence. He grew up on the streets, fighting for survival, before he pushed his way into one of the gangs. His initiation was killing a young woman who was walking home from work. He was fifteen at the time. She was nineteen. You know of his violent six-year rise to the top of that gang after that."

Lt. A'ja was making notes.

"He has weaknesses, like all criminals. He isn't as smart as he likes to think he is. He tends to shoot first and plan second, which is not a great management technique. He rules by fear and intimidation. He has no wife or child of which Interpol is aware. Mistresses come and go." She paused. "He does have one weakness: he has a sister, or half-sister, we're not sure, whom he adores. She's in her early 20s. We don't have pictures and we don't know where either of them is living right now, but it is likely that they are together. He dotes on her. Protects her. Keeps her isolated from all but a few of her friends."

"How likely is it that they are in our jurisdiction?"

"With great respect to the fine city of Port Manatee, it is not a high probability. He seems to like the larger cities with more, uh, action. No offense implied."

"None taken. However, is it possible he is doing business in our area?"

"Oh, yes, that is most likely. Almost a certainty."

"Well," continued Perkins, "if he is here sometimes, could he have a residence of some kind?"

There was silence from the FBI. "Well," said the Intel Agent in Charge, "his pattern is not to take a one-bedroom ground floor apartment in a modest building. His ego would demand something more…suitable…for his lifestyle." She paused for a moment. "Let me make an addendum to my prior answer. No, I do not think he and his sister are living in Port Manatee. But, yes, there would be a good probability of his owning some penthouse or estate for when he visits. He would want the personal security of his own property, and the luxury and comfort of his own hacienda. Money is not a problem so he would have paid cash and therefore no mortgage to trace. Likely it would be registered under some company or false front. It is probable his sister would be with him, at least most of the time."

Everybody pondered that for another moment.

Lt. Stokes continued. "If he has property here, he will also have homes or estates in other cities?"

"Yes."

"Is it possible that he has developed his own network of safe houses for transporting his victims? Maybe keeps them in a locked room in the basement or something?"

"It is possible," came the cautious reply. "I'm just not sure that he would want to mix his own hacienda with his business. That is not traditionally how Mexican nobility would function. The home is sacred, to be protected. Family is everything. Separate from the world of business."

Perkins looked around his conference table. There were four very serious faces studying their notes. "Anything else?" he asked. "OK, James, we're done. Thank you, Agent Boothe, and please thank the other agents. We will stay connected on the case of Claudia Cabrera. We are not stopping our murder investigation. Let's pursue this sadistic son of a bitch and get him to face justice."

CHAPTER 39

THE TWO LEAD detectives hit the ground running. That translated to Cornice running and McMurray limping determinedly behind on his wonky knee.

They had been partners for nearly five years. There was complete trust between the two. They had each other's backs.

There are three major ways police get information. First is from the boots-on-the-ground cops and detectives pounding the pavement and talking to people, sniffing the air, studying crime scenes and acquiring forensic evidence.

Second is tips, sometimes anonymous, sometimes from concerned citizens or witnesses. Sometimes from criminals trying to take out an opponent. Sometimes from a criminal who has a moment of conscience. And sometimes investigating officers receive information from Confidential Informants.

Third is electronic research, and today that is becoming a key part of police investigations. There is a lot of information on the internet; happily for law enforcement, that is supplemented by really stupid criminals merrily posting their exploits on social media.

The two veteran investigators poked and prodded at all three options for two and a half days. They got nothing.

"It is so damn frustrating," exclaimed Cornice to Captain Williams. They were at their daily briefing session. "People on the street freeze when we mention Tiga Joe. It's like he's got their lips sewn together." He coughed. "Hearing about his methods of discipline, maybe that's what's happened."

"We've talked to our contacts. We've sent word out that there will be cash payments for information. We've muscled a couple of snitches. We've talked to hookers and hustlers, con men and thieves. Nothing. We talked to waitresses, because they hear everything. We've stopped cab drivers. Nada. Ditto with pizza delivery guys, street cops and a priest. Zero. Sometimes their eyes get big when we mention his name, but there is so much intimidation that if they know anything, they just clam up."

Williams spun his pen on his desk. He was equally frustrated. He had to keep going to the Sheriff with nothing. Unpleasant.

McMurray swallowed the dregs of his cold coffee and made a face. "We got nothing, Cap. We think we need to bring in some E-help."

"Wayne?"

"Wayne."

Chapter 40

WAYNE COOPER WAS a computer savant. His mind worked in peculiar and mysterious ways as it darted from concept to concept. He wasn't anti-social, but he did have some unique personality traits.

He was technically part of the Governor's special task force for forensic audits. He loved tracing arcane financial transactions and seeking hidden foreign bank accounts. He had become an expert at finding and puzzling together complex webs of hidden assets and corporate intrigue.

This ability to see different patterns in data, and the clues they offered to his unusual mind, often produced startling jumps in logic that resulted in completely different ways of looking at a situation. He was skilled at digging up deeply buried, clandestine items of information that could open new lines of investigation. Perkins' office had used him on a few occasions; the results had been impressive.

"Madam Governor, how are you?"

"I am managing to fight off the alligators and the opposition party, Sheriff, although the alligators' bites are not as vicious."

Perkins chuckled. He had developed a personal relationship with the Governor when she was a rookie in the state legislature. He had been of help to her in a particularly nasty situation involving some pictures of her as a young coed.

"I have to tell you, Perk, I've become a little jaded running our great state. For example, I don't believe in the laws of physics anymore." Perkins cleared his throat, not quite sure what the response should be. "If something's full of hot air, it should rise, right?" "Uh huh." "So then tell me, why isn't the Minority Leader floating in the ionosphere?"

Perkins laughed.

"OK, that's off my chest. What can I do for you?"

It took him nearly five minutes of the Governor's valuable time to explain the situation.

"Wait," she finally interrupted him, "you're telling me that we've maybe got a modern sex slave trade going on in my state?!?!"

Perkins paused. "Well, ma'am, we think so. Our investigation is in the early stages. But it is tied to a murder in my county. A young woman. She'd been beaten and abused."

The Governor sucked in her breath. "How brazen can you get? Doing this in today's social…well, let's rethink that statement. OK, what do you want from me?"

"Wayne."

"You got 'im. What else?

"Our investigation will probably reach into other jurisdictions. I may need you to run a little interference."

"You got it. Yes, yes, I'm coming. Sorry, Perk, my Chief of Staff is waving at me to…for a what? The Boy Scouts of where? Well, they're tough kids, they can stand for two minutes. Perk? You need anything, you call me. You've got my private number, right? OK, good. And keep me in touch. Sex trafficking! The things that go on in this…"

The call ended.

Perkins gently replaced his own receiver and turned to the two detectives. "We've got him. I'll call now."

Cornice looked at his partner with relief. Maybe the computer genius would find an opening.

CHAPTER 41

WAYNE COOPER WAS wearing an Alanis Morrisette T-shirt. XXL. She looked hot in the photo, although Cooper did little to enhance the sexy image on the shirt. He wore his usual black pants and boots. The boots had last been shined during the Obama administration.

Cooper's heavy black glasses slid down his nose so often that his pushing them back up became almost hypnotic. His voice was raspy, his patience was extremely limited, and his appreciation of beautiful female rock stars was now legendary. He had switched his T-shirt allegiance from his KISS devotion to gorgeous female rockers. There were lots to choose from.

His personal peccadillos were tolerated by smart bosses, mainly because his IQ was 166 and he had a seeming unlimited capacity to focus on a problem and see different patterns.

"Welcome back," greeted Perkins as he bumped fists with the computer genius. Cooper also had a thing about germs or touching most things. Or people. It made shaking hands or dating difficult.

Perkins was exceedingly polite to his guest for two reasons. First, he greatly respected Cooper's intellect and his ability to solve very complex problems. They had worked together in the past, quite successfully. Second, secretly, Perkins was terrified that if he ever pissed the guy off, Cooper would strip his on-line financial assets and bank accounts, install child porn on his personal computer that would be leaked to the FBI, and send dirty messages to Samantha that would cause her to flee from his life, screaming.

Wayne had met Samantha once. He liked her. A lot. Perkins kept hoping that a promise of dinner with her would be enough to keep Cooper sort of in line during his visit.

"We've got a cooler of Dr. Pepper on ice for you right here," Perkins pointed out. "Several packages of M&Ms. A nice hotel suite. Anything else you need, just tell the detectives. And I'm here anytime for you."

Cooper nodded, already hooking up his special high-capacity computer outfitted with apps and programs, many of them legal, that big corporations could only dream about. It was possible that the US Space Force Central Command had computers more sophisticated, but it would probably be a toss-up.

The sheriff left and the two detectives began their briefing. Cooper absorbed it without taking a note. He fidgeted with his computer and didn't ask a question.

"Find Tiga Joe. Find some local connection. Right?"

Cornice and McMurray looked at one another. That pretty much summed up their weeks of fruitless work and their 23-minute briefing of the nerd.

"Right"

"OK. I'll need a couple of bacon cheeseburgers at three o'clock. No dill pickles. See you."

With that he turned to his keyboard and started pounding away.

The detectives left the board room quietly, shutting the door and making sure the DO NOT DISTURB sign was taped securely on the pebbled glass window.

CHAPTER 42

"WE NEED ANOTHER big thangy. Some demonstration. Huge. Scare the shit outta that bitchy mayor. Keep our winning streak alive, like the…the…oh hell, like one ah them big teams." Jed let out a huge belch. Birds fell from the trees.

Jethro reached deep into the ice chest for another can. He tossed it to Jed who fumbled it briefly before gripping the icy can and popping the tab.

Jim Crandall looked on in disgust. The J-Men were drinking more than ever these days—he hadn't thought that was possible—and talking louder. Their perceived 'win' just by driving some pick-ups down Main Street, holding torches and Molotov cocktails, had emboldened the already sloppy, undisciplined group.

He was having fun screwin' that sheriff, though. The fireworks had been epic. They'd got the community buzzin'.

His own life was also buzzin'. He was still tiptoeing around Beulah, trying to figure out where their relationship might be heading. So far there had been no clear signals. He figured she wouldn't encourage him to bring the J-Men home for supper anytime soon; she was not a fan of Jed and the boys. He realized that he needed to figure out his own future, because his domestic situation was precarious.

That was all a lot of figuring for one man in one day.

Jacob Pew was deep into the shot-and-beer technique. Some rot-gut bourbon washed down by a long slug of beer. He didn't come to these little soirees very often. Crandall guessed even a loner like Pew got tired of his survivalist mentality and needed a night out with the boys occasionally, before somebody dropped a nuke on his cave.

The man could hold his booze though, Crandall thought with respect. Unlike a couple of the other members of this little cabal.

Jeb was already half-way to la-la-land. He was never much of a drinker, and the extended practice sessions with the J-Men hadn't improved his game very much.

"Yeah, less' do a biggie. Schare 'em. Oopsh. Scare 'em shumore. Yeah. Hey Jimmy, whaddyagot?"

Crandall, who had hated being called "Jimmy" since Grade 4, just gave him a hard stare.

Jed rushed to fill the awkward silence. "Workin' on a big plan now. Jus' wait a bit. We'll do a number on those yokels at city hall, jus' you wait." He nodded in satisfaction and inhaled more Schlitz.

Pastor Jenner looked up from his Diet Coke. "I'm going to be on The Major's Report again soon. I could announce something for you. He gets that big national cable TV audience."

Jed glanced at him. "Good, yeah, thanks, man. We'll let you know." Jed wondered again why and how the creepy little minister had gotten into this group. It wasn't as if the boys were big churchgoers. Especially at that weird evangelical church out on the side-road where Jenner preached.

One of the wives, he supposed. God knows what went on in that temple—well, no, perhaps that line wasn't advisable to pursue.

Crandall had had enough. He got up stiffly. His joints cracked. "Gotta go work on the next attack," he announced. The boys nodded wisely. Jenner paled even more.

Jethro opened another can of beer.

CHAPTER 43

WAYNE COOPER WORKED pretty much through the night, into the next morning, crashed for a couple of hours, devoured several cheeseburgers at different times of the day and night, sucked back a lot of Dr. Pepper, popped M&Ms, went to his hotel suite once more for some sleep and a shower, changed T-shirts twice, and pushed his glasses back up on his nose about 800,000 times.

The two detectives had made occasional forays into the boardroom that Cooper had converted into a mad-scientist lab of computer geekdom. Their conversations had not been lengthy: "Get out." "More Dr. Pepper." "I'm working on it." And, hopefully, eventually, "Yeah, got an idea."

Friday morning Cooper was slumped in his chair and sprawled over the keyboard when Cornice and McMurray cautiously entered the boardroom. They looked at one another.

"Do you think he's dead?" Cornice asked softly.

McMurray quietly approached. He bent down and listened. He straightened up and shook his head. "Still breathing." He moved away. "Breath smells like a hyena's." There were cheeseburger wrappers scattered around; empty cans of Dr. Pepper had been stacked neatly in a Blue Box—Cooper was a fanatic about recycling cans and bottles—and there were papers strewn across the table.

"What do we do? I'm scared to wake him up."

McMurray nodded agreement. "I guess we just—." He paused as the large, limp form began to stretch and move.

After a moment Cooper's head rose, he pushed his glasses up, he yawned, took his glasses off to rub his eyes, put his glasses back on, and peered at the two men. "Gotta pee." He pushed past them to the bathroom. He was wearing a Pat Benatar shirt. It was several minutes before he returned. His hair was sort of combed. His face looked washed. He had put on another T-shirt, this one adorned with a sultry picture of Sheryl Crow.

He yawned and scratched himself, then shook his head.

"Tiga Joe doesn't live around here," he announced. "But he has expanded his business into this area in the past two or three years. His real name is Jose Sanchez."

Cooper cracked open his last Dr. Pepper from the cooler. He looked at the melted water sadly. He drank deeply.

"Everything is buried under two or three or four different corporations or names. He owns nothing personally that I can find. He must have a clever lawyer. He seems to appear around here every couple of months. You know about the shoot-out on the street last year with that rival gang? He was behind it. What were there, four dead?"

McMurray nodded. It has been bloody and was still formally unsolved, even though the cops knew the players and who shot first.

"He was claiming territory. He's ramping up activity in your city. Look out for more bloodshed."

Cornice was frantically jotting notes. Cooper continued his ad lib report.

"Tiga Joe nick-named himself when he was shooting up the ranks in Mexico. Ha! Shooting! Good one!" He chuckled. "The lad does love his Uzi. Anyway, he picked the name to instill fear in the villagers and his own gang, I guess. He's ruthless. Had the mayor of a little Mexican town assassinated. Machete. They at least found the head to go with the body in time for the funeral." He paused for another glug.

"It was after the subsequent shoot-out with the Army that that he headed for Cuba. Word is he pissed off El Jefe. Something about not paying enough tribute to him. El Jefe likes gold. Sees it as a hedge against inflation. Actually, that's not a bad financial strategy—for a Commie bastard," Cooper offered as an aside. "Tough to carry much of it with you if you are fleeing the country, though."

"Anyway, your boy. Tiga. He doesn't allow photographs, but I found one small picture of him from some charity event four years ago. It was in a little community newspaper around here. It took some deep digging to discover. My guess is he was trying to buy respectability when he first came here, but the picture got snapped by mistake. He had no gracious way out. It's the only picture that I could find."

McMurray and Cornice lunged for the printed sheet. It showed two women beside Jose Sanchez at a charity reception. Tiga Joe was short, strong, thick-chested, had a lot of black hair and a short beard, and was wearing an ill-fitting suit.

"I guess the paper published a page of people attending the charity cocktail party. They probably never thought anything about it. No other paper picked it up. My guess is that by the time his lawyer would have tried to suppress the picture, it had already been published. Nobody's ever looked for something like this."

It was a tribute to Cooper's complete commitment to his digging and research that he could find one small picture in an obscure little newspaper that no longer existed.

"Great, Wayne. The Sheriff is going to prize this. Thank you."

Cooper nodded. It was what he loved doing. The intellectual challenge of digging deep into illegal business deals or corporate shenanigans was juice for his system. When he got called into a murder investigation, it was an even bigger charge.

McMurray kept studying the copy of the picture in the paper. The typeface was so small he had trouble making out the names in the cutline.

"Who are...can you...the names of..."

"The two women? Yeah, thought you'd want 'em." Cooper pushed over a piece of paper with two names scribbled on it. McMurray looked at them, paled, and shoved the paper to his partner. Cornice stared in disbelief.

CHAPTER 44

"WELL, WHEN YOU surround yourself with clowns, you're going to end up in a circus," Perkins commented bitterly as he surveyed the page of pictures from the society fundraiser. He read the two names on the list his two detectives had just handed him. "And Tiga Joe and these women just created one big, steaming pile of elephant dung that is going to get hurled all over our tent." He flung the paper down in disgust.

Cornice and McMurray snuck a glance at one another, then at Captain Williams, who sat glowering at them and the world in general. Their progress report on the murder case was not being greeted with unbridled enthusiasm by the brass.

On the other hand, the Sheriff hadn't said they were being transferred to kindergarten patrol. Yet.

Perkins checked the list again. The names hadn't changed. He blew out a huge puff of air. Once more his eyes flitted down to his desk. The names on the list still hadn't changed:

Veronica Wilson.

Inez Rivera.

The Sheriff moved his eyes up to lock Captain Williams' big dark eyes. "We follow the evidence," Williams said.

Perkins nodded. Cornice and McMurray nodded.

"Yeah, that's what we do. No favoritism. Justice for all." Perkins studied the list one more time. "Start it off, gentlemen. Just be...careful."

The two detectives nodded and left the office. Williams and Perkins just stared at one another for a long moment.

"Going to be ugly," said Perkins.

"You're right—it'll be a circus," Williams nodded.

CHAPTER 45

"LAS TRES AMIGAS. The three friends. They've been leaders in what passes for high society in our little burg for seven or eight years."

McMurray listened on the speaker phone as Cornice talked to the Society Editor at the Port Manatee Observer. "Three?"

"Yeah. Just wait a damn minute." The cops could hear ice being put in a bowl or pitcher. A glass tinkled. Finally, she returned. "They each have an interesting back-story. Why do you want them?"

An awkward pause. Usually it was a newspaper getting information from the police, not the other way around. Suellen Carter had been writing society news and women's features for about a hundred years. In an era when other newspapers had long since dumped that kind of weekly column, the Observer's owner kept Suellen on the payroll. No editor was quite sure what Suellen had on the owner, but a couple of them had been fired for trying to find out. There was late-night speculation amongst two senior editors that it probably involved dwarves, donkeys and dancers.

She had her own work schedule and her own ideas for columns. Her weekly scandalous report about 'celebrities' in Port Manatee and their goings-on was still required reading for the societally conscious and the wannabes trying to elevate their status.

Suellen had last picked up a restaurant check in 1979. She was known to be not unsympathetic to 'sampling' products. Grey Goose, Louboutin's, gourmet food baskets, Bordeaux wines, and designer fashions had accumulated in her closets and pantries over the years. An invoice was never included with the delivery.

The Wives at Sapphire Blue made it a point to have a weekly wine-and-snicker event as they read the latest goings-on. When one of them made the column, it was an occasion for buying drinks for the entire afternoon. It made no difference if the item was positive or negative. Publicity is publicity. Pour me another.

Port Manatee still had some deep societal roots anchored in the Old South. The debutante balls had ended just a few years before. Their demise had ruined the plans of many avaricious mothers, who had been reduced to lawn parties and—lord help us—casual barbecues to attract young gentlemen to meet their darling daughters. As one horrified doyen had reported to her friends, "The caterer served sausages in a bun!"

The shame had lasted for months.

There were homes in the South, and the hostesses in them, that were still judged on the quality of their sweet tea.

While Suellen's power to make or break a woman (usually) or a man (occasionally) in local society had dimmed, she still knew all the players and their back-stories. Sometimes she had been cruel in her writings, and occasionally quite wrong. None of it had stopped her. Nobody had sued her in years, because no one had ever won. There was a rumor that Suellen and a Superior Court judge had a long-standing, uh, friendship.

Now deep into her seventies, she only came to the newspaper once or twice a week. Everyone knew that once she died, and someone had driven a stake through her heart and rubbed garlic on her forehead, that there would never again be a Society Editor at the paper.

"It's just background for us, research for a situation."

Suellen sniffed. "Sure." She sipped something with tinkling ice cubes. "Well, boys, here's my proposition. I give you the background, you give me the real story when things start popping. Deal?"

Suellen hadn't risen to her position without making lots of deals and breaking lots of scoops. She still had a reporter's instinct for a hot story.

Cornice looked helplessly across the desk at his partner. McMurray coughed and leaned forward. "Suellen, it's Fred McMurray."

"Well, hello there, sweetie. Oh, wait. It's the cop, not the movie star. Different spelling." She paused. "He was hot in his day." She smacked her lips loudly. "He was on a press junket years ago and we spent a very fun afternoon in his hotel suite. Just chatting, of course!" she hooted into the phone.

The officers could hear her taking another long sip.

"Ah, that first mint julep of the day is so important. Do you know how to make one, Freddie?"

"Uh, no, no I don't."

"Well, you come over here some afternoon and we'll play the movie star and the innocent young newspaper reporter, and maybe drink a few juleps."

She sipped again and chortled to herself. Finally she leaned into the phone. "We have a deal, boys?"

McMurray shrugged. "As long as we have control of the situation, we'll give you the first tip," he proposed. "If it gets out of our hands, nothing we can do."

"Not much of an incentive, boyo, but since you're lying to me anyway, I'll just take it as another man's promise to me that will be broken. I could tell you stories." She sighed. "Well, you're lucky. You caught me on a slow news day and right in that sweet spot between that first pick-me-up julep and the third lay-me-down julep. Break out the limes and the mint leaves, boys, and I'll tell you the story."

Chapter 46

"VERONICA WILSON WAS trailer trash. Her real name is Maggie Schlitz. Yes, like the beer. Mother worked as a grocery store check-out girl. Father worked at being a drunk and an asshole and was successful at both. Some talk about domestic violence. Maggie got sent to live with her aunt in Savannah when she was about 12. Came back a few years later all refined and with boobs 'n a new name. Her dad had passed away from liver cancer a couple of years before that. Surprised he had any liver left. Her mother died a year later. Her aunt left her a chunk of money when she passed, and suddenly Veronica was a hot item in town. She married Steve Johnson. He was a third-generation retailer; family owned a bunch of real estate downtown. She was smart enough to have a couple of kids to lock in the payoff in case of a divorce, which miraculously happened about three years later."

There was a pause, then a long slurp over the phone. McMurray just looked at his partner.

"Who'da seen that coming?" The laughter over the phone was coarse. "Veronica did real well in the settlement. Poor Stevie, not so much. She got some real estate downtown and a pile of cash. He was dumped hard. He's still around town, but bitter about it all."

Another long slurp.

"Anyway, Ronnie. A nickname she hates, by the way. Guess it doesn't go with her nouveau riche role, so I get a hoot out of callin' her that. Then she got her tits done and some facial work, and ended up with George Wilson, the realtor. Big house, big car, big bucks. What she always wanted." A pause, then grudgingly, "Gotta give the broad some credit. Where she came from to where she got to…well, a lot of people have done a lot less with a lot more."

The two detectives swallowed this piece of social philosophy.

Another pause. "Word around town is that the money has been drying up in the last coupla years. Cash flow ain't great anymore. George isn't selling much and she keeps spending."

A yawn down the phone line.

"Who else? Oh yeah, Inez Rivera. Rumor in the country club locker room is that she gives the best BJs in town. Maybe that helped her land Chico. He's always played on the edge of the law. Automobile dealerships. Used car lots. Garage over on 14th that your stolen property guys figure is a chop shop. He says he doesn't own it, of course. Ha! He's a rough-edged guy. She gives as good as she gets in the relationship. Volatile, I think is the word for that marriage."

A coarse chuckle, then a rattle of ice cubes.

"Anyway, they've got two kids, both away at school somewhere. Leaves Inez time to play around town. 'course Chico does as well. They show up at social events dressed to the nines, she's hangin' on his arm, then one or both gets drunk or high on cocaine, and they sometimes provide an unscheduled bit of entertainment. They don't necessarily go home together."

McMurray looked at his partner, who shrugged.

"Inez has expensive tastes and a checking account that won't fully pay for her desires. She's got some other income or something lately, I dunno from where. But the lady does like spending. She and Ronnie are wonderful shoppers. Store clerks fall all over themselves when they enter a store."

The death rattle of old ice cubes at the bottom of a glass. "Come to think about it, they both live in the same area down on Bayside Drive." More rattling and then the pouring.

"That leaves Charlotte Martinez. She's the third of this trio of tawdry. Surprised she wasn't on your list. They're in cahoots all the time. Charlotte is quiet compared to her two pals. She aspires to be in the same category as they are for the money and social standing, but she's always the third one in the group that few notice—Gummo to Groucho and Harpo." She paused. "You boys remember the Marx Brothers?"

McMurray responded with a yes. Jamal Cornice mumbled a no. There is a generation gap that some entertainment acts just can't span.

"Ah. Well, Charlotte is divorced. Hasn't remarried. No kids. She lives in a luxury condo downtown with a nice view of the harbor. She works part-time as an interior designer. She didn't get a big cash settlement. She's condo rich and cash poor. She tries hard to play in the big leagues, well, the big leagues socially around here, which ain't the big leagues at all, ya' know…"

The two detectives looked at each other with bewildered eyes. They were not privy to the upper echelons of society in Port Manatee. This was a unique peek behind the drapery of the nearly rich and almost famous leading ladies in Port Manatee.

"They're all money-hungry, if you ask me. All three of 'em want the big bucks. Big. They talk about making large donations, but I hear the charity doesn't always get the money from their pledges. They are pretty snotty to other women; they suck up to men. Just their nature I guess, predators that they are. As a result, other women don't like 'em. They suspect they're always after their man," she wheezed into the phone. "Well duh."

A pause. Cornice and McMurray looked at one another. "This is really useful background, thank you," Cornice broke in suddenly. "You ever heard about Tiga Joe? Tiger? Anything like that name connected to these ladies?"

The veteran columnist drew a deep breath that the detectives could hear over the dingy phone line. "Tiga Joe. Yeah. Bad dude. You wanna stay a long way away from that cat."

Nobody spoke for a minute. Suellen finally added, "I've heard stories about Tiga Joe using, uh, a couple of people for, well, things. I don't know anything, you understand. Just a little whisper that I've picked up a couple of times."

"About what?"

An uncomfortable silence.

"This could be important, Suellen. Point us in some direction."

"Shit. Look, I know nothing. But I've heard some rumors, a couple of murmurs, about illegals passing through here. Sex trafficking. Somebody said once that Veronica had a lot of gardeners at her place. Somebody said Inez had a bunch of cousins visiting but they always seem to look different. But I know nothing, you understand? Nothing from me about that."

"OK, we got that." A pause, a head shake. "We appreciate this, Suellen. We'll keep in touch," McMurray said.

"Sure. And don't forget to come up and see me sometime." A throaty chuckle as she hung up.

McMurray furtively wiped his sweaty palms on his pants. "Geez, my wife would cut off my…" He shuddered.

The thought hung in the damp air of the detective's bullpen.

CHAPTER 47

"WHAT YOU'RE SAYING is, these three society ladies just might be in cahoots with Tiga? For what? Harboring illegals? They'd probably claim they were rescuing refugees and giving them shelter."

Captain Williams was not a happy man as he listened to the report of the two detectives. He banged a big fist on his desk. The desk quivered but held.

Cornice and McMurray side-eyed each other. Wasn't there some line out there about 'don't poke the bear'? Apparently, they each had a sharp stick and a dumb idea.

McMurray harrumphed and cleared his throat. "Well, Cap, thing is, we've done some poking around..." Poking. Damn. Bad choice on so many levels. "...and we think there might be a bit of truth in this thing. We've been surveilling the homes of Ms. Wilson and Ms. Rivera. Ms. Rivera seems to be getting a number of visitors. Male. Several days a week. We just don't see them leave."

"Yeah? So what happens, they sit down for a nice long cuppa tea?"

Cornice shifted uncomfortably in his chair. "Well, that's the problem. We don't know what happens."

Williams blew out air. His cheeks puffed. He rolled his eyes. "Maybe they're playing darts. Come on, guys, you're not giving me anything! These three ladies are supposed to be well respected in town. Why on earth would they get involved with Tiga Joe?"

"Our speculation, and it is only that right now, is that the ladies are all short of cash. They are big spenders. They all live a lavish lifestyle. Word is that family cash flows may be drying up. At least that's one rumor out there."

Captain Williams stopped fidgeting at that and looked more interested. "Huh." He paused. "But what if it turns out these three women are just the bowl of bran flakes on a Las Vegas brunch buffet."

The two detectives mulled that metaphor for a moment. Cornice cleared his throat. "What we need is more support on surveillance so we can try to knit this whole thing together."

McMurray unrolled a map of the city. "The three ladies all live close together. You can see Charlotte's condo here, overlooking the harbor. Then just down a couple of streets are the estates of the two others. They both overlook the water but from different parts of the Crescent that goes around this part of the inland waterway. We can't keep watch all the time."

The big captain cooled a bit. "What do you need?"

"Give us two teams. We'll figure out a schedule, rotate surveillance, try to get a full scope of whatever is going on. It just feels like there's something we don't understand yet."

Williams looked steadily at the two detectives. "We're short-staffed right now. Shit. When aren't we?" He rolled the pen in his big left hand. "OK," he finally said, "you get two teams for three days. I'll send a quick note and clear it with Sheriff Perkins. You'd better make it good, though. Unless you like all-night shifts for a month." He waved them out of his office.

CHAPTER 48

PERKINS AND SAMANTHA were sprawled comfortably on her couch. Country gold hits played on the speakers. Rosie was curled in a ball at their feet. Her paws twitched occasionally as she chased imaginary squirrels off the manicured lawn at Whispering Palms Seniors Residence, where she and Mommy and Auntie Kim volunteered.

Samantha was reading the latest novel from one of her favorite authors; Perkins was buried in a bound report from the Sheriff's Association on crime statistics. He sighed as he closed the document, stretched and looked at the beautiful woman to whom he was deeply committed.

"Some days I'm not sure we're winning," he grumbled. Samantha peered at him over the cover of her book. Her eyes dropped down to finish the page. She inserted the bookmark, closed it and looked at the tough, rangy man in her life.

"You're winning," she reassured him. "You and all the law enforcement personnel who risk their lives every day…you are winning. And I for one am very grateful for what you do and for the risks you take out there."

She leaned over and kissed his cheek. It was stubbly at the end of another long day. He patted her thigh where her shorts ended. Wisps of passion began to stir.

"Oh!" He suddenly jumped up, leaving her a little askew on the couch. Rosie woke up. "I have something for you. Hang on."

He stretched stiffly and nudged Rosie. "Come with me," he said as he headed for the kitchen. Rosie was instantly alert; the kitchen was where yummy treats were stored. She trotted after him as Samantha rearranged herself into a more lady-like pose on the couch. She crossed her long, elegant legs and idly noted that it was time for a pedicure. She checked her fingers—make that a mani-pedi.

She yawned and ran her fingers through her tousled hair. She could hear rustlings in the kitchen. She finished her glass of ice water and looked out at the dark skies over the Gulf.

Perk reappeared and sat down on the couch. He looked at her intently. "I've been thinking a lot about this lately," he began. Samantha sat up straighter. A fluttering began in her tummy.

"I really love our life together," he continued. "You have brought some light and joy into my life that hasn't been there before. I treasure our time together; I love the passion we share."

Her palms began to sweat. This was suddenly serious. *Dammit, why didn't I shave my legs today?*

"Rosie!" She came trotting in and stopped near them. Samantha looked at her. Something was different. Something was—Oh. My. God. There was a ring-box attached by a ribbon to her collar. *Wait! What was happening??!! I'm not ready for... but what if...was this...why hadn't she worn a pretty dress tonight?*

Perkins grabbed Rosie's collar. He had trouble untying the little box. He finally got down on one knee so he could loosen the ribbon. Samantha sat there paralyzed, mind spinning and throat dry.

Perkins took the ring-box in his hand. Rosie beamed up at Samantha. Perkins remained on one knee as he turned to her.

"Rosie and I have talked about this, and we both feel this is the right thing to do."

What?

"So we wondered if you would accept..."

This is the weirdest propo—

"...what's in this box..."

Wait. Propo-what? What is happening? Will I say YES? Will I—

"...so that we can become even more of a family..."

Am I ready to get married again? I love the big galoot, but do I LOVE him beyond—

"...and make us both really happy..."

WHY DIDN'T I THINK ABOUT THIS? WAIT! WHY DIDN'T HE AND I TALK ABOUT THIS?

"...because we both love you and when we're all together..."

OH, BROTHER. IT IS COMING. I'M READY. NO I'M NOT. I WANT THIS. NO I DON'T, NOT YET. YES YOU DO, YOU IDIOT. HE'S A FINE MAN. A DECENT MAN. A GOOD LOVER. NO, USUALLY A GREAT LOVER. WE FIGHT SOMETIMES. THAT IS OK I GUESS. WE—

"...I think we are all better. So that is why we want to..."

SO OF COURSE YOU DIDN'T FIX YOUR HAIR TODAY, AND THERE IS THIS LITTLE STAIN ON YOUR BLOUSE FROM THE PIZZA SAUCE. OMG. YOU DIDN'T EVEN COOK DINNER FOR HIM TONIGHT! YOU ORDERED FROM 'NAPOLI RISTORANTE.' THAT WILL BE A HORRID STORY FOR HIM TO TELL OUR GRANDCHILDREN. WAIT!!! OUR WHAT??? DOES HE WANT KIDS?? DO I?!??! HOLY COW, WHAT IS GOING ON? HOW DO I STOP THE MERRY-GO-ROUND FOR A MINUTE AND—

"...offer what's in this little box as a token of our love together."

With that he handed her the little ring-box. With shaking fingers she gently opened it to find a shiny, beautiful—key. *A KEY??? HE GAVE ME A FREAKIN' KEY!! IN A FREAKIN' RING BOX??? I'LL...I'LL—*

"It is a key to my house," he went on as he straightened up with a little groan as his knee cracked. "Rosie and I think it will be better for you to have a key, although not as much fun for the neighbors to watch when you have to squirm through Rosie's doggie door to get in." He grinned at her. Samantha flushed as she recalled the humiliating experience of squeezing her thousand-pound butt through that little flap in his kitchen door as Rosie danced around smirking at her.

Her numb fingers held the ring box. She looked down one more time. *Yeppers, it was still a key. A flippin' shiny new brass key. In a ring box. With him down on one knee. WHAT ELSE COULD SHE HAVE THOUGHT???*

Rosie came over to nudge her knee. Absently she patted her.

Perkins slid over on the couch. Absently she patted him.

The ring box—yeah, the one with the key, that one—lay in her lap. Here she was, all aflutter, heart racing, her man on one knee, a ring box...*WHAT THE HECK WAS SHE SUPPOSED TO THINK WAS HAPPENING?*

"Tha...thank you. It's...lovely."

She sat there, totally drained.

A KEY. A LOUSY KEY.

CHAPTER 49

JIM CRANDALL LEANED back in the rocker on Beulah's front porch. She was inside finishing some paperwork. He had finally figured out a way to get back at city hall and those nasty people who had raised her taxes so much.

He wanted to make a huge splash, something that would disrupt and embarrass the city and generate national headlines. He was convinced that even if there was no hanky going on at city hall, there was certainly plenty of panky.

After a couple of weeks of research and planning, and a mysterious phone call from some guy in Arkansas or somewhere, never got his name, Crandall thought he had the answer. If he could pull it off it would paralyze the city, garner huge media coverage and probably end the political career of Mayor Rodriguez and at least a couple of council members. Kim what's her face. And the old guy who'd been there for a hundred years. Maybe even see that smart CAO get his ass caught in the mess and have to resign in disgrace. Yeah, that might just happen.

And the Sheriff. It would be great to see him get his butt kicked from here to Tallahassee and back.

Beulah appeared on the porch, rye and ginger in hand. She slumped tiredly on the other rocker.

She stretched her legs out with a groan. Her feet were pale white against the dark brown tan of her legs. There was no polish on her nails. She drank deeply and put the glass down on the wobbly table between them.

"Could use a little help in the morning on the south field," she said.

"No problem. What do you want me to do?"

"Fence is starting to go along the north and west sides."

"OK, I'll take care of it."

She nodded. Took another gulp of the strong highball. Closed her eyes. A moment later she reopened them. Farming is a job for the strong and the smart. Some days she wasn't sure she was either.

She finished her drink. "I'm exhausted. Heading for bed. You ready?"

"Not quite. Got a bit of figurin' to do." She looked at him quizzically. Nothing else was forthcoming.

"OK, g'night."

"Sleep well, Beulah. I'll be quiet coming to bed."

She grunted. "Bring a brass band. I'll be out cold." The screen door slammed behind her.

She is a good woman, Crandall thought as he finished his beer. She doesn't deserve all this crap from city hall she'd been getting. Her property taxes are just too high. Well, he was going to do something about that. He'd brief the morons in the J-Men group tomorrow night. He'd impress upon them the need for secrecy, so the event didn't leak out and give the authorities time to prepare.

After knowing the J-Idiots for a few months, he wasn't optimistic about their understanding of urban insurrection and the need to conceal intelligence. In fact, he wasn't all the certain they really had the balls to help pull this off. But sadly, they were the only troops he had in this war.

He shook his head, ran through the details in his mind one last time, locked up the house and headed upstairs to bed.

Chapter 50

"IT'S BEEN REALLY weird lately," reported the CI to Captain Williams. "A lot of huddling together by this little J-Men gang. Seems that Crandall is running the show now. He shuts up every time anybody gets close to them. All I've overheard is 'semi' and 'freedom' and 'convey' or 'confer' or some word like that. Can't put it together. Semi what? Semi-conductors? Some kind of computer attack? I don't think these clowns have that expertise, but…Ransomware? Freedom? Shoot, that's all these morons blab about after a few cold ones."

Williams drummed his big fingers onto his desk. These tips weren't adding up to much. Still, you never knew what would trigger some other clue.

"Alright, stay on top of them. Keep me informed. Call anytime. Stay safe."

The voice on the phone grunted and hung up.

The sheriff wandered into his office a moment later. "Got a sec?"

Williams nodded as he shuffled some papers into a pile. He looked at his boss. He looked tired, Williams thought. The pressure of this situation was stressing all of them in upper management at headquarters.

"I keep thinking that something big is coming, but I don't have a clue what it might be," Perkins began. He gnawed his cheek. "I just don't think these J-Men are done with us."

The two officers contemplated that threat for a moment. Williams updated him on the latest. It was thin gruel.

"We have been investigating the three ladies, as I told you," he said to change the subject. "I've got teams doing surveillance. They just told me that men get dropped off at Inez's house a few times a day, but they never seem to come out. It's weird." He shook his head in frustration.

"What about this Tiga Joe character?"

"Well, that's the other problem. We strongly suspect he's running drugs as well as women. But we can't directly tie him to the whole scenario. We're not sure if they are coming in by ship or sneaking in at night on little boats or whatever. Sometimes women show up at Inez's house at odd hours. Then they just…disappear."

Perkins thought about that one. "Any way to get into her house?"

"No reason to send in officers. No threat or danger. No complaints. Nothing."

Perkins shook his head, pushed out of his chair and left the office. The entire case was a debacle. He was due at Samantha's for dinner.

CHAPTER 51

HE AND ROSIE arrived a few minutes before 7. Rosie had been fed and had a walk. Perkins was hungry and horny. He was hoping to find a solution to both problems at the Sapphire Blue condo.

Samantha kissed him deeply upon their arrival. Rosie got a tummy rub. Perkins kind of wished for one as well but was too embarrassed to ask.

Wine poured and appetizers spread out on the coffee table on the lanai meant time for relaxation. Rosie paced around, staring down at the big oval pool in the center of the condo complex. Perkins sighed, swallowed some wine and chewed on a cracker that had blue cheese and some kind of jam on it. It was delicious. He grabbed two more and sort of gestured with his free hand.

"It's a soft gorgonzola with orange-fig jam," she said. "I invented it this afternoon. Do you like it?"

"Great. Yeah. Love it." He swallowed more of the mellow Cab-Sauv and grabbed two more of the crackers.

The evening sun was dropping in the western sky. Perkins moved a pile of mail on the coffee table to make room for his small plate.

"Some social invitations," Samantha commented as she gathered the envelopes. "After my Martinis & Manicures party, all of a sudden I'm a hot commodity in the ladies social circle."

Perkins grunted, focused on the cheese plate. It really was a fabulous blending of flavors. Rosie wandered over to negotiate a snack.

"I guess the ladies heard about how exclusive it was. Now they want to invite me to events, like fundraisers. Yeah, right." She snorted delicately. "I got one today from somebody I've never heard of, Inez something, lives by the bay. Don't know her from—what?"

She paused as Perkins suddenly jerked upright. "Inez. Inez. River, Ramirez, something like that?"

"How on earth would you know her?" Her eyes narrowed. "You sneaking around on me, cowboy?"

"Good lord no! But her name, or a name like hers came up today in an investigation. Inez is not a common name. It just clicked for me."

Samantha gave him a long, cool stare before dipping into the mail. It was never a bad thing to keep him on edge, she smirked to herself. Especially after the key incident.

"Here it is. Inez Rivera." She quickly perused the card. "She's having a cocktail party Thursday. 5-7pm. Ah, here it is. A fundraiser for something. $500 a pop."

She went to toss it into a discard pile when Perkins reached over to grab it. He studied it carefully. "Is this for two?"

Samantha found the envelope, re-read the invite, and looked up. "It says 'and guest,' so I guess that's me and one of my boyfriends."

Perkins felt his heart clench for a moment before catching her grin.

"OK. Good. Can you RSVP for us? I'd like to get inside that mansion."

"Why?"

"Can't tell you."

"Oh. Well, too bad. I'm busy that night."

Perkins sat there. He sighed. He knew when he was beaten. "Alright, the deal is we have suspicions about something strange going on in their mansion. People come, but don't go. We'd like to know more."

Samantha thought that one through. "Well, that should make the party more interesting. Let me check my diary. Oh, wait, I am free that night."

CHAPTER 52

THE EVENING OF the party was a blustery one. Perkins and Samantha arrived at the Rivera mansion to find valet parking out front. Perkins traded his keys for a numbered token. The pimply-faced teen looked excited about driving an official sheriff's vehicle. Perkins made a mental note of the kid's features so he could identify the perp after his SUV was stolen.

Samantha glided gracefully on her four-inch heels. She was wearing a tight silver dress cut above her knees. Her burnished gold hair gleamed in the soft light of the main foyer as they advanced into the party.

Perkins caught his breath. "You look spectacular," he whispered into her ear.

She turned towards him and rewarded him with a dazzling smile. "Thank you. And please try not to shoot any bad guys until I've had a couple of glasses of champagne. It looks like Cristal." She sniffed. "Have to love the nouveau riche, trying so hard to impress." She paused for a moment. "Still, I'll enjoy it. Sorry you can't."

She turned abruptly to introduce herself to Inez Rivera, who had suddenly appeared in the doorway that led to a large living room. You certainly could not fit an entire football field inside the room, but a medium length field goal would work.

Inez Rivera was a hard-eyed brunette. She was wearing a fixed smile, perhaps because her plastic surgeries had left her skin without a lot of elasticity. Some baseballs have a looser cover than her face. Her dress was a garish orange; her designer shoes matched the dress. She wore a lot of jewelry and a pound or two of makeup. She gushed over Samantha, who was now the prize catch for any hostess.

Samantha took it all in with a couple of expert flicks of her eyes as she extended her hand. She then introduced Perkins. Inez's eyes widened.

"Wel...welcome," she stuttered. "I, uh, didn't know you two..." The sentence ended awkwardly.

"Oh, yes," Samantha picked up smoothly, "he seems to follow me everywhere. Sort of like my own personal bodyguard." Perkins grinned.

Inez didn't seem to find much humor in that. She hesitantly shook hands with Perkins and then turned to snap her fingers at a near-by waitress. "Champagne! Quickly!"

The young girl turned red as she extended her tray. It was shaking just a bit. Samantha took one. So did Perkins. He didn't drink while on duty but having it in his hand made him look more a part of the party. Besides, he could keep Samantha's glass refilled more easily.

"An interesting house," Samantha ventured cautiously as she studied the replicas of sculptures and gargoyles that adorned the front part of the house. Some large modern artwork hung on the walls. Perkins couldn't see much to appreciate but then he wasn't a connoisseur. The splotches of colors and the random strokes of the brush seemed rather gauche to his eye. He smiled internally; what a great word, gauche. He paused to stare at one wall: was a urinal tilted upside down on a smeared black canvas really art?

"My husband is around here somewhere. You'll meet him," Inez declared. "Please. Go in. Enjoy yourselves. Thank you for coming."

With that she turned to greet another couple arriving at the door. Samantha grabbed Perkins' arm and they stepped deeper into the living room. A pair of doors at the far end opened onto a large terrace that overlooked the bay. They headed for the view. They were both aware that they drew a lot of stares; Perkins knew why Samantha got the looks, but he figured his own presence was a startling addition to the usual guest list.

Samantha sipped as she perambulated through the crowd, nodding to a few people she had met before. Perkins was taking in the house's physical lay-out.

They switched glasses when they stepped onto the terrace. The view was lovely. The soft evening light and the colored lamps around the terrace and the torches that burned along the cobblestone paths down to the water glittered like sparkling gems as the sun set.

A waiter circulated with a tray of baby lamb chops. They each tried one. Perkins snatched another as the waiter turned to go. "These are really good."

Samantha nodded as she finished chewing and then gave the bone to Perkins to hold in his napkin. A moment later another waiter offered seared scallops. This time Perkins didn't even pretend as he helped himself to two. He managed to sneak the lamb bones onto the edge of the silver platter.

They were soon engaged in conversation with other party guests. Perkins continued to glance around the house and yard, mentally configuring the mansion and its floor plan. Finally, he excused himself and returned to the house. He carefully looked around and then swiftly went up the curving stairs to the upper floor.

He peeked into the half-dozen bedrooms, and lost count of the number of bathrooms. Opulent.

He didn't see anything out of the ordinary. Still holding an empty glass, he returned to the main floor and was caught up in a group of guests debating the Florida governor's race. Dumb and Dumber were the two leading contenders.

After a moment he waved his empty glass at the group and exited down a corridor. At the end of the hall was a room with a closed door. He tried the handle; it opened into a lavish office. Slender taupe chairs. A white desk with curved legs and an elaborate phone. Dark peach paint covered the walls. Soft ivory inlaid tiles on the floor. Perkins studied the layout. It was an odd—

"It's my wife's office." Perkins whirled at the interruption. A short, swarthy man holding a cut glass tumbler with what looked like expensive bourbon in it was standing behind him. There was no smile. "Can I help you?"

"Oh. I'm just exploring the house. It is so beautiful. I like architecture," Perkins lied with a smile. "We haven't met yet. I'm LeRoy Perkins. You must be Chico Rivera?"

"Yeah. So, you're the Sheriff? Escorting that spectacular redhead? She is a knock-out," he said appreciatively.

Perkins bristled just a bit. "Yes, she is. We have been dating for more than a year now." He set down his markers very clearly.

"Yeah. Well, enjoy the party." He waited for Perkins to retreat down the hall. With that he firmly shut the door to the office, turned away, and disappeared into an adjacent room. He closed that door firmly as well.

Perkins walked back into the party. Samantha was engaged with three other women as he moved towards her. He heard "designer," "Paris" and "fashion" so he figured his presence wouldn't elevate the discussion. He snagged a fresh glass of champagne, exchanged it for the empty one in Samantha's hand, got a smile, and fled the conclave of couture

A moment later he was quietly patrolling the back of the house. The large kitchen predominated; it was busy with chefs and servers. He chose an ahi tuna roll from a passing waiter. When the coast looked clear, he took a chance and opened the door at the end of the hall. Stairs. Stairs? He slid in, shut the door and walked down. A basement? Nobody in Florida has a basement.

This basement had a man-cave. Giant TV. Leather recliners. A bar with three taps for draft beer. A suede couch against the back wall. A couple of framed Miami Dolphins signed jerseys. A picture of the Heat cheerleaders at center court. Two Playboy centerfolds, also signed.

There were the expected laundry rooms and HVAC controls down a side hall, and a storeroom. Four locked doors. A hallway that seemed to go nowhere. The basement had an odd feel to it. Most Florida homes don't have anything below ground because of flooding and water table concerns. This house seemed to have quite an infrastructure in the basement.

Perkins checked his watch. He'd been down here too long. He walked quickly up the stairs and slid into the corridor, and soon rejoined the main party. He found Samantha surrounded by three men. She looked as if she was enjoying herself.

He rushed over to the group. "Hi, I'm Sheriff Perkins," he introduced himself to the trio. Two of the men took a half-step back. The other man, wearing a mustache and a fog of cologne, shook his hand. "Hey. Marco Martinez. Great to meet you. I'm in sales."

"Ah. What kind?"

"Whatever the market needs," he grinned as he turned to his two pals. "We'd better go. See you another time," he nodded at Perkins and winked at Samantha.

It took a moment for the aroma to clear. Perkins looked at her. "That's what you come up with when I leave you for a moment?"

"Hey, here I am, all alone, nobody to get me Cristal and hors d'ouevres, a girl's gotta take what's out there." She gazed fondly at him. "Remember that next time."

"I was working," he hissed quietly. Then he paused. "Martinez? That the guy's name? Why have I heard that before?"

Samantha drained the final sip of champagne. "He was married to some poor woman named Charlotte. They got divorced. He was quite forceful about making that point to me."

"Hmmm. That's the connection. You ready to go?"

"Heavens yes. I'm thinking you owe me big time for tonight." She took his arm and steered him to the front hall. Samantha waved thank you at Inez and they walked down the front steps. Perkins proffered his valet token; to his considerable surprise, the vehicle seemed undented.

In his own office, Chico watched on the big monitor as the two drove off. The hidden security cameras kept rolling. He cackled with amusement as he watched a pious Congressman with the Christian-right grab the ass of his neighbor's wife. That clip would go into his private vault in case he needed some leverage for a piece of legislation.

Chico puffed on his Montecristo. He was going to have to talk to Inez about the Sheriff snooping through their house. His visit downstairs was concerning.

He clicked the monitor. A new camera angle showed two men in a dark corner groping one another. Chico made a mental note: one of their wives might be interested. Or the gentleman might prefer to do Chico a little favor or two to keep the tape private. He grinned into his cigar smoke: isn't technology grand?

CHAPTER 53

"IT IS A big house," Perkins reported to his investigators early the next morning. "The proportions seem a little off to me somehow, and there's this elaborate basement, sort of a male frat house. A long hallway that seemed to go nowhere."

"A basement?"

"Yeah. I've never seen one in Florida before." Quiet around the table.

"We are still confused by the men, and it is usually men, who go in. And always the side door. But they don't seem to come out," said Cornice. "First, why are they there? Second, what happens to them?"

Willie Williams thought for a moment. "It seems odd to me that they're going in through the side door. Heck, even my mother-in-law gets to come in the front."

Snickers from the married men.

"Inez seemed a pretty tough cookie," Perkins continued. "Samantha didn't like her, which is a big strike against her. Her husband is a little guy who thinks he's tough. I'm not so sure. He gives off a nasty vibe, just something...I'm not sure. But I think he's been stacking the deck for a long time."

A number of Chico's used car customers would agree with that statement.

He drummed his fingers on the conference table. "Both of them give off this hard edge. Rich, I guess. But crude. Between the two of them, you could write a list of their social graces on the back of a postage stamp."

Chuckles from around the table. "Keep the surveillance going for a couple more days. Let's see if we can get some drone coverage. Oh. Be aware that Chico has what I suspect is a rather elaborate hidden camera set-up on the property." Stokes made a note. Perkins looked around the table. Nods all around as the meeting disbanded.

Chapter 54

"I'M JUST TELLING you, the fuckin' sheriff was snooping around the house!" Chico erupted.

Inez was exhausted and hungover from her big party. "What did he find? Nothing, el stupido! You think I'm crazy?"

Chico chose not to answer that one. "I'm just sayin', why would he be in the basement pokin' round?"

"Maybe he was looking for the wine cellar, how the hell do I know?" She flung a coffee cup at him. He ducked and it broke on the tile floor. Her aim was never very good, particularly on the morning after the night before. It wasn't the first cup to meet its demise.

A maid scurried in with a broom and dustpan. The domestic staff had learned to keep them handy.

"Get me a Bloody Mary," she shouted at the maid. The young Latina reddened and rushed out.

A few moments later an older Latina woman returned with the glass of tomato juice and a double Grey Goose. Inez snatched it from her hand and gulped greedily.

Chico finished his chorizo and scrambled eggs, drained his coffee and pushed back his chair. "I'm jus' sayin', you and Veronica think you've got this foolproof thing goin' on. I'd be real careful. You're the one who invited him into our house with that luscious redhead just so you could play grand society dame. Now you'd better watch your ass, baby."

He dropped his napkin on his dirty plate and stomped out. Inez took another angry swallow and thought about his words. Their marriage had evolved into a mutually deterrent partnership. If the cops ever came knocking, each knew enough about the other's dirty deals to blow the other one to Timbuktu. But, like the Soviets and the USA during the Cold War, they both knew that mutually assured destruction awaited if either went too far. It did, however, provoke a rather volatile foundation for their relationship.

On the other hand, the sex was great. Chico was spectacularly endowed. Inez liked it rough. Besides, she loved the house she'd built with his money. She coveted the ever-higher social status to which she was now addicted.

Still, she thought as she finished her first drink of the morning, she'd better talk to Veronica and Charlotte. God, Charlotte's ex-husband was a creep: Marco Martinez. She'd have to have the fumigators in to get rid of the odor of his cologne.

She thought back to the party. It had been a real coup to get Samantha Summers to attend. She was the talk of high society in the city after her now-famous exclusive "Martinis & Manicures" party. She hadn't been very warm to Inez, however. A little snooty, really, which had hurt. But who knew she would bring the flippin' sheriff?

He was pretty cute, in his rugged, cowboy-tough look. Inez squirmed a bit.

Inez decided Perkins and Samantha were not a very good match. Their relationship wouldn't last. Then maybe Inez would console the poor man. She knew a few tricks in the sack that that skinny redhead would never do.

She smacked her lips as lascivious scenes flowered in her tired brain.

She pushed aside her muffin and hollered out to the kitchen. "Hey! Bring me another drink! I'm going up for a hot bath."

A couple of minutes later another maid appeared with a big, icy glass. She carefully put it on the side table by the huge tub in the master bathroom, turned down the lights to a soft glow, and quietly shut the door.

CHAPTER 55

"THE BLUEPRINTS SHOW several rooms in the basement," reported Detective McMurray the following day. "They had a lot of trouble getting a basement approved because of flood plain concerns, but I guess somebody at city hall got paid off. What is peculiar about these plans is that the hallway in the basement that you told us about, Sheriff? You're right. It just seems to dead-end."

Silence around the conference table. Nobody in the Sheriff's management team was particularly knowledgeable about architectural plans.

Finally Perkins shrugged. "Maybe talk to a planner or somebody? See if they've got any idea." McMurray nodded; Cornice made a note. "What else?"

"We've been getting some action from our street visits," Cornice reported. "We're chasing down some tips from a couple of the ladies of the evening we've talked to. We've got another meeting set up in the neighborhood this morning. Somebody called in a tip and wanted to meet. Tip said it will tie Tiga Joe to the Cabrera murder."

It was, in fact, the first clear lead they'd had in a while on the murder of Claudia Cabrera. Captain Williams nodded approval. He was a big believer in old-fashioned leather boots pounding the pavement. While he acknowledged the benefits of electronic data mining, there still wasn't anything as good as talking to people.

"Hmm. Yeah, pissing off Tiga is not a very smart way to last long enough to collect your Old Age Security," acknowledged one Lieutenant. "I wonder what his real body count is up to by now."

"A dozen or more."

"Then let's get him for this," snapped Perkins. "I want a lot more progress a lot faster than we've had. Let's make it a priority and get the thing solved."

His stern direction straightened up the room. Williams jumped in. "Sheriff's right. We haven't been totally focused on this. I'll assign extra resources. Fred, Jamal, let's meet with our Intel people right after this and plot out the next couple of days."

They both nodded. Perkins asked if there was anything else. There wasn't. McMurray's knee cracked alarmingly when he pushed himself up.

"When do you go under the knife?" Perkins asked.

"A week Friday," McMurray said through gritted teeth. As much as he worried about the surgery, the pain level in his leg was elevating every day.

"Good. Your knee sounds like a bag of marbles rattling in the back of a pick-up truck driving over a rutted road."

"You should try how it feels," McMurray replied. "Thank God Doctor Al-Hindi pushed me through the system and found me a date for the surgery." He shook his head. "I'm not sleeping much at night. And I won't take opioids."

"Smart. Now, get this murder wrapped up before you go in, and there'll be a nice bouquet of balloons for you in the hospital."

McMurray snorted in disgust. "There'd better be a bottle of Canadian Club hidden in the balloons."

Perkins grinned at him as they left the conference room.

CHAPTER 56

THE BULLET CAME out of nowhere. It pinged off the chrome on the window on the driver's side of the detective's car, just missing Cornice's head. The next shot cracked the windshield. Cornice reacted after a split-second, swerved hard and accelerated down the street. The car was weaving to make it more difficult for the shooter. Another bullet exploded the side mirror. Cornice came to the first intersection and squealed around the corner. McMurray had drawn his service weapon and was squinting through the car windows.

After another block and another turn, Cornice stopped the car and looked around. "What the fuck!!?"

McMurray shook his head. "How do I know? We got set up." He pulled himself up from where he'd been hunched. "You OK?"

"Yeah." Cornice called in the situation and requested back-up and an armored vehicle. Both detectives were breathing hard, hearts racing. Being ambushed will do that.

"Ninety seconds," promised the dispatcher. Cop shootings get top priority.

They both got out, popped the trunk, and put on bullet-resistant vests. McMurray grabbed a rifle and racked a round. They stayed behind the car because they didn't know if the shooter was pursuing them. Their heads swiveled as they tried to spot a sniper in an upper floor or a shooter tracking them on the street.

The neighborhood stayed silent. Nobody was on the street where the shooting had taken place, or even here, two blocks away. No noise of kids playing; no banter between neighbors. The whole neighborhood seemed frozen.

"Word got out in advance," McMurray grunted. "Place is dead." He winced over that word. "This was an ambush."

"Yeah." Cornice tilted his head at the faint sound of sirens approaching. "Let's go. We'll rendezvous at that old shopping center parking lot."

Four patrol cars screeched into the parking lot. Another detective's car swerved around the corner to join them. Two minutes later the SWAT team arrived.

"It was a total bushwhack," McMurray reported to the captain in charge of the SWAT team. "They or he or what the hell were waiting for us. Bullets came down at the car. Jamal did a helluva job getting us outta the fire zone. Not sure how many shots, three or four at least. Not sure where the shooter was but it was probably an upper floor in one of those abandoned buildings at the end of the street."

The captain nodded and pulled up a map of the street on the computer screen. He and the sergeant swiftly planned the counterattack.

The armored unit trundled back to the incident location. The SWAT team in full gear followed, protected by the armored skin of the beast that no rifle bullets could penetrate.

No more bullets flew. Nothing moved on the street.

The SWAT team soon invaded a shabby red brick building with a lot of broken windows. A moment later they came back. "Clear." They headed for the next one. It was a longer wait for the captain; every time he sent his men into danger, he sweated it out until they returned.

Finally the radio crackled. "This was the shooter's nest," reported a SWAT member. "We've got shell casings and you can see where he knelt to get his rifle out the window. We've also got a body on the ground floor."

"Any ID?"

"Nothing on the body. He's a little guy. Old. Wearing a dirty vest."

McMurray's head shot up. "Omigod, that sounds like Freddie!" He took off at a fast limp towards the building. Cornice hustled to catch up.

"You mean the guy we talked to in the alley a few days ago? Rather pungent, as I recall."

"Yeah. He called me two nights ago. Said he had some info on Tiga and some murder. Sounded real nervous." He slowed to a walk, flexing his knee painfully. "I think he got set up. By Tiga, looking for a leak in his organization. And then we got ambushed when we came here to meet with Vest Man."

They arrived at the building's shabby foyer. McMurray approached the body lying on the floor, careful not to disturb the crime scene. It only took a glance for the veteran detective to stop, shake his head, and then retreat.

"Yeah. It's Freddie. Looks to me like a double-tap."

Cornice looked at his partner. Two in the head was a professional execution.

The forensic unit took over the crime scene. The Medical Examiner was called to check the corpse.

The SWAT team finished clearing the adjacent buildings. No other signs of a shooter. The officers and the two other detectives fanned out, trying to talk to local residents.

Nobody had seen anything. Nobody knew anything. Nobody had heard anything.

"Isn't it mysterious how they were all inside their apartments, watching "The Price is Right" on morning television," said one of the cops after being shut out by yet another family. "Tiga Joe's got the whole street, the whole neighborhood, scared shitless."

Nobody said anything for a minute.

Finally, McMurray looked up, pain on his face. "Well, wouldn't you be?"

CHAPTER 57

THE PACE OF the investigation quickened. Nobody from the neighborhood was talking. Forensics had identified the rifle as being built in Finland. The shell casings were being checked for fingerprints. None were expected; this was a professional shooter.

"Whadda ya wanna bet that rifle's in the harbor by now?"

McMurray nodded. "Yeah. Listen, let's try to find Adele's apartment. Remember she first identified Claudia. Maybe she'll be ready to talk."

Cornice grabbed the keys to their newly assigned car and headed down the stairs. The garage staff was assessing the damage to their previous vehicle. The sergeant in charge of the fleet made some rude suggestions about taking a remedial driving course. Cornice made some rude hand-gestures in reply.

McMurray limped behind his partner. His knee had been especially painful this morning; his leg was hot and stiff and swollen.

It took them some time to find Adele's apartment. It was a small walk-up. The urban renewal folks had not visited her neighborhood.

"Adele. Adele!" Cornice knocked firmly. Eventually they heard sounds inside.

"Who is it? Fer Chrissakes, it's only 11 o'clock."

"Adele. It's Detective Cornice and my partner. You remember old fart?"

A double lock was unlocked. The door cracked open, but the heavy-duty safety chain was still firmly attached. One bleary eye peered out through the crack. It looked carefully. The door shut. A moment later they could hear the chain being unlatched. This time the door opened.

"Better be something' big, boys. Like, maybe I won the Powerball? That'd be nice."

"Sorry, no. May we come in for a minute?"

Adele hesitated. She finally shrugged. "The maid hasn't made it in this week, so things're a bit messy." With that she stepped aside and waved them in.

The maid certainly had not visited this week. More likely not so far this year. Possibly not this decade.

Clothes were strewn across the small couch and an old armchair. Cigarette butts filled a couple of ashtrays. The light coming in from the three small windows displayed a variety of dust motes and whatever else was circulating in the air.

Adele was dressed casually in a short bathrobe. Green once, now faded to dull silver. Bare feet. Hair tousled. She yawned and ran her fingers through her hair. The movement lifted the hem of her bathrobe, revealing more of her anatomy than the nuns teaching Grade 9 at St. Pius would ever permit. Much more.

"I need coffee. You boys bring any?"

Cornice looked at his partner and raised an eyebrow. "Sorry."

"Not very nice to call on a lady without a hostess gift." She yawned again, turned and went into the small kitchen. They remained standing in the small living room, mainly because there was no place to sit. A boxy TV from the last decade sat on a little table. Her bedroom door was open, revealing a mattress and box spring, an old chest of drawers, and more clothes scattered everywhere.

Her microwave beeped. A moment later she returned to the living room with her mug of coffee. No offer of hospitality.

She flung herself on the sofa, crushing some clothes. She curled one leg under her thigh; modesty was not top of mind. She swallowed a couple of big gulps and finally looked at the two.

"Ok, boys, what's up? Whatever it is, I didn't do it."

"We are still putting the pieces together on Claudia's murder," Cornice said, "and now Vest Man. "We are pretty sure it ties back to Tiga Joe. We are—"

"Don't get me into any shit with Tiga! No sirree! Not me. You wanna go there, get out right now."

"This is not about you or tying you to him. Promise. We just need to link up some loose ends. Just a bit of info, that's all we want."

"Yeah. Where'd ya park?"

"Outside the building."

"Well, that's gonna get noticed in about five minutes, so you got four minutes left to wrap this up and get out."

"Gotcha. Here's the thing…have you ever heard about a couple of society women, rich, living on the water, maybe in the biz?"

Adele waited for a minute, thinking. "Maybe."

"Good. We are pretty sure they are all connected with the women being shipped in."

"Ain't my problem. We all got issues down here. One minute left, boys."

McMurray threw a Hail Mary pass. "Please. Anything."

The hooker shook her head in despair. "Yeah. Tough." She waited, then looked up at the two detectives. "Word on the street is somebody named Inez. You never heard anything from me. Now get out."

The ride back to headquarters was somber.

Finally Cornice sighed. "The shooter's probably half-way to Venezuela by now. But I can't figure out why Tiga Joe wanted to attack us. He's gotta know that shooting at cops is just going to bring increased attention."

"Yeah. But he's not playing with a full deck. He's scared the neighborhood into submission. He's terrorized his competitors. We've had reports that he is ranting more, drinking more; God knows what drugs he's on. Remember somebody picked up that hooker a couple of months ago. She'd been beaten but still wouldn't admit it was Tiga." He paused as another thought hit him. "Hey. You think that Chico was involved in this? After the sheriff's visit to their mansion?"

Cornice shook his head in frustration. "I don't see the connection."

McMurray leaned his head on the headrest. He was depleted from lack of sleep and the agony from his knee. People never understand how exhausting pain is.

"We're not going to get close to him by chasing him directly. What if we tried to get to him the other way? Through these society women Adele told us about."

Cornice thought for a moment. "Sure. Good to try. Her tip might open something. We're just pissing in the ocean right now. We need a break."

McMurray nodded. He was still shocked by how efficient Dr. Al-Saadi's clinic had been. X-rays, blood tests, her examination of his leg, all in one hour. Then, stunningly, he had been prioritized for surgery. It was amazing. He flexed his knee. How many hours to go?

CHAPTER 58

THE SAMS CLUB was meeting at Kim's condo. Rosie oversaw circulating the snacks, as Rosie always did. She was a
devoted connoisseur of snacks. Anything with bacon was always a smart choice. Sharp cheddars were good. Meat from
the barbecue ranked high. Well, meat period.

Kim and Samira reclined elegantly on the couch. Samantha
draped herself over the matching armchair. A very pleasant
Sauvignon Blanc was being served. Rosie paced anxiously between the three women and the tray of snacks.

"What are we watching tonight?" Samira asked.

"An oldie and a goodie," Kim announced. Samira and
Samantha weren't surprised. Whenever Kim hosted movie
night, the odds were that it would be a classic war movie. She
had a fondness for them. Of course, her time in the Army and
her war experiences overseas gave her a unique perspective.

The Great Escape," Kim said. "Starring Steve McQueen,
James Garner, Richard Attenborough. Oh, and that tough-guy
hottie, Charles Bronson. A classic film. It won a bunch of
awards."

Samira didn't exactly roll her eyes at Samantha, but there
were definite twitches.

"Oh, come on, you'll like it. Lots of fun. Lots of action. The
good guys sort of win. Rosie will like it, won't you sweetie?"

Hearing her name, Rosie instantly switched her snacking
allegiances from Samira to Kim. She licked Kim's hand and was
rewarded with a very nice little piece of salami.

"We got wine, let's go," Samantha urged. She leaned over
and topped up Samira's glass, then her own. Kim hit some
switches, her TV lit up and the memorable music filled the
screen.

Two hours and 52 minutes later, the final credits rolled.
Rosie was curled up, sleeping. Kim had a couple of soggy tis-
sues beside her. Samira was engaged but not passionately.

"

Samantha had become quite fascinated by the story of Allied POWs trying to escape from a German prison camp.

"Yes, it is based on a real story," Kim assured her. "I love the movie. The humor, then the drama of the escape and the chase." She sighed and then looked around. "Geez, you guys drank all the wine."

"That's what we do," Samira announced as she stood and stretched. "I've got to go. Early rounds at the hospital tomorrow." She bent to hug Kim, waved at Samantha, patted Rosie and left.

Samantha wasn't far behind. She helped Kim clean up, then leashed Rosie for her walk to Samantha's condo. Perkins would probably be there by now.

He was. He was relaxing on the couch watching the late-night sports highlights. Rosie bounded over to say hello. Samantha dropped on the couch beside him, kissed him on the cheek and leaned into his shoulder.

"You OK?"

"Yeah. Well, you know. Frustrated with this case. People arrive at Inez's and then disappear. Then this shooting at my officers. This whole Tiga Joe case is getting ramped up, and we're running way behind. Drugs. Pimping. Smuggling."

Samantha patted his hand and they sat quietly for a long moment. Rosie was tired after her long nap at Kim's, so she dropped off in the corner.

Perkins finally stirred. "How was your party?"

"No party. Really, Perk, you should know that the three of us just get together to solve the world's problems in a sophisticated salon of knowledge."

"'Bout the only thing you guys solve are the questions about increased wine consumption," he grinned at her. "What was on the agenda tonight? Famine in North Korea? The GDP decline in Sri Lanka? The currency crisis in Brazil?"

"Oh, those were the easy ones," Samantha replied with a yawn. "Then we solved the issue of why men are so much dumber than women. Then we watched a great old movie about POWs escaping from a German prison camp. All that tunneling." She yawned again. "You about ready to go to bed?"

Perkins was gazing out the door onto her terrace. The night sky was dark; the lights around the giant pool in the concourse below offered muted red, blue and green points of light.

"I remember that movie," he said slowly. "Gosh, I haven't thought about it for years. But you're right—great action. They tunnel out. How they got rid of the dirt, dropping it down their pant legs." He stopped for a moment, deep in thought. "Hey, you remember Inez's house?"

Samantha winced, recalling the raucous decor. "Sure."

Perkins waited for another moment, his mind whirling. "What if there was a tunnel from that strange hallway in the basement that we thought dead-ended?" He sat up abruptly. Samantha stared at him. Perkins rose, then paced the room. "We couldn't figure out why they had a basement next to the inland waterway. What if they were building a tunnel?!"

He pounded his right fist into his left palm. "I need to talk to Roy Crawford. What's his number?"

"Honey, its 10:45pm. City hall is closed."

"Why? I need them."

"What you need is a few hours' sleep. Then you can chase city hall in the morning. I promise."

Perkins looked at his watch one more time. It was 10:47pm. City hall still wasn't open.

"Rats. I need to get site plans, zoning, whatever else for that property. Where would the tunnel open out? Wait! What's her name, Veronica, um, whoever, doesn't she live right there? I think that's it! What if the tunnel goes from Inez's house to Veronica's house, and that's how they move the women and men in and out without our knowing! Man, these pieces are just dropping into place!"

He was pacing the floor even faster now. She could see his brain computing the complex equations of this confounding crime.

"We need the information from the city's planning and engineering departments. Wait. We need to do a map of possible tunnel routes. We need to, well, lemme see, how would we— wait, that's it. We can get ground-penetrating radar to scan the property. Wait, how do we do that without tipping them off? I don't want them running away, I want to catch them red-handed. I want to see them in handcuffs and behind bars."

He continued to storm through the condo. Samantha sat, fascinated. Rosie opened one eye, assessed the situation, and went back to sleep.

"And I want them to lead me to Tiga Joe and I want him for the murders as well as the trafficking. Women. Drugs. Money laundering, I bet. Probably a few other things. I like this. I like it a lot."

He looked at his watch again. 10:59pm. City hall still wasn't open. Damn.

CHAPTER 59

"MORNING, SHERIFF."
Like a lot of successful executives, City Manager Roy Crawford answered his own phone whenever he could. He glanced at his watch: 7:14am.

"Roy, listen, I need help. I need to see the site plans and the zoning details and the approval process for a couple of properties. Pretty urgent."

Crawford could hear the imperative in the sheriff's voice.

"You've got it. Addresses?" Perkins shared the two street addresses. "OK. I'll have my Planning Director get back to you this morning. Uh, want to share the why on this request?"

There was a short pause. "Well, OK, for your ears only. We might have a lead on a human and drug trafficking situation. It involves, well, might involve, a couple of high-end properties on the inland waterway. We need to keep it quiet for obvious reasons."

Crawford grunted. "Understand. Wow." He thought for a moment. "Anything specific you're looking for?"

"Yeah. A tunnel."

Crawford blinked. "Uh, Perk, the city has never approved a tunnel between two private properties, at least that I know of. Or even between public buildings, when I think about it. Unless somehow it got grandfathered many years ago. But it would be highly unusual, particularly with the water table issues around here. Dangerous."

"Yeah, well, the pirates used to do it. I think we're dealing with modern-day pirates. They are smuggling drugs not barrels of rum, and women slaves, just like two hundred years ago. They will take any risk, break any law, to enrich themselves. No conscience about the lives they destroy. Greed. The excitement of outwitting law enforcement. Well, not on my watch!"

Crawford shrugged. "Wow. I still don't believe the tunnel thing, but whatever you want, we'll provide. I'll have our Planning Director call your office as soon as she gets the plans."

"Thanks, Roy. Later."

Perkins disconnected. Crawford hung up more slowly as his mind raced. A tunnel? In Port Manatee? For drugs? For human trafficking?

No way.

And that's what his Planning Director told him an hour later after she had pulled the files of the two properties and reviewed the specs.

"I just don't see it. Certainly there weren't any approvals for a tunnel for either property. With the water table so high, it would be perilous. I'm surprised the houses got approval for a basement four years ago. That was the Smithfield mayorship, of course." She rolled her eyes. "Before you arrived, but you know how corrupt city hall was at that time."

Crawford nodded. The former mayor and two city councillors from that era were still enjoying the hospitality of the state.

"We don't even consider basements in new buildings," she continued, "and increasingly we are demanding buildings be raised so the parking is under the first floor but still above ground or just barely sunk into the soil. With the concerns about coastal flooding and hurricanes, it just wouldn't be prudent to approve below-grade construction. Besides, I doubt they could get insurance for flooding if they had basements." She paused. "It's already difficult to get insurance in coastal areas, especially for flood damage. But underground development near a bay? Never."

"I agree. But the Sheriff's got a burr under his saddle. Will you call him right away and brief him?"

"Of course."

Chapter 60

"THE CITY SAYS there has never been a tunnel approved," Perkins fumed to his task force. "We need to think like the pirates we're dealing with. Pirates don't wait for a permit. They just create havoc. Pirates used caves and secret tunnels. Why couldn't they be doing that again today? But tunnel to where? And why?"

The site plans were strewn across the conference table. A couple of officers spun them around to look. The district featured a curved street around the edge of the Intracoastal Waterway system. Lots near the shoreline were designed to maximize exposure to the water. That was gold to developers, and increased the value of the property by multiples.

Wayne Cooper took the maps and tried to put them together. He was back in town on an investigation into a corporate Ponzi scheme, and had dropped in to see Perkins, who promptly dragooned him for a free consult.

He was wearing a vermillion T-shirt adorned with a voluptuous Katy Perry.

As the conversation buzzed around the table, he stared at the table. He moved one set of blueprints closer to the other, then overlapped the bottom sections. He kept moving the blueprints in peculiar angles. Finally, he looked up at Perkins.

"Sheriff?"

The room quieted. Cooper's insights were legendary. "When you juxtapose the plans at this odd angle, you can clearly see the proximity of one back yard to the other woman's yard, even though the addresses of the homes are on two different streets. Nobody would think of a tunnel, because a tunnel is almost by definition a straight line." The officers studied the plans again. "But if you make a right angle in these backyards, you could connect their two properties underground." He swiveled the site plans. Everyone looked with fresh eyes at the blueprints. "It would be dangerous to build, but while the city has not *approved* a tunnel, they have no idea if there actually *is* a tunnel."

Perkins got it immediately and so did his team. "Of course. If these two modern-day buccaneers are in cahoots, then…" He thought. "I did see that dead-end hallway in the basement of Inez's mansion, but I didn't go down to check out a blank wall. Who would?"

Nods around the table. This case was suddenly about the dog who didn't bark.

"What we need is to check their yards. How do we do that without alerting them?"

Captain Williams had that one covered. "We just had some surveyors in my neighborhood doing a check of underground conduits and utilities. I think that is routine, so the city's maps stay updated so that contractors won't dig and sever phone and cable lines, or cut into water or gas mains. What if we inserted our own crew into that area?"

"I like it," Perkins said enthusiastically. "But we need to do it surreptitiously. We don't want to alert these ladies. They might shut down the operation."

"We could have the city send letters to all the homeowners along that block, notifying them of the survey. That should relieve any anxieties," Williams suggested.

"Good. I'll phone Roy Crawford and get his support. We'll need what, ground-penetrating radar or something? It's got to look authentic.:"

Williams nodded. "Leave it to us. You get the approvals, and we'll work out the technology."

Half an hour later the City Manager phoned Perkins back. "I can have letters delivered to all the homes in that neighborhood tomorrow morning. We'll just tell them that city crews will be doing routine surveys of utility corridors, and that the crews will have official city ID and they won't bother the homeowner."

Perkins paused. "Uh, I was going to have my officers do it."

"I don't think that will work. They will need official identification and will have to know how to do underground mapping. You want it to look authentic, right? Why don't you include a couple of officers with our crew? I'll get IDs and coveralls for them, and they can work with my people. I'll get the union onside. Nobody's going to notice if the crew is 4 or 6. Couple of city trucks. No big deal."

"Great, that'll work. You let me know when and where and I'll have two officers ready to go."

"Don't make them too eager," Crawford warned with a chuckle. "They're city employees for that day!"

(HAPTER 61

AT 8:48 AM two days later, two city maintenance trucks rolled onto Bayside Drive. It was a very upscale waterfront boulevard with big estates, the six-person crew noted as they parked in the shade of two tall palm trees that were swaying gently in the breeze. Big houses, big properties, big taxes. Their boss had told them not to bother the homeowners other than to introduce themselves and show their ID. Standard procedure.

Four of the crew were sipping coffee as they unloaded a bunch of equipment—some electronics, some wands, a couple of metal detectors, many charts and clipboards, and cell phones. The other two chugged energy drinks.

They started at the west end of the street. The foreman rang the doorbell, politely produced his city-issued ID, explained they would be on the property for about fifteen minutes, asked about dogs or other animals, and thanked the homeowners for their cooperation.

The crew then went over the sidewalks, sewer systems, curbs and gutters, water pipes, back yards and the electricity and telco connections. The same process was repeated at each house along the street.

Notes were made, charts were studied, water was sipped as the morning heat upped the temperature inside the union-approved overalls. A couple of bright lines were sprayed onto the sidewalk to identify utility conduits underneath the pavement.

There was one incident when the homeowner forgot to bring in his dog. The German Shephard didn't appreciate a bunch of strangers arriving in his backyard. The crew retreated hastily until the big dog was lured inside by bacon-treats. Nevertheless, they kept a wary eye on the backdoor in case Brutus burst through it.

One homeowner wasn't very enthusiastic about their visit. He was a hard-headed New Jersey businessman who was a big believer in property rights. He exercised those by going outside with the crew to film their every move.

Another homeowner, a Mrs. Wilson, offered them iced tea. They thanked her but declined. "Union rules," explained the foreman. Why that was, no one seemed very sure, but the nice lady smiled brightly and retreated into her home. They finished her property and returned to the trucks.

The last two properties offered no surprises. The crew finished their surveys, completed notes on their charts, packed their equipment into the trucks, took off their hard hats with their names and the city crest on them, and drove off. It had taken most of the day to complete the work. They had had a bagged lunch while sitting on the tailgates of the trucks and took a bathroom break at a nearby fast-food restaurant.

Few noticed their arrival, their work, or their departure. Overalled workers with ID badges and hard hats were pretty much always ignored. In fact, in several of the mansions, owners pretty much ignored their own household and outdoor staff.

The two trucks returned to the city works yard. The equipment was locked up and the computers and clip boards were brought inside by the crew. The door in the squat brick building swung shut.

Chapter 62

IT WAS NEARLY 6pm by the time the two young officers returned to HQ. The Sheriff and his team were waiting impatiently.

"We are pretty sure we found it," breathlessly reported Deputy Bronstein. He flipped open the laptop, punched a few buttons, and then connected his computer to the intelligent white board in the conference room. Eyes darted to the screen.

"You can see the backyard of the Rivera property. We scanned it and our pals from the city marked the gas main and the telecommunications conduits. Then we found this faint track. The foreman said he'd never seen anything quite like it. Two parallel lines we are speculating are walls, maybe concrete or brick." He hit another command and another backyard appeared. "The Wilson property. We did the same procedure there. And we found similar lines underground. Then we put them together in a computer program that overlays the mapping of the area and—voila."

The evidence on the screen was compelling: a distinct set of parallel lines between the two properties and a sharp right turn that joined up the lines exactly.

"A tunnel." Williams barely breathed it out. "Son of a gun. I never would have thought that was possible in this water table."

"The city crews felt the same way," added Bronstein. "In the truck going out in the morning they didn't actually say we were nuts, but you could tell that's what they thought. Once we got the mapping completed in their office, the foreman couldn't believe it. We had to include him," he added hastily as Williams glowered, "but we just told the others on the city crew it was a drug deal. They all believed that. And we made the foreman promise not to tell anybody else."

"Secrecy is crucial to getting this done," Williams reminded everyone at the table. "If these people get tipped off, they can collapse the trafficking operation. They could flee our jurisdiction. They've probably got some hideaway in the Caribbean or somewhere. We could end up with nothing." He glanced at Perkins. "I say we go in."

"How are we going to raid them?" asked the L.T. in charge of operations.

Perkins sat back and watched with pleasure as his management team began to discuss the various operational options and risks. He had worked hard to elevate some young talent to the team, and they were responding to the challenge.

It took an hour to sort out the logistics. Williams declared himself happy with the outcome. Everyone looked at Perkins. "I like it. Good job, everybody. Tomorrow we go after the search warrants. Say, who are we going to?"

A brief pause. Different judges had different standards for granting warrants to crash private property.

"Judge Green? She's usually cooperative," suggested McMurray. There were nods of agreement.

"OK," Perkins continued. "Jamal, you and Fred take care of getting the warrants. You are the ones who got the tip about the names of these two women. Make sure the DA is in the loop and approves the application because this take-down is going to create a lot of headlines. There'll be lawyers representing these women storming our front door as if there was a free single malt scotch tasting going on inside. You can count on high profile attorneys, and lots of them. They'll be looking for anything to argue against our charges, so be careful about dotting every i."

A young lieutenant stuck his hand up and looked at Perkins, who nodded. "This works for Veronica Wilson and Inez Rivera. What are we going to do about Chico Rivera? And Charlotte Martinez?" He paused. "And then what about this Tiga Joe piece of work?"

A long silence. McMurray finally spoke up. "We still haven't tied those two into the trafficking and whatever else is going on in there. The evidence against Chico and Charlotte is…slimmer." He rubbed his throbbing knee. "Tiga Joe is different. We think we can get him on the drugs and several murder charges, but we are still building that case because he has so many levels of crooks and lawyers—sorry, I repeat myself—protecting him. If we go after him for the trafficking of women right now, I don't know if we can convict. Yet." He paused. "Again, we think he is doing it, but we haven't got enough evidence or eyewitness testimony. Yet. Sheriff?"

All eyes turned to Perkins. He took a deep breath. This was why the job of leadership was defined by some as the privilege to make tough decisions.

He took his time. Everybody at the table understood that if he made the wrong call now, the entire case would likely be defenestrated by the courts.

Various permutations ran through his head. He thoughtfully stared at the table. Sadly, no ideas were sent to him by the scarred wooden top.

"OK. This is how we're going to play it. First, we get warrants to raid the Rivera and the Wilson properties. I want our crews filming the raid and documenting the activities. If we can't get the tunnel door unlocked or however you open it, we're going to break it down. We arrest Inez and Veronica on the spot. We're also going to arrest Chico, because I just don't think you can live in the same house where something like this is going on and not know about it. Maybe his lawyers will claim that line of defense, but I don't believe it. I think Chico is dirty of something besides chopping up cars. He flashes around too much money. Maybe he and Tiga Joe are doing a side-hustle in cocaine. Anyway, we isolate all three of them immediately upon arrest. Separate police cars, separate cells. No contact. We interview all the domestic staff, because they must be aware of something. We need to keep options open for charging some of the staff with aiding and abetting if our investigation leads to that."

Perkins ran his fingers through his hair in frustration at the lack of hard intel.

"Look. The reality is we don't know what we don't know. We may be into a drug smuggling operation. Could be human trafficking, and that means the sex trade. Could be some kind of ring that harvests human organs. It is weird that our surveillance teams have seen men, well, mostly men, walking into Inez's house but rarely coming out. But we've seen other people come out we never saw going in. We've seen unmarked vans delivering people, sometimes just a man, sometimes a couple of women, who go in that side door. Is there some kind of secret cabal having meetings? Political insurgency or treason being plotted? Domestic terrorism? This is Florida, after all." He gestured angrily. "The truth is, we aren't sure what we're going to find. That's why we prepare for everything. We don't know about weapons on site, so we're going in with a SWAT team leading the way. I want our troops to be protected, so they will be in full gear. Everybody else wears vests."

Several officers were making notes.

"I want the raids to be executed meticulously. This will get a lot of media coverage. You should expect scrutiny from ten different angles." He paused as his senior staff jotted down things to be double-checked.

Perkins took a deep breath. "Now, as to Charlotte Martinez. I agree with Jamal and Fred that the case against her is weaker. At this moment, anyway. I suspect she is as deeply involved in whatever this mess is as the others, but if we don't have a case now, we need to keep building it. If she is involved and hears about the raids, she might freak and run. That would be good because we can grab her then and it will pretty much prove her involvement. I want a third warrant from the judge, but we won't execute it at the exact same time as the other two raids. We'll assign a unit to watch her condo. If she hears something from Inez or Veronica and then flees, or if we get something about her from the other two women, and let's face it, these two rather pampered ladies will be panicked and scared at being arrested, then we radio the watchers and they can execute the warrant and arrest Charlotte. Willie, you organize the two raids on the homes. Yvonne, you lead the apartment building surveillance and possible raid. Make sure you coordinate communications and the go-trigger for the second raid. We'll need to move fast so she can't destroy evidence if she gets tipped off. If we don't bust her condo, we'll follow Charlotte for a couple of days and see what she's up to. It might lead to other conspirators. In case she tries to leave the country, let's give a heads-up to the TSA at all the airports in our region. Get her passport flagged. They can detain her until we take custody."

Perkins looked around the table. "Questions? Comments? Improvements on this plan?"

"Are we filming the potential raid at the Martinez condo as well?"

"Good question. Yes, let's do that. I want this all by the book. Yvonne?" The L.T. nodded as she made a note. "Geez, we'll have more film crews working than Spielberg."

"Sir, what if there are children involved?"

"Huh. That never occurred to me. Excellent point. Let's see if we can get one of the church relief agencies to provide some help. Make sure we have toys and things for the kids. Diapers, clean clothing, anything else you think of. Make sure we include a couple of Spanish-speaking officers."

"Are there guard dogs or armed security on either property?"

Perkins side-eyed Williams. "Our crew that did the ground surveillance found one dog two doors down, but no dogs at either property," replied the big Captain. "Both properties have security services that do regular rounds plus electronic monitoring. They shouldn't be a problem because of our legal warrants and the heavy presence we'll have on the block."

"How do you want the media handled? The location of the raids on Bayfront is going to generate huge social media commentary. The TV trucks will be all over this," warned the Public Information Officer.

"Yeah." Perkins was not a fan of social media, let alone the traditional media, but he grudgingly understood their role in 21st century law enforcement. "Just before the raid begins, we'll block street access and keep the media outside that perimeter. You prepare a statement about the raid for use on site. I'll be available if I must to do a brief comment."

The PIO made her own notes. "OK, thanks. What about media drones filming?"

Everybody sat back at that one. Drones were ubiquitous in Florida. Some of the trashiest media and social media sites used them to gain access to once-private homes, estates and events.

"I'd like you to shoot 'em down, but I suppose the law might frown on that. Wait, we are the law!" It got some laughs around the table. "Really, I don't have a clue. You figure it out."

The PIO nodded unhappily.

"Anything else? OK, good improvements, thanks everybody. If you have other ideas, coordinate with Willie and Yvonne. We'll get the warrants tomorrow and execute the raids on Thursday. That will give us one day to get rehearsed, equipped and organized. 8am tomorrow, folks. And keep this thing quiet."

With that the meeting broke up with an energized hum. This was a big action for any law enforcement agency. It was high risk, with a lot of moving parts; if any of them didn't mesh, the entire operation was in jeopardy.

There were a lot of big ifs, Perkins knew. They still weren't positive what—if any—illegal operations were going on. The half-tunnel might just be really old, long forgotten, or not operable, or they got false readings from the ground radar. There was still uncertainty over how or if the two properties were connected. Some lawyers might find an error in procedure or police actions. A media leak could blow the entire raid before it occurred. His department may have misread the entire situation, and Inez and Veronica were simply nice ladies hosting a book club in their homes for widows and orphans.

There were a lot of uncertainties in this police action. So public a raid, especially in that genteel, old-money neighborhood, was high risk. But Perkins knew one thing was certain: Failure would come crashing down on the Sheriff's shoulders in a very loud and public way.

CHAPTER 63

JUDGE GREEN WAS proving to be intransigent. Detectives McMurray and Cornice were standing before her desk and were starting to feel like the pinatas at a kid's birthday party.

"Your request for these search warrants seems to be based on some rather flimsy evidence," she declared as she studied the documents. "Some ground radar's vague pictures of two parallel lines that don't seem to connect to anything. I've never heard of tunnels by our waterfront. Mysterious vehicles entering some property? Men walking into a mansion but not coming out? A murder of a woman found in a grove of trees many miles away?" She sighed heavily. "This seems like a reach, Detective."

McMurray decided to lay down his king. The risk was that the judge held the ace. If she trumped him, and they didn't get the warrants, the entire raid would fall apart. Then it would leak somehow. That would jeopardize the entire investigation and let the three women escape. Worse, Tiga Joe would find out and laugh at the cops while becoming even more brutal on the street.

"Judge, Detective Cornice and I also interviewed a young woman who is in the sex trade. She was scared and didn't want to talk to us. We finally convinced her, but she demanded complete confidentiality from us. We committed to that, which is why we did not include her information in the application. She gave us the name 'Inez.' She said there was a connection with Inez to young women being forced into the sex trade. Inez Rivera is one of the owners listed on the deed for one of the properties in question. We believe this is the critical first step in building a case on sex trafficking."

Judge Green stared at him for a long moment. "Alright, that is more compelling. Now I understand the connection you are trying to verify. Still, you are on thin ice. Give me a little more."

"Your Honor," he began slowly, "I have had the privilege of appearing before you several times requesting a warrant. You have always been tough but fair. Detective Cornice and I have been working on this for several weeks. We believe the situation is getting worse. There are more bad drugs appearing on the street and they are killing users. Too many of those are our kids. We have had reports of sex trafficking of women from Central and South America, and certain Eastern European countries, who are enticed here and then enslaved in a life of prostitution and drug abuse. We are worried about domestic terrorism. We believe there is a convergence of concerns that dictate the police urgently investigate these premises."

He flexed his knee unconsciously as he stood before the judge. She observed it.

"We understand that the evidence at this moment appears to be slightly underdeveloped—and you're right, it is. But this raid is our department's foundational effort to build a larger case and put a stop to this shameful and dangerous happening on our streets. I am asking you, Judge, to grant these three warrants to help protect women put into the sex trade, or to help stop domestic terrorism, or the drug trade locally, or whatever else is going on in these premises."

His knee cracked as he bent it. He staggered a bit and grabbed Cornice's shoulder to steady himself.

"You're in bad shape, Detective. Time to get that knee fixed."

"Yes, Your Honor. Next week. Friday."

"Good. The loud cracking is waking up my staff." She smiled as her staff laughed. Even a poor joke by a presiding judge draws a big laugh. "Well, your supplementary information about a link with an Inez and her ownership of one property in question for these warrants gives an added preponderance of rationale that is sufficient for the court to believe there may be illegal activities involving innocent women at this residence that may result in endangerment to this community. As your bon voyage present, Detective, I'm going to sign these three things. But you'd better be right in your assessment, or it will be the last warrant I sign for you. I'm going out on a long limb. In fact, I'm so far out on it that I can see your Sheriff's butt even further out, and he's quivering on the very shakiest end of that limb. If he crashes down, I don't intend to follow him."

With that she carefully scrawled her signature on the three warrants. Her clerk took them, stamped them, and handed them to Cornice.

"We appreciate it, Your Honor. And if that limb breaks, I'm sure the sheriff will be happy to provide a nice soft landing place for you."

The judge gave a wintry smile and waved them out of her office.

CHAPTER 64

THE SHERIFF'S DEPARTMENT struck at 6:03am. It was a carefully planned time. People are usually asleep or just getting up. They are not very sharp. They are scared and disoriented at the arrival of many large, helmeted, stern and unyielding officers carrying search warrants and weapons. The homeowner is unlikely to have easy access to their lawyer. Residents are frightened and nervous, and that usually means they talk too much. And, most cruelly of all, they probably have not had their first cup of coffee.

Perkins and Williams were in the Mobile Command Center. They watched in real time through cameras on the helmets of some of the officers as they crashed through Rivera's door as soon as a maid opened it, waving their search warrant.

Chico Rivera was wearing only pajama bottoms when he came thundering down the stairs. The maid was terrified and fled into a back room. Chico was incensed and stomped into the foyer. He screamed about invasion of privacy, discrimination, illegal search and seizure and the sexual proclivities of the mothers of several of the officers.

His invective was perhaps less effective because of his man-boobs jiggling and his hairy bare toes squishing on the cold marble tile. The little toe on his left foot was crooked.

The raid participants remained focused on their objectives, although two of them flinched at the insults to their sainted mommas.

Two officers immediately rushed down the hall to Inez's office, while four others poured into the basement to check for 'aliens'—as the US government designates foreigners.

Inez Rivera followed Chico down the regal staircase a moment later. She had thrown on a yellow robe that ended at mid-thigh; it didn't appear that she slept in any bedclothes at all. She too was screaming at the officers, demanding to know what was happening. She nearly stumbled in her high-heeled

mules with sassy pink tassels. She had her cell phone and started recording her own version of events.

The warrant was formally served; officers immediately separated the two and took them to different rooms. Inez screeched
threats and curses when they took away her cell phone.

The tension rose in the command vehicle as the officers
searched. "Nothing here, Sheriff," soon came the report. "The
man cave like you saw before. Four bedrooms, empty. Some
weird decorating, but I guess there's no statute against bad
taste. A lot of red velvet and a round bed in one. A hot tub and
a four-poster bed with silk ropes on the posts in another. Weird.
No idea."

Perkins sagged. The officer was correct—there were no
legal objections to what people did in their homes or how to
decorate bedrooms. If they didn't find something, this was
going to be a huge embarrassment to him and to the
department.

On another monitor, Perkins watched as the second team
raided Veronica Wilson's home. Same procedure. Same outraged screams and threats from the lady of the house. Same
teams rushing into the basement. There the similarities ended.

"We found two young women in the basement," reported
Staff Sergeant Eddie "Bull" Brock. He was a devoted body
builder who looked like he ruled the pasture. He was leading
the raid.

"Veronica Wilson has been served the warrant. She is demanding her lawyer and for us to get out. She, uh, phrased that
request a little more directly," he chuckled. "We declined to
leave," he said as he hustled down the basement stairs.

His helmet cam revealed a bar area with soft couches and
some erotic art on the walls. Brock caught up with his team that
had cleared the basement. Two sleepy young women dressed
in skimpy nightwear were rubbing their eyes as they stood in
the doorway of their rooms.

There were three other doors in the hallway. Brock peered
in each one. "Empty. Wow. It's like a, well, a hospital suite.
Looks fake." He shook his head as he took one more glance,
then strode to the next room.

"Also empty. What the hell? This room is decorated like
some, well, some kind of Arabian tent or something. Weird."

He moved to the next room. "This is, oh my God, this is
some kind of dungeon."

Perkins and Williams looked at one another as the same thought struck them. "Holy Crap," exclaimed the big captain. "It's not a human trafficking ring—we just busted a brothel!"

CHAPTER 65

PERKINS SAT BACK in dismay. A full-blown raid, SWAT team operation, guns drawn, the whole shebang...for a freakin' cat house. He could already imagine the mocking and derision that social media posts would inflict upon him.

"It is still a good bust," offered Williams, who instinctively knew the anguish Perkins was feeling. "These things are illegal, after all. And who knows, maybe they traffic some women who are forced to serve as prostitutes."

"Yeah," Perkins replied bleakly.

A quick interrogation of the two sleepy young women confirmed that they were high-priced call girls. "Fantasy granters," one of the girls explained, "to men who are, well, men who like that sort of thing. We're like therapists."

One of the girls was a third-year student at the college. The other was a young housewife whose husband was a long-distance trucker. Both women had stayed over after a long night. Both cheerfully admitted to what was going on. "For a thousand a night, it's great money for doing something I like," explained the housewife. "My husband and I use the money to pay down the mortgage."

The student said she'd seen other women brought into the basement in small groups but didn't know them or what happened to them. She pointed to the last room in the hall. Officers quickly forced the lock. Inside, they found a dorm room with six metal bunk beds and a small bathroom. Two terrified women from Venezuela huddled together on the lower bed.

A female officer who spoke Spanglish squatted down, took off her helmet and began to quietly speak with the women. They finally stopped quivering and crying and began to respond. They chatted for several minutes. The officer reassured the women they were now safe and had been rescued.

She then stood up and quickly reported to Perkins. "They were brought here to make money for their families, except they had to pay the 'transportation fee.' They were going to be sold or put into the sex trade." The revulsion in her voice was clear.

Brock was still exploring the basement. He paused to collect his thoughts when one of his officers waved him to the smallest room at the end of the corridor. It was double-locked. He waited as his team broke the locks. Inside they found…nothing.

"Why would you double-lock an empty room?" Nobody had an answer.

Puzzled, Brock took his heavy Maglite and turned its powerful beam on the walls. They were wood-paneled. Nothing there. He studied the ceiling. It was painted drywall. No secret openings. Nothing. The two officers in the room also looked carefully. They stomped on the concrete floor. No cracks to show a secret vault below. No hidden trap door. Nothing. This was turning out to be one weird raid, Brock muttered to himself. The sheriff was not going to be happy. The department was going to look foolish. Crap. All this action for a couple of hookers and the two madams, or whatever the broads upstairs called themselves.

"Let's move on, boys," Brock finally said. They left the room; the door lock would need professional repairs.

They started down the hall. Brock suddenly froze. "Hey. Wait. Why would you panel an empty room in a basement that had concrete floors but no carpet? The room wasn't finished or furnished. A double lock on the door? I don't think so."

With that he spun around and re-entered the basement room. His two officers followed, puzzled. Brock looked around the room again. "They had a false door for the tunnel. What are the odds there's another one in here?"

With that they began a meticulous search of the walls. One of the officers found it. "Hey, Sarge. C'mere. Feel this." He pointed to a tiny slit down one seam of the paneling. They both pushed and pulled for a minute, trying to find the secret way of opening the space.

"Hell with it, let's rip 'er down," Brock said. He was in no mood for careful protection of the wall. In a minute the three men had torn off the wood panels. A recessed vault was revealed.

"Get me Abbott!" Brock ordered.

Tony Abbott was an expert on locks and safes. His father had been a locksmith, and Tony had picked up his old man's expertise. He entered the room a moment later.

"Crack it!" was Brock's terse order.

Abbott nodded. He studied the vault and its electronic lock. He extracted a sophisticated digital codebreaker and attached it to the dial. The old way of using a stethoscope to break into a safe was long past. The red LED numbers flashed, spun for a minute and then froze. Abbott removed it and dialed the numbers that had been revealed. The door swung open on oiled hinges.

The officers crowded around the open door. Brock was the first to reach in and grab a vial. He opened it and shook out the contents into his big fist.

He grinned at his colleagues. "I think we're about the make the sheriff very happy."

CHAPTER 66

A FEW MOMENTS LATER Brock keyed his mic to finish his preliminary report. "Sheriff. Captain. We have found what we believe to be a very large stash of illegal pills. Opioids. Fentanyl. Steroids. Several others that will need to be tested. We are photographing them now and will document each vial carefully. It is a significant cache."

Perkins sagged back in his chair. The stakes had been raised in the last hand of the night, and with the final card he'd drawn into a full house.

Williams grinned at him. "Got 'em," was all he said.

S/Sgt Brock started his officers carefully photographing and cataloguing the contents of the large locker. He then resumed his trek down the hall while still broadcasting and reporting to the command center.

"The door at the end of this corridor is in fact the tunnel entrance. It had some code lock on the door that the woman upstairs wouldn't share, so we used appropriate force to enter." He grinned. "The door may have to be replaced."

Williams snorted. "The boys enjoy the beat-down of the innocent door?"

"You know it, sir."

"Does the tunnel connect to the Rivera house?"

"Roger that, Sheriff. The B team had to kick it in on their side. The entrance was concealed behind a false wall. No wonder you never noticed a door when you were down there. Our guys found out later that the entire wall opened with a remote. Tough. Anyway, the tunnel makes this right turn half-way down, which I guess is what fooled everybody into thinking that there couldn't be a connection between these two properties because there was no straight-line access."

Williams and Perkins nodded at each other. The gamble of the raid had proved to be a winner. Judge Green would be comforted.

"We are speculating that johns would come in the side entrance of one house and then go through the tunnel into the other one, depending on their fantasy. They would then leave by the other property onto a different street, thus protecting their privacy. Pretty clever, in a way."

"I guess. Any office or files or anything at the Martinez house?"

"We're just finishing the sweep upstairs. We haven't found much yet. We'll keep looking."

Perkins sighed in satisfaction. The raid wasn't what they had expected, but it was still a good bust. "OK, book the three primaries. Separate cars, separate cells. Oh. You might do the initial booking at the Fourth Street station."

Yes, sir!" Brock responded with enthusiasm.

Perkins could see the grins on the faces of Williams and Brock. The lawyers for the three people in custody would naturally go to the Sheriff Department's Main HQ to see their angry, scared clients. Booking them at the secondary sheriff's station would delay any lawyerly contact for a while longer. And sometimes it was amazing what somebody under arrest, and still with no coffee, would blurt out.

Chico attempted to phone his lawyer. It took three calls because Chico couldn't remember his lawyer's latest mistresses' phone number. The legal beagle said he was coming and not to say anything. His mistress pouted at his departure. His wife was unavailable for comment.

Inez and Veronica made their own panic-stricken phone calls for legal representation. Each of the three then sat for long, lonely hours on a concrete bed in separate cells and cursed the others for getting them into this mess.

The mopping-up of the raid began at both houses once the primary suspects were transported to jail. The two young women were identified and dismissed. The two aliens were moved to a secure hotel where church leaders comforted them.

Lots of pictures and videos were taken at the two properties. The offices of both Inez and Chico Rivera were thoroughly scoured. Several boxes of evidence were filled. It was sort of like the FBI at Mar-A-Lago.

There was a surprising lack of any paper at the Wilson house. No office. No filing cabinet. A computer was seized.

The few staff on site denied any knowledge of anything. Officers were taking statements and confirming identities.

"The big question is, do we trigger the raid on Charlotte Martinez," said Perkins.

"Could," Williams agreed, "but maybe if we let her run for a day, we'll stumble across some interesting stuff somewhere. We need to go through the files we captured. Interrogate the women. If we've got eyes on Charlotte at all times, I think we're OK. And hearing about the arrests of her pals might scare her into doing something stupid or contacting someone."

Perkins thought for a moment. If Charlotte somehow escaped, the black eye on his department would be very large and extremely public.

"Neither of the other women phoned or texted her this morning?"

Brock shook his head. "No indication of that, unless Inez called from another phone before she sashayed down the stairs."

Perkins looked at the floor of the Command Center. "Tough call. Let's give her a few hours and see what happens when she hears about the raids and the arrests. Maybe she'll panic and lead us to Tiga' Joe. Him I would really like to nail. Tell the team on her surveillance what's happened. And tell them if they lose her, you'll kick their asses from here to Sarasota."

Williams nodded and reached for his cell phone. Perkins congratulated the planners and the officers who had executed the raid so flawlessly. The PIO came to get him. Perkins grimaced, but he knew how important media relations and public information were in today's complex social media world.

It had been a good day for the Sheriff's Department. That wasn't always the case.

Perkins sighed. Now came the most dangerous moment—facing the cameras.

Chapter 67

SAMANTHA HAD A headache. She was grumpy. She had probably overdone it at the gym yesterday because her glutes and thighs ached. She hadn't had a glass of wine in three days because of some stupid cleanse thing she'd let her trainer talk her into. It involved gagging back glasses of some thick, disgusting green liquid.

She hadn't heard from Perkins or seen Rosie in the last three days. No fun in the sack with her sheriff since the previous weekend. Life pretty much sucked.

Besides, it was a gray, rainy day. No pool or beach time this afternoon.

She knew that Perkins had been consumed by some big investigation for the past few days. Samantha had been consumed by dealing with her investment advisor in New York as they conducted her annual review and strategy session. Samantha cared a whole lot about her financial situation now, so that she wouldn't have to worry later in her life. She had become a shrewd investor who paid attention to global market trends. She had grilled her team of advisors and tax planners very precisely for most of the day. Everyone was exhausted by the conclusion, but she insisted on the detailed review. A girl had to look out for herself, she had learned very quickly during her divorce.

The results this year were quite satisfactory. Samantha had been quietly moving some of her investments into big international infrastructure projects like seaports and toll highways; it was proving to be a smart decision with very gratifying returns and steady dividends.

She poured herself a third cup of mocha blend and flicked on the local TV news channel to catch up on what had been happening in town.

It took a few minutes for her to understand the frantic commentary of the young news reporters. She vaguely recognized one house. She sipped—wait. Wasn't that the home of whodoyoucallher, that bitchy, social-climbing wannabe where Perkins had made Samantha go to her party and—Holy Cow, was this the raid Perk and his staff had been working on? This was big. This was interesting.

She cranked up the volume and put down her coffee.

"These are the two homes that have been raided. They are both located in the exclusive Canal District, which overlooks the inland waterway system. Prices for homes in this block start in the $4-5 million range. We are still waiting for the press conference from the Sheriff's Department which has been scheduled for 11am. Lesley, back to you at the desk."

A rather surprised news anchor attempted to smooth her facial expression as her camera's red light flashed on. She would have needed a trowel and putty.

"You are seeing the live images of this dramatic early morning raid by the Sheriff's Department on two mansions in the Canal District. Two vans just left one property. Our reporters could not see inside them. A large number of police personnel remain on site at this time. Street access remains blocked. We will take a commercial break and be right back with more of this emerging story."

Samantha's coffee kicked in at that moment and she departed hurriedly for the bathroom. She glanced at the wall clock in her dining room on her return: 10:54. OK, let's see what Perk and his people had to say. She curled up and called Kim to turn on her TV. As the ward Councillor, Kim had already been made aware of the police activity.

There were nearly a dozen microphones set up at the end of the driveway of Chico and Inez's property. Samantha thought briefly that a week ago, Inez would have given her left kidney for such publicity.

Perkins was in his dress blues, as was Captain Williams. Three other officers joined the group as they walked toward the media.

"Good morning. I'm Francesca Goncales, the Public Information Officer for the Sheriff's Department. Thank you for joining us. In a moment Sheriff LeRoy Perkins will update you on this morning's activities. Captain Willie Williams will provide any background you need. Lieutenants McCray and Steppings, who coordinated the activities this morning, are also here. The Sheriff has an opening statement and then we'll have time for a few questions. Please remember that this is an on-going investigation, so we are limited in what we can say at this time. Sheriff."

Samantha watched intently as Perkins moved behind the phalanx of microphones. He looks tired but pleased, she thought.

"The Sheriff's Department early this morning executed search warrants on two homes on Bayshore Drive. Three persons of interest have been taken into custody and are now on their way to a secure facility. Charges are pending for all three in what we believe to be multiple crimes. We expect to lay charges concerning smuggling, prostitution, keeping a common bawdy house, and possession and distribution of illegal narcotics. We are investigating possible human trafficking. There may be other charges as our investigation proceeds. We will also inform the IRS of possible unreported income, and the FBI of possible international money laundering and sex trafficking."

He paused to clear his throat. There was a buzz from the assembled reporters. In Port Manatee, this was the story of the year.

"The raid this morning was planned and carried out flawlessly by our personnel. There were no injuries to anyone, no excessive damage to either property. Two women from a South American country who had been brought into the US illegally have been rescued. They are now in a safe haven and are being guarded by my officers to ensure their privacy and safety."

Perkins paused for a moment to stare icily at the reporters. "Any attempts to find or photograph these innocent women, who have suffered enough, will be met with swift action."

He let that linger in the morning air.

"Finally, we are aware of other persons of interest in this complex case. Our investigation is ongoing. Because this case is so large and intricate, it will take some time to complete our work, gather evidence, and perhaps to indict other suspects and lay further charges. Officer Goncales will keep you up to date as new information becomes available."

He stepped back and Willie Williams came up to the mics. He enjoyed public speaking even less than Perkins, but he bravely outlined the details of the investigation, the warrants and the raids.

Goncales reclaimed the podium. "Questions?"

The media began to shout a dozen different questions. She pointed at one reporter.

"Who has been arrested? And on what charges?"

"We currently have three people in custody. Veronica Wilson, 41. Inez Rivera, 42. And Chico Rivera, 44. Details on the charges will follow in the next 24 hours."

There was a gasp from the reporters. The names of the three were well known in town.

Another frantic scrum to get the next question asked. The PIO pointed at a reporter in the back.

"Sheriff, what were the women used for? Why were they brought in here?"

Perkins reluctantly stepped forward. "Remember that this is still very early in our investigation, but we believe this involved kidnapping, prostitution, unlawful confinement and some other charges. I emphasize that this is a rapidly evolving case and it may go in several different directions. Greg?"

"Thank you. Sheriff, how did the foreign women get into Florida?"

"I have already spoken to James Robertson, the Regional Director of the FBI in Atlanta. He is collaborating with Homeland Security and both agencies will be involved in determining answers to that question."

More shouted questions. Perkins pointed at a reporter in the front.

"How did the women end up here?"

"Through diligent intelligence work, we began to suspect that there was some sort of secret linkage between these two properties. That seemed highly unlikely, as the site plans for this area showed no connection and the city had never approved a connection. Our intelligence concluded that there most likely was a secret tunnel that was used to move the women and the illegal drugs and possibly other contraband from the property on this road under the backyard to the property that faced the other way around the corner. From that second house the women and the drugs were moved in secret to other locations. Once we determined the probability of such a tunnel, and using other investigative techniques, we were able to put together a likely scenario. Our City Manager and his staff were extremely cooperative in this investigation and provided critical assistance to us."

"Hey! Can we go in the tunnel?"

"No. Last question."

"Was the tunnel legal?"

"No. Thank you. We'll keep you informed of further developments."

With that Perkins and his officers walked back to Command Central.

Samantha immediately called Kim. "Wow. That's the house Perk and I were at the other night for that dreadful party. He was casing the joint." She giggled. "Golly, do they still say that?"

"This is big, big stuff, Samantha. Human trafficking? Drug smuggling? Running a bawdy house? In our little town? Good grief."

They thought about that for a minute. "This is in my ward," Kim continued. "Man, everything that goes bad in town happens in my district."

They both thought back to the previous ward councillor who had gone to jail for corruption; bombs exploding at the gorgeous new high-rise development that had put the city's largest-ever development in jeopardy; a murderous crazed nurse at a senior's residence who was killing residents; and now this.

"Hey, you're the one who ran for city council."

"No, you're the one who told me I was running," Kim laughed. "And then got me elected. Remember that vicious election battle? Whooee." She paused. "Well, I'd better get to city hall. I'll call you later."

Samantha slowly put down her phone. No wonder Perk had been unavailable for days—planning such a raid must have consumed everybody's time and energy. Well. She could certainly give him a little reward. After all, he'd given her a key to his house; she still remembered with exasperation that awkward moment: him on one knee and Rosie bouncing around.

She did have that new, flirty little sun dress that he hadn't seen. He would like it.

She called Mary, his assistant. She agreed to get him home by 7:30pm. That would give her time to organize a nice dinner, get Rosie all tuckered out, and then seduce the heck out of the poor, innocent sheriff.

Her headache was suddenly gone.

CHAPTER 68

"YOU LOOK A lot better this morning," Captain Williams observed in his blunt way.

Perkins grinned. "Yeah." Images of Samantha in an incredibly sexy little sun dress, some beautifully barbecued lamb chops with mint jelly and an arugula salad, and an action-packed evening in his bedroom had relieved a whole lot of stress. His back might not recover for a few more days, but it had been worth the exertion.

Williams began his update. "The techies just solved the password issues on the mobile devices. Our experts are poring through those files right now. There are a few boxes of paper that we're already going through."

He checked his notes again. "We have started interviews with the three of them. Lawyers finally found 'em, which kinda restricts the free flow of conversation because we have this Bill of Rights thing." He grinned. "Bottom line right now? Chico is saying it was all Inez and he wasn't involved in whatever might have been going on. He is a man without conscience. He'll flip to save his own ass. Inez is saying who, me? I didn't have anybody illegal in my house. What tunnel? It's the Sergeant Shultz defense—'I saw NUTT-ING.'"

He grunted in disgust. "Veronica is saying it was nobody doin' nuthin'; it was always somebody else misbehaving. Mind you, Veronica is having a little trouble explaining why two Latina women were locked in her basement." He paused. "So far, nobody is talking about Tiga Joe. They're all scared to rat him out."

Perkins understood. Fear is the water in which mob bosses swim.

Inez, Chico and Veronica had all requested bail, concluded Williams. The hearing on that would take place at 11am.

CHAPTER 69

JUDGE CYNTHIA GREEN swept into her courtroom with a swirling flourish of her robe. She understood this was going to be a difficult case that would draw a lot of media attention. She had a savvy legal mind as well as a finely tuned nose for media controversy. Her mother had trained her well and set her on a trajectory to become a Justice on the Supreme Court. So far, her plan was right on point.

"Good morning. Counsellors. Mr. DA. It has been a long time since you have graced my courtroom."

Doug Sanders rose from the prosecution table. "It has been, Your Honor. It is a pleasure to be back in the courtroom doing the legal work that I love, away from the tedious burdens of office paperwork."

Judge Green smiled to herself. The DA was a politically savvy operator who had his eyes on the Governor's mansion in the next election. It was impossible to believe he would pass up a high-profile prosecution such as this one.

"Defense counsel?"

Two women and one older man rose from the opposite table.

"Good morning, Your Honor. My name is Rhonda Black. I represent Veronica Wilson." She was a woman in her early 50s. She dressed and spoke in a no-nonsense way. Her pumps were black, her dress was gray and her jacket was dark mauve.

"Judge Green, nice to see you again. I am Ronald Terwilliger, and I am representing Mr. Chico Rivera, who has been so wrongfully accused of—"

"Yes, of course he has been. Let's save the arguments for later, Counsellor." Terwilliger was now in his mid-60s. He had long, wavy, silver hair and was dressed in a three-piece suit and bow tie. It was one of 17 suits he owned, all bespoke. His bow tie collection was legendary. He and Judge Green had sparred on many cases.

Terwilliger flushed a bit and nodded. Judge Green looked down at the third lawyer standing before her.

"Good morning, Your Honor. My name is Maria Sanchez. I represent Inez Rivera."

The Judge looked at the woman. She was wearing a crimson suit cut just above her knees. Her blouse was black silk. Her skin was flawless and seemed to glow with health or very good cosmetics. She was stunning. The high heels accentuated her legs.

Judge Green sighed. If this went to a jury trial, she'd have to assign bailiffs to keep the male jurors from slobbering too much.

"Ms. Sanchez. This is your first time in my court, I believe."

"It is, Judge. I look forward to the experience."

The judge studied her for another moment. This was going to be interesting. She wondered if it meant anything that both female defendants had female lawyers, and the male had a male lawyer.

"OK. Let's proceed. We are not arguing the merits of any case or charges today, simply conducting a bail hearing. Mr. Sanders? How are we proceeding?"

The DA rose quickly. The large media contingent of reporters sat up and opened their notebooks.

"These are extraordinarily serious charges, Your Honor. The People expect to file additional charges against all three defendants. The Sheriff's department is still conducting its very thorough investigation. The case is extremely complex. The People believe it has international connections and involves victims from several different countries. It already has the attention of the FBI and Homeland Security."

"Will you charge the defendants jointly or individually?"

"We are still determining that."

Maria Sanchez rose quickly. "Your Honor, if I may. We will be seeking to sever this case. Without knowing what the DA may file against my client and the others, it is our position that there may be significantly different situations involving the defendants. My client, for example, is totally innocent and will want to be tried separately, if indeed any charges are ever filed against her."

It was a nice opening shot, thought the judge. The reporters were scribbling notes.

"Ms. Black?"

"I would agree with my distinguished colleague. My client has done nothing wrong and looks forward to clearing her name if a trial proceeds. Which frankly, Judge, I don't think will ever occur, as the DA is overreaching so badly in this case."

"I'm sure Mr. Sanders will survive your dismay, counsellor," the judge commented drily. "Mr. Terwilliger?"

"Oh, certainly, Judge. I have never seen a weaker case against a client of mine, but we opt to sever the case from any others. May we discuss bail now?"

"Yes, that's what this morning is all about, if you remember?" She gave an icy smile at the defense table. No one was offended.

The DA rose. "Your Honor, as I said initially, this case is still evolving. I can tell the Court that there are very serious international implications to this horrific female sex trafficking case. Drug possession. Drug trafficking. As Your Honor would understand, charges are still being determined with other branches of government. My office believes that there will be multiple charges against several additional people. Very serious charges. Conspiracy. Perhaps kidnapping. Forceable confinement. Prostitution."

The media were scribbling frantically. The DA paused to give them time to catch up. He took a sip of water and continued. "Charges, that, on conviction, will result in many years behind bars. As a result, we oppose granting bail to any of the defendants before you this morning. Flight risk is extremely high. These are wealthy people with substantial personal assets. They are experienced international travelers. They have the means, and arguably the motive, to escape this court's jurisdiction. That is why the People urge you to not grant any bail request."

The three defense attorneys erupted like a covey of quail flushed from a bush. The judge let them talk for several minutes, then banged her gavel.

"OK. Let me see if I have this. All three of your clients are innocent and deserve a nominal bail to be set. I—no, Mr. Sanders, I've heard from you—understand the seriousness of the charges and the allegations that may become further charges as the Sheriff's investigation proceeds."

She watched for a moment as the reporters wrote down her statement. She wondered for a moment how her words would actually get reported.

"I understand that all three of the defendants have ties to this community, they own property here and they have a long history of supporting charities and other activities. I also understand that these are potentially extremely serious charges. As a result, I am prepared to grant bail"—Doug Saunders face tightened in anger, while smiles appeared on the three lawyers sitting at the defense table—"but only with severe restrictions. First, bail will be $2.5 million for each defendant. Second, each will immediately surrender his or her passport to my clerk. Third, each defendant is restricted to living at their residence except for medical appointments or visits to a house of worship. They will be allowed to return to their abode only after the Sheriff has completed the on-site investigation. Fourth, the three defendants are to have no contact with one another. That means Mr. and Mrs. Rivera will live separately. And finally, each of the defendants will wear an ankle monitor at all times. If any of these conditions are breached, the Marshals will bring them back to my court, I will revoke their bail, and they will be put in jail immediately."

Sanders face eased a lot. Terwilliger's face was bland—he'd warned Chico bail might be as high as three mil. The other two lawyers glanced at their clients. Both women grimaced but nodded.

"Any questions? No? Then we are done."

The judge banged her gavel, gathered her robes and swept down the steps to her chambers. She figured nobody was very happy with her ruling, which usually meant it was a good ruling.

The media surged forward to grab the four lawyers and the three defendants. It was chaotic, but a lot of good clips for that night's newscasts were captured.

CHAPTER 70

DETECTIVE FRED MCMURRAY had finally been captured. He lay there, naked, with only a frayed cotton cloth and a blanket to cover him. He was bathed in sweat, barely able to move. The harsh lights shone down without pity. His captors circulated, occasionally looking at him. They all wore masks; that was going to make it harder for him to identify them later.

His head was beginning to buzz. He could feel the drugs they had injected coursing through his veins. It was an odd sensation, as if he could feel the liquid surging every centimeter of the way through his body. He couldn't help but shiver at the physical pain he knew was coming.

He tried to breathe normally, but it was difficult. His head was spinning with emotions—fear, doubt, anxiety. The mental anguish was sending his pulse rate skyrocketing. He could feel his heart hammering at the thought of what was to come.

He envisioned the torture chamber he would soon be dragged into. He could see the axes and saws and swords and hammers and whatever other implements of pain hung on the walls. He could see the rivers of blood spurting from his body. He could feel the bones breaking in his leg.

He tried to wet his lips. He hadn't been allowed food for many hours. It had been a cruel time. Finally he heard the words he was dreading: "OK, it's time. Let's do this."

His wife leaned over the gurney as the nurses grabbed the bars at the end. "You'll do great," she said as she kissed him lightly and then stepped back.

The gurney moved quickly down the hospital corridor. McMurray stared up as they passed under each fluorescent light. They hurt his eyes. He wanted to close them but couldn't resist watching. They burst through the swinging doors leading to the Operating Theaters. The temperature inside was much cooler. A wide right turn and they entered OR #4. Several nurses grabbed corners of the sheet under him. "One, two, three."

They shifted him onto a harder, colder table. A large light hung above him.

A nurse wrapped a warm blanket around him. The intravenous line in his left arm was hooked up to another catheter.

Samira Al-Saadi wandered over. "You good, Fred?"

McMurray hacked out an OK.

"OK, then let's roll, people. I picked out the new knee for you myself, Fred. It's only been used twice before." McMurray went even paler on the table. "Just kidding. Gosh, that usually gets a big laugh." It did from the nurses and anesthesiologists assembled in the OR. "Nothing, Fred? Remember, I'm the one with the sharp scalpel. Still nothing? OK, then we're going to put in a new knee and transplant a sense of humor. Good one, huh Becky? No? Geez, tough crowd this morning. Alright, Fred, we'll put you a little further under now. You won't feel anything. Just relax."

As McMurray faded he could hear hits of the 80s cranking up. Huh. Aretha Fran—and he was out.

***

IT WAS ANOTHER room. Big room. Cold. More bright lights and beeping machine sounds. Many beeps. Many machines.

McMurray blinked his eyes several times and tried to shake his head. A nurse appeared, looking down at him critically as she appraised his condition. She eyed the electronic monitors attached to his body. "Fred." She spoke loudly. "Fred. You're out of the OR. Everything went really well."

He tried to speak but it was more of a croak. "All...good?"

"Yes. All good. You did great. The doctor will be in to see you soon. Here, suck on this ice chip."

Few things had ever tasted as good as that ice chip. She gave him another one. Boy, if they could make these bourbon-flavored, they'd have a real hit.

The nurse continued to bustle around his bed. She again eyed the monitors. Did the blood pressure cuff. Took his pulse the old-fashioned way. Made notes on his chart.

"You are doing great. I'm going to let your wife know. She's outside. So is your partner, Detective Cornice." She paused. "He's kinda cute." She tucked another warm sheet around him and waited for a response.

McMurray looked at her. Now that he was able to focus better, she was kinda cute herself. Dark blonde hair. Trim figure. Purple scrubs. Nice face. Light brown eyes.

Then he thought about the last time Cornice had stuck him with the check for lunch.

He had three possible answers to the nice nurse: Cornice was married. Cornice was gay. Cornice was available.

He recalled the lunch tab. Cornice had ordered the $24 lobster roll. $24!

McMurray had promised to get him. He opened his mouth.

"And Sheriff Perkins' office called to see how you came through surgery," she continued. "Everybody seems concerned about you." She made more notes on his chart. "You must be a nice guy."

Well, damn.

"I'll go and get your wife." She turned away from his bed.

"He's hot too, and he's a good guy." McMurray croaked out. "He's available."

She stopped, looked back at him, and smiled.

Chapter 71

"SHE'S RUNNING!"

The shouted call over the police radio echoed in the Communications Center. "Charlotte Martinez?" asked the dispatcher calmly.

"Yes. We just spotted her car speeding towards the freeway. Her license plate is confirmed. She's on 21st North. We're in pursuit!"

"Acknowledge. I am assigning other patrol cars to join the pursuit." The dispatcher looked at the electronic map and immediately found three patrol cars that could be diverted. She made the calls and then circled the vehicles in red on her board. The supervisor quickly joined her.

The four patrol cars converged rapidly on the suspect vehicle. Lights and sirens were activated. The dispatcher continued to feed data to the pursuing vehicles. The fleeing car soon hit the freeway and accelerated. She informed the state police of the chase. Two Florida Highway Patrol cars joined.

Five miles down the freeway, the police surrounded the sedan and guided it to the right shoulder. Guns drawn, three officers approached the car. "Hands on the steering wheel! Do not move! Do not move!"

The driver put her hands on the steering wheel. She didn't move. Cautiously the officers surrounded the car. One of them opened the driver's door, gun extended.

"Oh," said the woman in a distinctly island patois. "Was I speeding?"

The officer stared at the young Jamaican girl clutching the steering wheel.

CHAPTER 72

"CHARLOTTE CONNED OUR watch team," Williams reported angrily to the sheriff. "They got fooled by the car and the hat and the speeding towards the highway." He was disgusted that his officers had been bested.

"OK. She beat us. Question now is, where is she?"

"My guess would be south, because her fake was heading north. Maybe she's got a friend with a boat at some little marina. A private plane out of a private runway; there are lots of those around here. Maybe a commercial flight from somewhere. Drive down to the Keys, head to the Bahamas from there. She's got lots of choices. And probably lots of money."

That was a big concern to the investigators. Money can buy a lot of secret passages. They were still figuring out what role Charlotte Martinez was playing in the scheme, but with the papers impounded so far revealing no banking information, it was increasingly likely that Charlotte was the financial pivot.

"If she is doing banking in Grand Cayman, or some other cozy little island without much regard for international banking regulations, she could have bought some political protection," offered Lt. Stokes. "That could make extradition difficult."

This observation was received glumly. It was accurate, but it didn't make the situation better.

The interrogation of the young Jamaican woman had produced nothing. She was a soph taking biology at the college. There had been a notice on some private chatroom offering $200 cash to drive a car to Orlando and back. It was easy money, and she could use the cash. She had followed instructions to pick up the car key from a magnetic box under the front left quarter panel. The envelope with the cash was on the passenger seat. She never met with nor spoke to anyone.

The officers quickly organized an APB blitz. They sent out pictures of Charlotte to local TV stations across Florida. They notified marinas. They pushed TSA and local airport authorities to be on the lookout for her. They notified other police departments. They blitzed ride-sharing companies.

Nada.

There was no activity on any of Charlotte's known credit or bank cards. Her passport was flagged; no action. Talking to condo neighbors had revealed a loner who was polite in the elevator but never socialized. No one they interviewed had any leads to a Caribbean hideaway or a favorite destination.

None of them had ever seen strange women going in or out of her condo. A few recalled an obnoxious, cologne-scented man showing up a couple of times; he was soon identified as the ex-husband.

"It's as if she didn't exist. She made no mark on her condo neighbors. She had no presence in the community. She is like a wisp of smoke in the wind," concluded one detective.

It was the third morning of the fruitless search that they caught a break.

"Sarge," reported a young officer, "I think I saw something about the Martinez disappearance."

It took the Sergeant three minutes to call Lieutenant Stokes, who listened and then took one minute to call Captain Williams. He moved even faster, dragging the entourage into the sheriff's office after an impatient knock at the door.

"This is Officer Sara Blackwood," introduced Williams. "You met at the last induction ceremony." Perkins nodded politely. He made a point of attending the swearing-in of new officers and greeting them and their families. It meant a lot to them and was an important statement about how he ran the department.

"Sir," she said.

"Officer Blackwood has an interesting observation about our search for Charlotte Martinez," announced Williams. "She told Sergeant Guerrero, who informed Lt. Stokes, who brought it to me. I think you should hear it."

"You have impressed some smart people," Perkins said with a smile to make the young officer feel more comfortable. "I'll try to keep up."

"Yes, sir. Uh, well, I noticed this morning that there was a crack in her curtains."

Perkins cocked an eye at Williams. He wasn't keeping up. "Well, Sheriff, Officer Blackwood rents an apartment ten blocks away from the Martinez condo. She drives by it each morning coming to work. She figured out which condo Martinez owns.

Every day she's been looking at it. Today, she noticed the curtains weren't fully closed."

"Ahh. Got it. Do you think—"

"Yessir," replied Lt. Stokes. "She might have fooled us all by hiding in her own condo while we ran around the state looking for her, waiting until the heat dies down and then making her escape."

Perkins cocked his other eyebrow at his big captain. "I like it," nodded Williams.

"Officer Blackwood, am I to understand that you showed this initiative on your own? Figuring out the condo location, checking it every day?"

"Yes, sir."

"Outstanding. Great initiative. Sergeant Guerrero, we have a bright one here. I don't know if she's correct, but that doesn't matter. Officer Blackwood, well done."

The young officer's face shone with pride and pleasure at the commendation. Perkins made a mental note to send a formal letter to her file. It would help her at promotion time.

"What are you waiting for, Captain? Let's see if Ms. Martinez is receiving visitors this morning!"

Williams grinned and turned to leave. "Oh. Captain." Williams turned to look at the sheriff. "Do you think your team would have room for one more officer?"

Williams got it immediately. "Sergeant, suit her up. Let's go."

Chapter 73

CHARLOTTE MARTINEZ WAS arrested that morning. As one of the detectives laughingly told Williams later, "When we burst into her condo, she got that same look on her face that Wile E. Coyote used to have just after he'd run off the cliff and his legs were still churning, and he realized he was about to plummet to the canyon floor."

Investigators quickly found a large bag of shredded documents hidden in the back of a closet. They were beyond resurrection.

There was a secret safe they eventually discovered behind the kitchen pantry. It revealed three sets of books. Officer Blackwood was chosen to take those records, and Charlotte's laptop, into custody.

It took Wayne Cooper and his team of forensic auditors one day and most of one night to ferret out the money trail. His Adele T-shirt was badly wrinkled during the process.

"She set up three off-shore accounts in Grand Cayman, then three more in Liechtenstein. No names, just codes," reported Cooper as he yawned and chugged another Dr. Pepper. "We and the DA have a lot more work to do."

Charlotte appeared before Judge Green the next day. The same bail terms as she had imposed on the other defendants were set for Charlotte. Unfortunately, she had never read "Bail and Jail for Dummies." She was faced with a $300,000 retainer for her lawyer, who saw this as a lengthy, complicated trial. Then she needed to come up with another $250,000 as 10% of the bail.

She couldn't do that. Her condo was owned by a corporation based in Grenada. She was simply a tenant, which meant she had no equity to draw upon. The fact that she owned the corporation in Grenada was not helpful at that moment.

The irony, Charlotte thought bitterly, was that she had millions in cash and investments in foreign banks. She just couldn't access the cash because that would set off gigantic red flares at the IRS.

She had tried to live a quiet life and live on modest investments and some alimony from her sleazebag husband, whenever he decided to write the check.

It had never occurred to her that she could be caught and charged with serious crimes and would therefore need large amounts of cash.

It all added up to panic attacks and a lot of crying. She learned that she wasn't as strong as she thought she would be when facing adversity. She wept in court, she sobbed in jail, she cried in front of her lawyer, and she whimpered in her cell.

That drove Big Bertha crazy, and she was not known for her patience and civility. Big Bertha was Charlotte's cell mate. She was a veteran of the prison system. This time she was in for beating up a tough bouncer at the gay bar she frequented.

"Stop crying, bitch, or I'll smack you from here to Albuquerque" Bertha warned. That caused Charlotte to cry more. And harder.

Officials in the jail observed all of this. A message was sent to the interrogators from the Sheriff's department. They began to press harder at their interrogations. Charlotte's eyes were red and swollen. During some interviews she was shaking from exhaustion, terror and the thought of spending the rest of her life as Big Bertha's bitch.

The officer leading the interviews promised a cell of her own and certain privileges and protections.

"It took a couple of days, but she finally cracked," reported Sergeant Gabrielle Garcia, who was lead interviewer, to Perkins and DA Doug Saunders. "And have we got a story for you."

Chapter 74

"LAS TRES AMIGAS have been friends for years. They are also greedy bitches who learned never to trust their husbands or exes. As a result, they each wanted to build their own private, secret nest egg. They just didn't want to do much work. Or pay any taxes."

The sergeant shuffled her notes and glanced at her colleague who had also been part of the interrogation. "Tiga Joe met them at that charity event years ago. He had just come into town and wanted to make a social splash. He thought he could buy respectability and saw these women as patsies. Originally it was to run drugs into their social groups, but Charlotte got antsy. Veronica liked the money but didn't like the drug business. Inez was already half into drug dealing with her husband, so she was cool. After a while they started talking about sex trafficking. Lucrative. Inez was into it because she is one freaky bitch and thought she could build her own little harem of female slaves. Veronica liked it because she wasn't involved other than somebody used her basement. The house of ill-repute was almost a natural offshoot. Some madam ran it. We're still looking for her. In addition to forcing some of the aliens into sex work, they found lots of local women wanting to make some money on the side. They set up those fantasy suites. Kinky," she muttered softly.

She paused and then shrugged.

"It was pretty clever," she admitted grudgingly. "The johns would usually get dropped off by a van at the side door at one of the houses, go downstairs and have a drink or two, watch a little porn on the big screen, choose their partner and walk through the tunnel into their fantasy suite. They would exit out the door in the other house so no one could track them, and no nosy PI could get pictures of them being unfaithful. No cars were left near the properties that could be identified. It was cash-only, of course, so there were no electronic transfers to trace. And no names for the johns. We will be trying very hard to get those…gentlemen…identified," she said with steely-jawed determination.

"Charlotte became the corporate secretary-treasurer, so to speak. She did the books, set up ways to hide the money, created shell corporations, controlled the banking and payments, made the investments. She made them all a pile of money in European currency futures. Hmmph. Anyway, she never touched the women. Tiga Joe just sat back and enjoyed his half of the money while his tough guys ran the women. It wasn't a big deal for his people to slip a few women into the country every couple of weeks, along with a shipment of drugs."

Perkins looked at the assembled team. All eyes were riveted on Sergeant Garcia. There was anger that such an enterprise had been developed and operated in their jurisdiction without their knowledge.

"The tunnel was Veronica's idea. She was worried about the women being seen going into her house. It was all vanity for her, to protect her reputation. They hired some Mexican laborers under Joe's control. The soil was soft, they shored the tunnel with timbers that Veronica told her neighbors were for a reno in her house, so nobody thought anything about it. There was no building permit, of course."

Captain Williams rolled his eyes.

"They did a test run on sneaking the women into the homes a couple of years ago. Nobody blinked. The women thought they were getting good jobs in America and could help their families back home. Instead, most got hooked on drugs and were fed into the sex scene as strippers and prostitutes, or work in illicit massage parlors. The ones who weren't attractive enough got placed as domestic workers. From all reports they were usually treated badly. Long hours, no days off, sleeping in a tiny room. The housewives who bought them suddenly thought they were now some duchess running a palace."

The sergeant grimaced. "The money started to roll in. Charlotte set up foreign bank accounts. She'd only dole out a little money to her two partners so nobody would have a big windfall to blow, which would get talked about by their socialite friends. As I said, she also invested wisely." She shook her head and sighed. "They've each got over five million dollars in accounts overseas."

Detective Cornice spoke up. "The girl who was murdered. Charlotte claims she and the two others knew nothing about that. She says she heard that the girl had become a discipline problem for the couple who bought her. Tiga Joe handles discipline problems. The couple who bought her was into S&M; she wasn't. We have the names of those two. Fred will be back tomorrow from his knee replacement. I'll take him and some back-up to their home. He won't be moving too fast, but I thought he should be there for the bust."

Perkins nodded approval.

"Where is Chico in all of this?" asked DA Doug Saunders. His two associates were taking frantic pages of notes.

"Our view? He knew about the scheme. We suspect he got involved in some kinky sex with several of the victims, sometimes with Inez participating. We don't have much hard evidence yet that he was involved with the daily actual…uh… operation of the, uh, bawdy house. The drugs? He ran that."

Discussion continued for another half hour. Finally Saunders brought it to a conclusion. "OK, good job, everybody. Sheriff, great job by your team." He turned to his associates. "Now we need to start sorting out what charges and against whom. And who wants to make a deal. Charlotte is already rolling over, I hear. What's on the table?"

Sergeant Garcia looked at one of the ADAs in the room. "We've been working with Mr. Goldman."

The young lawyer grabbed some papers. "What's on the table is full testimony from Charlotte against her two co-conspirators for the brothel and the trafficking of the women. Complete revelation of their foreign banking assets. Information on Chico and his drug dealings." He paused. "We are hopeful that Inez might crack and rat out Chico if she's offered a deal as well. We don't think there is a strong passion to protect him if flipping will reduce her sentence."

Saunders glanced at his colleagues around the table. "You all like it?" Goldman nodded. So did the other two attorneys. "OK, draw up the papers." He thought for another moment. "Chico?"

"He's a crook and a pervert, but that's also true of most Florida politicians, many of whom have not yet been charged," replied Goldman. "Chico's good for possession and distribution of huge quantities of illegal drugs. There will be other charges. Money laundering. Trafficking. Hey, maybe some of the women got sold to people in other states, that would mean federal charges for interstate." He thought some more. "I don't see any of them directly involved in the murders. That seems to be Tiga Joe and his enforcer, but we'll keep an open mind."

Nods of satisfaction from around the table as the judicial process was refined.

"OK, anything else from anybody?" Perkins enquired. No one responded. There was elation in the room, but also exhaustion. Big cases suck energy out of the police once they are resolved. There is a gigantic exhale by the officers involved. It is a natural emotional release from the danger and intensity that drives everyone during the investigation. "OK, then, great job everyone. Now…let's get Tiga Joe."

CHAPTER 75

FINDING TIGA JOE and gathering more evidence against him became the focus for the Sheriff's department. The stories and denials from the three ladies about their knowledge of Tiga Joe's residence, travel and criminal business activities were murky and confusing. All of them seemed terrified of saying anything about the crime chieftain.

Chico flatly denied ever meeting him, or talking to him, or having anything to do with Claudia's murder.

He then proceeded to finger Joe for the murder of The Vest Man. "What I heard was that the word on the street was that he was squealin' to the cops 'bout somma Joe's shit. It was just discipline. Nothin' personal." He shrugged indifferently. "Gotta keep the troops in line. Nothin' to do with me."

Detective Cornice gripped the corner of the desk when he heard the story. His partner would be distraught by this confirmation of the reason for the murder, even though he had suspected it.

Veronica and Inez both waffled more than a presidential candidate during a nationally televised debate. Each said she had met somebody who might have been this Joe character once at a social event a few years ago, but who could remember?

They maintained that this Tiga person, whomever that might be, never met with any of these three sophisticated ladies after their first get-together—if indeed that had even happened, but, after all, at cocktail parties one meets so many sycophants and one must be polite to the little people who would want to meet them so they could brag to their dull little friends that they had actually met one of these three fabulous, famous, society women. So maybe, just maybe, it might possibly perhaps conceivably feasibly be in the remote realm of possibility that it could have happened. But one couldn't be sure.

It was a nice evasive story. The interrogators didn't believe a word of it.

Explaining the picture in the newspaper was rather more awkward for Inez and Veronica.

As one of the detectives said to Perkins, "Inez's story has more holes in it than a rusty colander."

The one lead that finally came out was a rumor about a private marina on a waterfront estate in a small town in the south-west part of the Gulf Coast.

Small boats are the easiest way to sneak people into or out of the long Florida coastline. There are lots of darkened ships that sail silently in the night; many small, private docks dot the state's jagged coastline.

Perkins promptly briefed the FBI. ICE and Homeland Security sent two teams to the area. They soon reported that Tiga Joe was known there. So were his thugs, who had had a couple of run-ins with locals who had had the misfortune to stumble across mystery boats arriving at the darkened marina late at night.

The local Chief of Police in the small town only had a staff of three. He had no resources to stake out any of the marinas. He did point the feds toward a rickety marina in a small harbor on a private estate as the most suspicious.

An elderly woman and her personal homecare worker lived there. She was in a wheelchair. It seemed unlikely she would be using the marina, which was out of sight of the house. The focus turned to the marina. A Coast Guard helicopter did a low-level fly past that afternoon. "No sign of people," reported a Lieutenant, "but one small cruiser tied to a dock."

The joint raid struck that night.

As the intel from the copter promised, a 36 foot boat was found tied to a shaky wooden dock. It flew a Panamanian flag. Two phone calls later it was confirmed the boat was registered in Panama under a corporate name: Tigre Sociedad Anonima.

No one was on board. The boat was promptly impounded and a quick search for forensic evidence was expedited by order of James Robertson.

Investigators worked through the night and got lucky—they found hair samples that matched the two women discovered locked in Veronica's basement. The evidence was clear—those women had been on that boat. Not voluntarily.

They also found massive residue of cocaine, fentanyl and other drugs. It was clear the boat had also been used for drug smuggling.

It gave Perkins' team compelling links to the human and drug trafficking they had suspected. Now they were connecting Tiga Joe to the entire criminal empire; the noose was drawing tighter.

Perkins smiled grimly at the final notation in the FBI report: the boat's name was El Tigre. Meanwhile, the media frenzy continued unabated. It had even been mentioned on 'The Major's Report' on COYOTE. Michael Majors and Sophia Roberts criticized the DA for persecuting these three upstanding local families who were obviously just trying to assist the poor and downtrodden.

Pastor Jedediah Jenner made another appearance, this time to lament the lax laws that allowed these godless alien women from Central and South America, who probably supported a woman's right to choose, God help us, into the country. Then he warned of a thunderous crusade that was coming.

Captain Williams resisted throwing his beer at his 65" TV, but it took a lot of willpower. He muttered to his wife that he was surprised the hosts weren't criticizing the poor women who ended up as prostitutes or sex slaves of "stealing jobs from hard-working American citizens."

Compassion for the innocent female victims or the horrific fate that awaited them was in short supply on COYOTE.

The people of Port Manatee were still buzzing about the entire case. Perkins had imposed drastic traffic control measures on Bayside Drive because so many people were going by the crime scene to have a look-see. Neighbors fled to avoid the media attention and the pitiless public scrutiny of their area.

Everybody wanted to see inside the now-notorious tunnel. The city was buzzing with lewd and lurid fantasies about the suites and hooker heaven.

The local paper tried to sneak a reporter into the basement by sending him in as a safety inspector. He got thrown out.

One of the maids still working at Inez's house was captured by an alert deputy sheriff after he heard a click. The maid had smuggled her cell phone into the tunnel and snapped a picture. The phone was confiscated, the maid fired, and the DA was deciding whether to charge her with trespassing.

There were rumors that TMZ was offering big bucks for a video of the tunnel and the fantasy suites. Speculation was rampant over what had suddenly become a buzz-worthy national story.

"Perk could make a lot of money selling tours," Samira al-Saadi laughed as she hosted a Sams Club meeting the night before. The ladies enjoyed an exuberant Portuguese red that had deep notes of violet and blackberry that produced a great finish.

"I'll tell him," Samantha promised. "He'll find that really funny." The ladies giggled at that thought. Samantha then told the other two about the garish interior decoration inside Inez's house. "Some nice snacks, though," Samantha admitted. Rosie perked up at the word; she was certainly interested in that part of the conversation. The description of the ceiling gargoyles, not so much.

"Well," Kim concluded with a yawn, "I guess it all won't be over for another year or two."

That was a sobering reality. Justice can take a very long time in American courts. Lawyers deliberately drag out cases, hoping witnesses will die, or forget important details, or just disappear. Evidence might go missing. DAs can change and have a different focus on prosecutions. The media attention would die down.

But, most importantly, hourly billings would continue to accumulate.

CHAPTER 76

A S SO OFTEN happens in a difficult case, it was good old-fashioned police work that finally got the lead on Tiga Joe's location.

Perkins spread the word that officers should be talking to all their street contacts and confidential informants. The Intel Unit cranked up electronic surveillance. The FBI cooperated by tracking members of Tiga Joe's entourage.

But it was loose lips about a birthday party that cracked the wall of secrecy.

It was his sister Isabella's 23rd birthday. Tiga Joe and his gang would be in Port Manatee that night. He had rented out the entire Los Hombres Ristorante, to ensure privacy. It featured a very popular chef from Columbia.

Tiga Joe had hired one of the hottest Cuban rock groups currently touring Florida. His sister loved the lead singer, a hottie named Ernesto. He had smoldering black eyes, and a chest that was chiseled and gleamed with oil whenever he ripped off his puffed shirt during his performances, which he did with alarming regularity. His black pants were very tight. Truth be told, he had a rather mediocre singing voice. The women in the audience didn't care that much about his singing.

Tiga Joe had 'invited' Ernesto's band to play at the private party. A modest $65,000, most of it in cash, plus a new speedboat for Ernesto, had been sufficient to induce him to suddenly cancel one concert on his touring schedule and announce he needed two days off to allow his throat to rest. A compliant doctor produced a letter.

Female fans who had purchased tickets for the show were outraged. Comments on social media were nasty.

Secrecy about Tiga Joe and his sister's party was honored by all the restaurant staff. Very large cash tips ensured that.

However, nobody thought about the roadies, those over-worked and very much underpaid burly men who drag the heavy equipment and amplifiers out of trucks and onto stages night after night. They have their own code of conduct.

A crisp hundred-dollar bill proved to be an extremely good investment by one of the undercover detectives working the Latino community.

His report to headquarters sparked a frantic response. The party would start at 7 that night, dinner at 8. The concert was scheduled for 11. Big cake at midnight.

It was the first legitimate opportunity to arrest Joe and question him about the murders, the sex trade and his drug cartel. The DEA and FBI were keenly interested in joining the interrogation.

Questioning of Chico had slowly revealed details of the drug wars in Mexico; the DEA had confirmed Joe's involvement with the drug trade. But Perkins and his team most wanted him for the two murders that were still unsolved—Vest Man and Claudia.

The plan was to bring him in for questioning and then see what developed in the other cases. They finally had enough probable cause to make the arrest. However, Perkin's team only had a few hours to plan and organize the take-down of their most-wanted villain.

"It is going to be a highly volatile situation," said Lt. A'ja. She pointed at the blueprint of the restaurant on the screen. "You can see there's no easy access for us. Four doors, two in front for the public, one off the kitchen for the chefs to go in the back alley and smoke, and one delivery door. We're assuming fifty or sixty guests at the private party. Tiga Joe will have his own security, of course. Everyone there will know everyone else, and most of them will be Isabella's friends. We don't see a safe way to infiltrate the party. The waiters are old-timers who have worked together for years. The band is, well, the band. Even the roadies have worked together for a long time."

Captain Williams studied the layout. "That means either crash the party or take him after he leaves."

"Yes, sir. That is our assessment."

"Swarming the restaurant endangers a lot of civilians," said Perkins.

"Yes, sir, that also is our assessment."

The senior staff studied the layout some more.

"It has to be a vehicle take-down," the Sheriff finally offered. There were nods around the table.

"Yes, sir. We have developed a tentative plan based on that strategy. An unmarked vehicle near the restaurant to scope out Joe's arrival and departure. Eight police vehicles a block or two from the restaurant, surrounding it. Our helicopter hovering, ready to track Joe's route. The SWAT team in their tank and just off site, ready for anything. We are assuming he will have heavily armed security traveling with him, but we don't have much of a previous pattern for his travels and we still don't know his home base. We are assuming that after the arrests of Las Tres Amigas and Chico that he will be on high alert."

"Why would he even risk this party?"

"Word is that he loves his little sister very much. Their parents are both deceased, so it is just the two of them now."

Perkins studied the board again. "OK, good job. Let's do it."

CHAPTER 77

IT WAS MIDNIGHT when the band struck up "Happy Birthday." Ernesto led the singing while on one knee in front of Isabella. He was caressing her left hand. She was barely able to breathe from the excitement. The top of her low-cut silvery dress heaved.

Her closest girlfriends looked on enviously. Two of them wondered if Ernesto would be available later that night. Isabella wondered the same thing. She flashed a smug look at her friends; maybe a *menage a cuatro*?

Joe looked on proudly. He had enjoyed several mojitos, a bottle of truly excellent Argentinian Malbec, and a snifter of very fine XXO Napoleon cognac with his Montecristo cigar. The smile on his sister's face as the words faded were enough thanks for him.

The pile of elegantly wrapped presents on a side table meant Isabella would be enjoying this evening for days to come.

The room darkened, the kitchen doors swung open, and two waiters pushed out a cart with a big pink and white birthday cake on it. Everyone stood, applauding and cheering. Sparklers were sputtering their glitter onto the cake, while 23 big pink candles glowed in the dark.

Isabella loved pink.

She ran to the cart and dabbed a finger into the icing. She licked her fingers and raced over to Joe and kissed him. "Gracias, big brother! It is magnifico! Te amo!" And with that she grabbed a couple of her girlfriends and raced back to the cake.

They each dabbed a finger into the icing. Isabella grabbed a knife and started to cut pieces to be served. Playfully she flicked a little piece of icing at Lucia and Camila. They shrieked and flicked back their own dabs of icing. After that, chaos.

It had probably been, the restaurant owner thought ruefully twenty minutes later, inevitable. He stood looking at the residue of what would be forever known in restaurant lore as 'the great midnight cake fight.'

Icing and cake crumbs were, well, everywhere. Streaks of pink and white icing smeared the floor, the walls, the curtains, the table, the stage and from what he could see by squinting up, a couple of places on the ceiling.

You put a bunch of horny, drunken 20-somethings together in a highly sexual environment to celebrate, and it was likely that there would be collateral damage.

It had taken about five seconds after Camila hit Isabella with some icing for the rest of her girlfriends to rush the cake. Flecks of icing soon gave way to handfuls of cake. Boyfriends quickly got in on the fun, smearing chunks of cake onto the girls while grabbing appreciative handfuls of boobs and butts. The girls were squealing, the cake was flying, the band was ducking, the waiters were running, and Tiga Joe just sat there, laughing his head off.

Then a piece of cake hit him on the side of the face. Shrapnel has no friends.

The room went quiet. He sat there for a stunned moment. He lifted his finger, swiped some of the cake, put it in his mouth and swallowed.

"Good cake!" He clamped down on his cigar and then rushed to join the fight. Pandemonium broke out again as all the guests got involved, screaming with laughter.

It took the skirmish five more minutes before the icing ammunition was exhausted. So were the partygoers. They wiped down as best they could. A clean napkin was suddenly a prized possession. There were a lot of sticky hugs and kisses. Everybody was in hysterics.

The guests began to depart soon after. Expensive gift bags were given to each couple as they left. The band started to pack up. The bar never officially closed, but it was only a few hardened stragglers who indulged in a last nightcap.

Joe strolled over to the restaurant owner. He wiped a little more pink icing off his face. "It is possible there was a slight bit of damage tonight," he said with a smirk as he puffed a fresh cigar. The No Smoking sign in the restaurant obviously did not apply to him. "I'll expect it to show on the bill. Along with a large tip for all the staff."

Jorge bowed. "I will take care of it, Senor Joe." He looked around at the devastation. He shrugged. "Your sister seemed to have a good time."

"Si. Bueno. The food was *excellente*. The tapas *excellente*. And the paella!" He kissed his fingers in acclamation.

Joe looked at Isabella's boyfriend, who was sitting glumly by himself. No Isabella. He checked the room. Hmmm. Ernesto was missing as well. Probably just a coincidence, he chortled to himself. Whatever made his baby sister happy. She was his only family now. He had to look after her.

And for the cost of that damn speedboat, Ernesto had better make his sister toe-curling happy.

Jorge again surveyed the room. Well, it was time for the annual thorough cleaning of his ristorante. It was nice that Tiga Joe offered to pay for it. Still, he would be careful with the bill. A drunk and happy Tiga Joe was one thing; an angry and acrimonious Tiga Joe was quite another.

"I am glad the evening was such a success, Senor Joe. You are welcome any time. Please, travel home safely."

Joe nodded happily. He glanced around for his security team. Isabella's boyfriend was still pouting by himself. Fine. Joe had never been impressed with the kid. He needed to get a job, cut his hair, and grow a pair if he was going to play in Joe and Isabella's league.

He stuck his cigar into the side of his mouth and strode toward the waiting black Escalade.

CHAPTER 78

"THEY STARTED SHOOTING first." The grim faces around the Sheriff's conference table looked down at the after-action report. "We had planned to do the take-down as a routine traffic stop after his car left the restaurant." The Lieutenant in charge of the capture of Tiga Joe looked at his notes. He tried hard to maintain his composure. It was the first time something like this had happened to him.

He swallowed more water. "It was 1:30am by the time Joe left the restaurant. He had been drinking a lot. We just got the results of the tox screen from the hospital. Both his driver and his bodyguard were clean for booze, but both had been smoking marijuana. Joe's blood alcohol was 0.17. That's very high." He checked another sheet. "The follow-car had two more body-guards. They also had ingested marijuana."

Perkins sat still, listening to the report and observing the young officer. Willie Williams was on his right, stone-faced.

A pause. No one spoke. "It went bad right from the start," admitted the Lieutenant. "As soon as the first patrol car hit his lights, Joe's car took off. It was weaving down the street. Joe's second security vehicle tried to follow but was cut off by two police vehicles. It began to swerve; they were dodging cars trying desperately to catch up with Joe's car, but then it crashed into a telephone pole and flipped. Both men inside were hurt, but not seriously. They are in custody in the hospital and are being interviewed now." He paused. "One of our vehicles was damaged but the deputies are OK." He paused again.

"Two more of our cars picked up the chase. The SWAT truck moved to intercept. Another police car came from the west side. Joe's car started to veer. It scraped three parked cars. It careened off the side of a building when it turned left on El Camino. Traffic was light, which probably saved a couple of lives." He swallowed hard.

"Joe's driver was still trying to lose our vehicles. He cut down a back lane between El Camino and Manzanita Drive. A delivery truck was parked at the far end. It blocked the only exit. They were trapped. The three of them got out and realized they had nowhere to go. That's when they started shooting. There is no question that they started shooting first," he emphasized to the senior officers gathered in the room. "All of our officers agree on that."

Perkins breathed a silent sigh of relief.

"Bullets were hitting our vehicles. Our officers were in imminent danger. One was wounded. They had to shoot back. The SWAT truck arrived about then. Their sharpshooter took two shots at Joe's truck. Our preliminary report is that he got the bodyguard. Joe was killed by multiple gunshots. Bullets from several of our officers killed the driver. We'll never know exactly whose." He paused. "Doesn't really matter, I guess." He paused again. "It was over in about ninety seconds."

No one said anything. Perkins stirred. "You told me on the phone this morning that we had two injuries. What's the report on them?"

"Yessir. Both are fine. Both will be released later this morning. One in the left arm, a through-and-through. The other is the driver in that chase car. Broken leg. No permanent damage to either officer."

"Captain?"

"Sir, we've called in the Sheriff's Department from Hillsborough County to supervise the after-action investigation. We want it to be impeccable, because you know the media will be all over this. It will also cause a lot of ripples through the criminal community."

"Yeah," Perkins acknowledged. "Lieutenant, make sure our two officers in the hospital are taken care of. I will phone their wives this morning and visit the hospital. We'll give them whatever assistance they need." Nods around the table. The strong blue line came together in such situations.

"Now. My preliminary assessment based on what you have told me is that the shootings were completely justified. We'll wait for the report from Hillsborough, of course, but our officers had no choice but to return fire once Joe and his bodyguards started shooting. That will be the thrust of our communications to the public this morning." He looked at the PIO, who nodded briefly.

Perkins paused, sipped some coffee, and looked around the table. "None of us want anything like this to happen on our watch. But it did. Lieutenant, good job. Tell your team from me." The Sheriff could see the young L.T. visibly exhale in relief.

"Captain Williams, anything else for now?"

"No, sir."

"OK. We're done for the moment. Get me those preliminary reports as soon as they are ready. Get the public statement out there right now. And we cooperate fully with the Hillsborough team. We don't hide anything."

The meeting ended abruptly. Anytime there was a police shooting, it involved extensive internal reports and many questions from the public. That was the new reality of policing in the 21st century. With three fatalities, their every move would be scrutinized.

As Perkins left the room, his assistant Mary was waiting for him. "James Robertson wants you to call him right away. He said it's important."

"OK, thanks."

Perkins hustled back to his office and punched the numbers for the private phone of FBI Regional Director. He answered immediately and began to talk as if they were already in the middle of their conversation.

"Your officers are OK?"

"Yes, they'll be fine."

"Good. And you got Tiga Joe off the streets. We've got some ideas on shutting down his entire operation. We want to work with you on that. I'll have one of my people call you later today with a suggested action plan."

"Fine. We've always worked well together, except when your bloated ego gets in the way." As tired as Perkins was, he still couldn't resist the friendly jab.

"Nice," Robertson replied. "I see Samantha is starting to teach you two-syllable words."

Perkins couldn't help but laugh.

"Listen, Perk, we're getting some very odd intelligence that may involve your city. We're getting reports of a number of big trucks, semi-trailers and other big rigs, heading towards Central Florida. A few are coming from the mid-west, some from Texas, Louisiana, Oklahoma. They don't seem to be carrying loads. The chatter on their radios is talking about some big showdown with the authorities. Some comment about J-Men, whoever they are."

Perkins sat back. "Huh. We haven't heard much in the last few days from these J-Men crazies, but I'll go back to my people about this. Why would a bunch of empty trucks be heading to Florida? Weird."

CHAPTER 79

WARD 3 CITY Councillor Kim Sharpe, City Manager Roy Crawford, Sheriff LeRoy Perkins, Samantha Summers and Rosie the wonder dog were sharing a pre-dinner cocktail at The Krazy Kangaroo that evening. It was a new bar and restaurant that had just been opened by an ex-pat Aussie from Melbourne.

The girls were sipping something called a "Melbourne Marvel"; it was blue and shimmery and came in a tall lab beaker. The boys were downing draft pilsners in icy mugs.

Rosie sat beside them on the patio. She lapped some cool water from her saucer and sniffed appreciatively at the veeerrrry interesting aromas coming from the kitchen.

Samantha was wearing a short, faded, blue denim skirt that she knew Perkins liked. A lot. He tended to walk a couple of steps behind her when she was wearing it. She liked that. A lot.

Kim and Perk both ordered the famous 'shrimp on the barbie.' Roy opted for a rib-eye, medium-rare. Samantha chose the grilled fish. Rosie got a plain hamburger patty, medium; she would not have objected to a steak. Just another example of her sad and pathetic life, she thought; nobody loves her.

Everyone was tiptoeing around the obvious topic of conversation. No law enforcement officer wants to be involved in a shooting. As the top cop, Perkins was ultimately held accountable for the actions of his officers.

"It was unquestionably self-defense," he finally said. "My officers had to return fire after Tiga Joe and his two guards started shooting."

That broke open the dam, and conversation for the next half hour centered on Tiga Joe and his illegal operations.

"What will this do to the charges against Veronica, Inez and Charlotte?" asked Kim.

Perkins paused as he cut the last bite of his shrimp. They were very good. "That is something of a question," he began cautiously. "The DA is reviewing the human trafficking case. All the women deny knowing Joe or having dealings with him. We are certain he was the driving force, but can we prove it? The two women we rescued from the basement only dealt with low-level foot soldiers in Joe's chain of command. They can't identify Joe or say they ever saw him during their abduction. Homeland Security is now searching for other women he trafficked to other cities. It is still messy." He chewed the final morsel of shrimp.

"Charlotte is spilling the beans on her two gal pals, though. There's a deal for her to get just two years in exchange for turning state's witness. My guess is that now they will all make plea deals in exchange for lighter sentences. Inez and Veronica will probably just get three or four years. They will all plead guilty to the brothel and trafficking charges, as well as tax evasion. The money laundering issue will remain open until the FBI completes its investigation. They will also pay a big, big fine. I'm guessing the feds will claw back their money stashed in foreign banks. They will end up broke."

He quaffed more icy pilsner.

"Chico we've got on the possession of illegal drugs, plus sexual abuse, and the drug trafficking charges. He'll go away for ten to fifteen. We'll repossess the houses and fill in the tunnel. Maybe that'll stop the media from trying to shoot pictures of that darn tunnel." He shook his head at what had become a gripping national story.

That quieted the table. Perkins sighed. "Now we've just cut the head off Tiga Joe's criminal operation when James Robertson calls me this morning and warns me about rumors and radio chatter concerning some truck protest coming to town. Phew. What's next?"

"Why would that be a problem?" Samantha asked gently.

"We don't know who they are, where they are going, why they are traveling in our direction, what they might do. We don't know if they end up here and somehow get tied up with the crazy J-Men. Who knows what those nut cases will plan. Or do."

The waitress, who was very cute with dirty blonde hair and an Aussie accent, returned to clear the dishes. Rosie got a few pats and a scrap from the kitchen. "What about dessert?"

Kim and Samantha agreed to share a lemon tart. Perkins decided he had earned a treat, so he went for the Australian Lamington. It was a soft butter sponge cake dipped in chocolate and then coated in coconut. He tasted it and then declined to share. Samantha pouted. It didn't help.

Kim had been silent during the lemon tart tasting. She had been listening intently to Perkins' description of the reports of trucks and the J-Men. She finished her last bite, laid down the fork with a satisfied 'aaah,' and looked at Perkins.

"You said 18 wheelers? No cargo? Heading in our direction?"

"Yeah, that seems to be the rumor."

"It's expensive enough to roll a semi with cargo. Gas, depreciation, everything else. But to run it without a load? That is very costly. I wonder who's paying their expenses? This is very unusual."

"It is."

"So, if they aren't coming to pick up a load or for some other legitimate reason, then why would they be traveling towards us? And apparently becoming a convoy?" She sipped some coffee and looked over at Crawford. "What I'm wondering, Perk, is if they are getting ready to pull an Ottawa."

Crawford blanched. Perkins and Samantha looked bewildered.

"You might not recall it, but a couple of years ago, a huge caravan of trucks drove across Canada in the middle of winter to end up in their national capital. Ottawa. Cold as hell there, but they basically shut down the heart of the city for three weeks. They froze traffic movement downtown. Some pedestrians and residents were hassled and scared. Businesses had to close. It was a debacle."

Crawford nodded agreement. "It is now a classic story in municipal circles. Even though these trucks rolled across the entire country, the local officials seemed to be caught by surprise. They weren't ready for the, well, sit-down of hundreds of trucks and angry people. They blocked main intersections, parked in front of the Parliament Buildings, and everything came to a halt. They were loud, blew air horns, set up barbecues, and blocked vehicular traffic completely. It drove residents of their downtown crazy. Every level of government did a terrible job of planning for this protest and then handling the invasion. Well, I guess they didn't do much planning. The police were ineffective. The Chief resigned. It became a nightly headline on TV newscasts. It was a disaster. It cost the city 30 or 40 million dollars."

Samantha looked on in amazement. "What did they accomplish? How was it settled?"

"I don't know that they accomplished much of anything," Crawford said, "other than to disrupt a major capital city for three weeks. I guess the leaders of it would argue it was a political protest for freedom. Anti-vaxxers. Anti-government. Whatever." Crawford shrugged in anger and frustration.

"Maybe it was really all political to embarrass their Prime Minister. I don't know. But I do know that they raised millions of dollars online. Nobody is entirely sure what happened to all that money." He paused. "The police finally got some reinforcements and then the feds panicked and passed some emergency legislation. The police finally began laying charges and making arrests and hauling trucks away. But the protest scarred the city badly. I think it resulted in permanent changes to traffic regulations in downtown Ottawa in front of their Parliament Hill. It was a real blemish on the city."

"And you think they might be trying to replicate that here?"

Crawford looked at the Sheriff with tired eyes. "I think Kim might be right. If this is becoming a convoy of the far right, and they're reacting to some call by the J-Men to support a freedom march or something, it is a big threat. If they shut our downtown, it would really hurt our local merchants and the tourist industry—and the impact would linger for years. It could become a national TV story. People remember that sort of thing. A blockade would disrupt local businesses that are just recovering from the pandemic. But I can tell you right now, my city is not going to be unprepared! These thugs are not going to take over my town!"

Perkins fist-bumped the City Manager. Kim and Samantha did the same.

CHAPTER 80

PERKINS REACHED OUT to the Florida Highway Patrol and explained the possible scenario. The senior officer promised to contact her counterparts in surrounding states to track any truck convoys and to ratchet up their own intelligence gathering.

Information began to flow within hours.

"Officers from all over, Texas, Alabama, Georgia, Louisiana, Tennessee, Kentucky, Missouri, they've been noticing an increase in empty trucks traveling in loose convoys. Nobody thought too much about it. Trucks are on the highways all the time, and truckers tend to gather together. But when we asked the officers to cross-check the weights of loads, the number of empty trucks was striking. Your call about gathering for a possible protest or whatever consolidated the data," Lieutenant-Colonel Sheila Prudhomme told Perkins, "and the red lights started blinking." She was a deputy director of FHP.

"We don't want another Ottawa."

"Good lord, no," she replied fervently. "How embarrassing for them."

"How solid is the information about their final destination?"

"Um, sketchy for now. A few rumors out there. Not much yet that I could confirm, but something is certainly bubbling. Why do you think you are the target?"

"We had a bunch of little pick-up trucks do a run through our downtown recently. Torches and trouble. No great damage but it shook up the town. Then we've been watching some right-wing crazies called the J-Men doing odd little protests. And we've got a preacher who is sort of nuts and maybe a pervert spouting all kinds of stuff on TV. We've heard some chatter about demonstrations or something. It's frustrating because there isn't anything certain right now, but things seem to be coming to a head. We want to be prepared."

"Of course you do. That's smart. And as these trucks get closer to our borders, we'll be able to track them very closely. Our people are setting up a computer model now to follow their routes. We can stop a couple of them and see if the drivers will talk."

Perkins thought about that for a moment. "OK. I appreciate your quick action on this, Colonel. You have my number, 24/7. Don't hesitate."

"Will do. Goodbye."

Perkins turned to his management team. "I think we are the target. I'm not sure why, so get to any informants out there and see what you can find out. But in the meantime, I'm going to create a Task Force to manage this. Captain Williams, can you take this on?"

"Yessir."

Perkins nodded his appreciation. He knew how hard Willie was working now, but he hadn't hesitated to add more responsibilities.

"Thank you. You will have all the resources you need. Let's get a liaison with Roy Crawford's office at city hall, and with Mayor Rodriguez. If this comes down, we're going to need them."

Williams nodded.

"OK. That's a start. We'll meet whenever Captain Williams requires." The senior staff bustled out.

Williams stayed for a moment. "I think they're coming for us," he said in his deep voice.

"I think you are right, Willie. That's why I need you to head this up."

"Not a problem. I can sleep next month." With that he lumbered out the door, leaving a smiling Perkins behind.

CHAPTER 81

JIM CRANDALL WAS bursting to tell Beulah all about his plan to bring the city to its knees and get city hall to reverse its brutal tax increase on her farm. He had been quietly putting together his siege of downtown Port Manatee for the past couple of weeks. It was all coming together now, better than he'd ever imagined. He'd had a couple of phone calls from some guy in Wisconsin advising him how to pull it off.

Lots of truckers are indignant about tax increases for anybody, anywhere, by any order of government. They dislike city halls' rules about parking, restrictions on what hours they could deliver, and what routes they could access in a city.

Truckers generally dislike police and highway patrols. And many of them had heard about the Ottawa power grab by a bunch of truckers. Once Crandall's idea to replicate that in Port Manatee leaked on a private trucker's social media page, and Jim still wasn't entirely sure how that had happened, dozens of truckers began to respond. They figured it would be great fun to get together and bring a city to its knees. And it would show the power that the trucker community had.

Money was already flowing into an on-line funding site that some nice person had started for them. Crandall had Jed Boone handling that; he just hoped so much money wouldn't stick to Jed's fingers that there'd be little left to pay for the gas and expenses of their trucking buddies. He had appointed Jeb as the co-treasurer. The smart former developer whom the feds had driven into bankruptcy would be good at keeping an eye on Jed and the money, and he had an added incentive to screw the government.

So far an impressive total had been contributed; it was growing every day as word spread about the "Patriot Pilgrimage." That was the name he'd come up with for the event. It would appeal to good ol' 'mericans who believed in the red, white and blue, less government, more freedom and the good book.

"Hey, Jethro. Toss another beer, will ya?"

The big guy reached into the ice bucket and fired a can of Bud towards Crandall. He caught it, popped it, and sucked back half.

"We're counting on you to marshal all the truckers," Crandall reminded Jethro. "Once they start arrivin' we need 'em held outside the city until all the trucks are here and we parade the convoy downtown to take over city hall. Park 'em out at Jacob Pew's place, remember?"

Jethro nodded. The survivalist had agreed to have the trucks sit on his property until the convoy was ready. The first trucks were reported to be approaching the Florida panhandle and should be arriving at Jacob's retreat within the next several hours.

Jim Crandall leaned back on the rickety chair under the big oak tree. The pulled pork sandwich was particularly good today. He glanced around the yard that surrounded The Ugly Porker. Typical Wednesday crowd. He stared at the single guy with brown hair who seemed to be around this place a whole lot. Was he a leaker? A rat? The table of four women were often there but Crandall dismissed them. A couple of families. Some local businessmen. How did a table of tourists get in here? He cut his eyes back to the brown-haired man. Looked in pretty good shape. Sat at a table just on the edge of being able to hear their conversation. He'd certainly seen him here several times. Maybe it was time to have Jethro go and say hello. That usually scared the crap out of anybody.

He started to rise when the man also rose. He went to the little wooden shack to pay his bill. He went to a three-year-old Corvette and lowered himself in. A moment later the engine fired up and the cherry red Vette took off.

Hmm, thought Crandall. Maybe next time. He turned to Jed Boone. "Everything is getting ready for our blockade. It's gonna be epic." He grinned and finished the last of his beer. "We'll show this damn city who's boss! We're taking it over!"

The J-Men cheered. This crazy plan of Crandall's actually seemed to be coming together. The media were going to go crazy once the J-Men had the downtown locked up and in their control. It had become a headline story across Canada. No reason it couldn't in the USA.

Jed was already scheming how he could again become the face of the J-Men and deal with the media. Jim Crandall didn't seem interested in that role. They certainly didn't want Jedidiah

Jenner as spokesman. Jed still wasn't exactly sure how the creepy preacher had become one of their group. Something to think about after their demonstration had shown the city who the real boss was.

Besides, the money in their on-line account had grown to a staggering figure. It was already over $1.2 million. Jed figured he and Jeb could figure out some, uh, disbursements that would pad certain personal bank accounts.

Jim Crandall reached for one more beer. The convoy was becoming bigger than he'd ever anticipated. The black ops he'd developed had spread across certain web sites that were not known to most people. The response from certain groups was building. The phone calls from that strange guy in Wisconsin had been complimentary. Weird dude. He had talked about national political stuff and organizing chaos. Whatever.

The great thing about this whole deal, Crandall smirked to himself, was that once he got it rolling, he didn't have to do much. Hell, the streets and the downtown were there, just waiting to be captured.

Nah, once these big trucks arrived, there just wasn't a damn thing that that uppity sheriff and those snots at city hall could do until Jim Crandall decided to declare victory and get the big rigs to leave. That would happen only after he had brought city hall to its knees and they reversed that tax grab on Beulah. And then he would be vindicated, as well as having the pleasure of humiliating the city, and finally winning back Beulah's affections.

His name would go down in protest lore, Crandall thought in his beer stupor: he'd prolly get invited tuh speak at some o' them rallies held around the country, them ones that paid big fees to speakers. He'd be seen as a champion of freedom, and a big success story in crappin' on local government. It'll be Grrrrreat!

Crandall grinned in anticipation of this new and wonderful life as he sipped his last beer and wiped his mouth. Beulah would be so impressed. She'd be all over him. He'd be in the pink for as long as he wanted to stay with her. Now he just had to get his demands ready about city hall cutting Beulah's taxes.

He belched majestically. Life was good.

Chapter 82

THE PHONE RANG in Willie William's house late that evening. "The J-Men have organized some kind of truck rally downtown," the informant reported. "It is going to happen soon. In the next couple of days."

Lt. Stokes texted him that her monitoring of social media was flashing gossip about a big trucker's rally in Florida 30 hours from now.

He called Perkins. "OK. I guess we're the target. Let's meet at 7am. I'll buy breakfast. Aunt Betty's?"

"See you there."

Both officers spent most of the night rolling scenarios around in their minds. They were both early for breakfast at the iconic café. It featured home-made biscuits, sausage gravy, crispy hash browns, eggs and bacon, ham and sausage individually or collectively. Fluffy flapjacks, of course, with syrup that had once been driven past a grove of maple trees while it was in bottles. Pure Vermont it was not.

Aunt Betty's is pretty much where diets go to die.

The surprise was Lt. A'ja Stokes joining them. Perkins lifted one eyebrow at Williams. "She's been monitoring the internet for the past day and I guess most of the night," he said as he looked at her weary eyes. She nodded.

Coffee came in a large pot with large mugs. A'ja gratefully grabbed hers, poured and gulped, burning her mouth a bit. Ice water helped.

"It's us," she told the sheriff. "There is increasing chatter on some of the black channels. They've lost their on-line discipline as word gets out and more people join whatever movement this is. That usually happens. The short story is, I think it is going to happen here at noon tomorrow."

She swallowed more of the now-cooler coffee and rubbed her eyes.

Williams nodded agreement. "That's what my informant said last night. I think they are set up to attack downtown with this blockade thing."

"One more item," A'ja contributed. "Somebody's set up an on-line funding page. It claims to be all about protecting freedom and fighting local government taxation and more crap. Sorry. 'The Patriot Pilgrimage.' Who comes up with this stuff? Anyway, they claim all the money is going to pay expenses for the truckers." She sighed in doubt. "Well, it has raised nearly $1.7 million as of 6 this morning."

Perkins felt his eyes widen in shock. The waitress appeared at that instant and looked at him with concern. "Honey, whatever she just said to you, a good breakfast will help you get through the day." She laughed. Her name tag read 'Edith.'

Williams ordered the lumberjack breakfast. Why there was a lumberjack breakfast offered along the Gulf Coast of Florida was known only to Aunt Betty, and she wasn't talking because she'd died eight years ago. There were rumors that the kitchen had honored her untimely passing by not changing the grease in the deep fryer since her funeral.

Perkins did bacon and eggs with a homemade biscuit. He loved a warm biscuit, and Samantha, despite her many charms and accomplishments, was an NYC girl who didn't have that tender relationship learned at her grandmother's knee that one needs to bake a really fine Southern buttermilk biscuit. It's all about not over-mixing.

A'ja shuddered at the menu offerings and finally asked for one poached egg with one slice of whole grain toast, unbuttered. Edith had never had an order like that in this house of grease. She checked it twice before shrugging and writing it down. "Can't promise Wilbur will know how to poach an egg, honey, but I'll try to explain it to him. You cook it in water? Gawwllll-eee. If it don't come with a pound or two of bacon grease, he ain't much good."

"That much money? You sure?" Perkins demanded of the young Lieutenant after Edith rolled away.

She pulled out her smart phone and punched little buttons. "Sorry. I was wrong." Perkins relaxed a bit. "It's now $1.8 million." She snapped off her phone and drank more coffee.

Perkins and Williams exchanged stunned looks. "They've got more financing for this thing than we do!" The Sheriff looked over at his young officer in charge of Intelligence-gathering. "What else are they saying on social media?"

"Momentum is gathering. It started small about a week or ten days ago. We think it started with one of the J-Men. We've traced some early text threads back to a 'freemantax.' He appears to have started this whole thing. Now some of the right-wing political crazies have jumped on board."

"Freemantax? What's that supposed to mean?"

"I wondered that too. But if you break it down, it might mean 'free,' 'manatee,' 'taxes.' Some kind of rallying cry for freedom from high taxes in Port Manatee? Anyway, my team was working all night and we think this is the origin."

"Hmm. Willie, you got any thoughts?"

"Not on that stuff. I'm sorta focused on a few hundred semi-trailers arriving tomorrow to take our town hostage."

Edith arrived at their table. She put a large platter in front of the captain: three eggs over easy, crispy bacon, three sausage links, a piece of country fried ham, a pile of home fries and three large pancakes. "You want some toast with that, honey?"

Williams shook his head. "No, thanks. I'm cutting carbs." He enthusiastically grabbed his knife and fork. Any trees in town should be shivering in fear after his loading up on the lumberjack special.

Perkins got his plate of E&B. The large warm biscuit was on the side with butter and homemade crabapple jelly.

A'ja got a small plate with one piece of unbuttered toast and a little bowl with an under-poached egg sitting disconsolately in the bottom of the cup. It was moist and runny. Williams turned his head away.

It took several minutes before the conversation began again at the table.

"Willie, your informant is pretty sure?"

"Yes. I've been using this informant for years. Not very often, but once in a while. This will also be the last time. She's retiring."

"She?"

"Yeah. That's another reason I never told anybody about her. She's a very nice older lady, absolutely unmemorable. We were in the same rookie class at the police academy 25 years ago. Two blacks and two females in a class of 28. We all sort of bonded, just out of self-defense. She served on the force for six years, fell in love with a civil engineer, got married, had twins, and they moved to Peru for a few years for some water project he was doing. They returned about five years ago. Since her twins started college, she has been my secret agent. She goes with a couple of her girlfriends to things I need. Nobody's ever twigged to them, a few older ladies having tea or whatever. They listen well, however. She told me if she ever sees another barbecued spare rib again it will be too soon."

Perkins reflected. "Wait a sec. If you were both in the same rookie class, how is she an 'older lady'?"

"With great respect, Sheriff, shut it." Perkins grinned at the Captain; Lieutenant Stokes averted her eyes. Impressionable young officers with a fine future career path sometimes shouldn't hear anything when their superior officers are sparring.

Williams finished his last bites of pancake, the last half of a sausage, and the last bite of ham. He nodded happily. "That was good. I may last the day now. You ready to go?"

A'ja was still poking at the white and yellow residue in the cup. She had nibbled half of her one slice of toast. "Yes." She looked around. "I wonder what the cholesterol count is in here right now?"

Perkins checked the plates on the tables. "I don't think you want to know." He waved the universal 'check please' sign to Edith who delivered it a moment later. "You folks have a real nice day, now. Keep our city safe."

The three uniformed officers nodded their thanks. Williams grabbed the bill and Perkins dropped a ten on the table for Edith. He figured she'd earned it after carrying Willie's truckload of food. And speaking of trucks...

"We need to get Roy Crawford down to our office. And the mayor, I think. Time to finalize our strategy."

CHAPTER 83

"WHAT WE'VE FIGURED out from the Canadian experience is to not let them into the downtown. Period. If the trucks can't reach the downtown core, they can't blockade the center of the city. We need to scatter them and keep them on the periphery."

Mayor Rodriguez, Councillor Sharpe, City Manager Crawford and City Engineer Bolsanaro paid close attention as Captain Williams pointed at a map of Port Manatee and the surrounding county.

"Our strategy is to block them outside the city. We'll also have roving patrols in case they try to come in on secondary streets. The big problem is what do we do with the trucks? They will be angry at being shutout. Many of them will have guns. We're going to shunt the trucks into the Palmetto County Fairgrounds out on Highway 23. There's lots of parking there. The issue is if we get into a lot of confrontations with drivers. It could get ugly. Those big rigs can smash into pretty much whatever they want and win. The FHP and our county officers will all be heavily armed. It is a potential powder keg. We just don't have a better idea." He paused. The planning group thought about the implications for public safety. There were no really good and safe options.

"Assuming we get the trucks to the fairgrounds, it is much easier for law enforcement to patrol and keep order. We'll have a big representation from the FHP on all highways. We're also talking to both adjacent County Sheriffs about additional support as needed."

"That makes a lot of sense," began the mayor. "We can't afford to have our downtown occupied or held hostage. It would be a huge black eye for our city, and frankly we've had enough of those over the past few years. However, I'm really concerned about the risk of fights, property damage, even shootings between truckers and law enforcement once they are blockaded from getting downtown."

Silence at the board table. Williams finally spoke again. "It is a big risk, Mayor, no question. Our planning team feels it is better, and less risk to the public, if we bar them from the downtown and keep confrontations on the highway or at the fairgrounds. We just don't see a better option."

More silence. Finally Perkins said, "We share your concern about violence. All we can promise is to try to minimize danger to public safety. We may get the National Guard to help patrol the fairgrounds to keep order. But it is potentially an extremely volatile situation."

"How do we communicate this to the public?" Kim asked after the pause. Her ward was involved in this plan. A lot of traffic would flow through it into the core. "And when?"

"That is also a problem," admitted Williams. "If we make a public announcement right now, the truckers will start infiltrating immediately. The public will panic. We lose most of the control we have of the situation now. As far as we know, the truckers and the protest organizers don't know that we know. We believe they are expecting an easy and open route into the downtown tomorrow morning." He paused. "Lt Stokes has been developing a communications plan for us." He gestured at the officer.

"What we are proposing is waiting until 10:00 tomorrow morning. We then saturate the airwaves with announcements and blitz social media. The message will say that there is a possible gas leak in a downtown gas line and traffic has been barred until the situation is resolved. That should handle any local questions and buy us enough time to resolve the blockade attempt."

Williams nodded and then continued with the ops plan. "To halt the trucks, we are still assuming they will come in one big convoy. That's the showiest strategy and will be a media photo-op...and also be quite intimidating to people. The concrete blocks and traffic barriers for the main entrances to the city will go up promptly at 10:30am. The city's dump trucks will move out at 10:00 to be at each major intersection well in advance. We'll also barricade city hall."

"We'll have fifteen city dump trucks, loaded with gravel, lined up ready to go," reported the City Engineer, "plus eight garbage trucks and a couple of big graders and three bulldozers. I assume you want them parked behind your traffic control barriers as a more solid line of defense?"

"Yes. You can talk to our traffic coordinator about which intersections need the most help. Thank you."

"We are coordinating this from the Emergency Operations Center?" asked Roy Crawford.

"Yes. We'll go active there at midnight. We'll need you and the mayor and other senior civic officials there by 7am. We're informing the Fire Chief and Ambulance Service after this meeting. We're hoping to keep a really tight lid on our counter-strategy so it doesn't leak out and the truckers start invading early." This was Perkins' worst nightmare—to wake up and find the city already held hostage, the truckers and the J-Men in control.

A few more minutes of planning and confirming details; the meeting broke up. With the deadline inching closer, there was no time to waste.

Kim returned to city hall to finish her own preparations, then she and Samantha met for a drink. Kim figured she'd earned one.

The beach bar was already heating up when Kim arrived. Most of the girls wore swimsuit bras with swirly, gauzy, colorful cover-ups cinched around their waists, fashionable sunglasses pushed up into their sun-bleached hair. The guys were attired in a variety of ripped T-shirts, cut-off sweatshirts, baggy trunks, tattoos and flip flops.

"Do we even belong here anymore?" Kim said when she plopped down on the small banquette seat beside Samantha.

"Hope. Memories. Our lost youth. Whatever," Samantha sighed. "And it is within walking distance of our condos."

"That's barely a good enough reason," Kim told her as they watched two nubile 21-year-olds on the dance floor. "I couldn't move like that if you tased me."

Samantha laughed as she sipped her Singapore Sling. They both watched the action for a moment. Less than twenty years separated the two women from most of the people at the bar, but it suddenly seemed like a generation apart. Then it dawned on them—it was.

"Anyway, what happened at your big meeting?"

Kim took a slug of her Sauvignon Blanc and lowered her voice a bit. No soft words could be heard over the noise of the energetic but mediocre band at the end of the bar.

"A bunch of crazy truckers are going to try to take over downtown tomorrow at noon," she confided to her best friend.

Samantha knew how to keep her mouth shut. Confidentiality was not a concern.

Kim explained the plot and the plan by the city to thwart the invasion of the big rigs. Samantha listened intently.

When she finished they each ordered another drink.

"Lemme get this right. You're, well, Perk and his team and the city, are going to blockade the entrances to downtown and push all these trucks into the Fairgrounds?"

Kim nodded.

"Don't you think the drivers are going to be pretty angry and upset about their whole plan blowing up?"

Kim nodded.

"So, if you can force them to the Fairgrounds, what are you going to do with them?"

Kim stopped nodding. She suddenly looked as if she'd been hit on the back of her head with a shovel. She stared into the dimmest recesses of the bar's far corner, the one with two old and abused surf boards hanging down. One of the boards displayed a shark bite. Neither surfboard contributed any ideas

"There was some talk about the National Guard for security," she admitted. "Everybody is worried about the potential for violence. But what else can you do with them after they are blocked from downtown?"

"Well, it seems to me that you're going to end up with a few hundred very unhappy people who have driven for a couple of days to make a protest and shut down a city. Now suddenly they are shunted to some county fairgrounds by a bunch of cops and dump trucks. My guess is they won't be thrilled. They'll have big trucks. Guns. And a very unsocial attitude."

Kim blanched at those thoughts. "Yeah. Well." She halted in confusion. "What if..." She stopped again. "What would Miss Smartypants do?" she glared at Samantha.

"It's easy," Samantha replied with a grin. "We're going to throw them a party!"

Chapter 84

IT IS AMAZING how fear of an imminent crisis can accelerate normally sclerotic planning processes inside government. By the time Kim had thought the idea through, she and Samantha were hustling back to her condo at Sapphire Blue. She called Roy Crawford on her cell phone to explain the problem. He grasped it immediately.

"You're right, honey. If we just corral them, there will be trouble. Fights and probably gunfire will break out. And with those big trucks there will soon be somebody wanting to break through the fence or something. But where else can we direct them? There's no other—"

"Roy! Hang on! What we're talking about is to keep them there! So, we put on a party for them! Get a couple of bands. Get a truck full of iced beer. Round up every food truck in the city and rush them out there."

Crawford got it. "That is genius. You are a genius. Love you. Gotta go."

And he hung up, leaving Kim spluttering that it was really Samantha's idea.

"No, don't," said Samantha. "This is a great opportunity for you. If it works, you'll be seen as a real community thinker, somebody out front of civic issues. You take the credit." She shook her head as Kim protested. "No, Kim, this is why you ran for public office. To make a difference. It doesn't matter if somebody else had a bit of an idea, you're the one running with it." She paused, and then smiled slyly. "Besides, if it fails, then I had nothing to do with it!"

They both laughed. "I still don't feel great about this," Kim told her.

"The important thing is to just make sure there's no trouble downtown or anywhere else in the city," Samantha assured her. "This could become a violent protest. We need to avoid that, and this might be a solution. Now, get back to city hall and help plan the party."

Kim hugged her and ran out the door. An hour later she was immersed in the party details with the city hall staff who had been recalled. They arranged for the stage at the fairground to be available, including washrooms. Somebody knew somebody who knew somebody's aunt whose favorite nephew was the star of a popular country band. Texas Jack and the Armadillos. Stunningly, they had that day open and once the problems were explained, they agreed to put on a free show. Anything for Auntie Mabel. The band's manager was left sputtering in protest.

A local C&W band was hired to be the warm-up act. For $500, the band would happily do a three-hour set while standing on their heads. They seemed chagrined at only doing a 30-minute opener.

The local beer distributor thought he'd died and gone to heaven. A few hundred hot and angry truck drivers at a free concert? Yes. In fact, hell yes! He would be there with trucks and tents and pretty girls to tend the bar. Monthly sales bonus, here we come!

Of course, as the number of people who learned something was going on and that there would be a big surprise party tomorrow afternoon at the county fairgrounds, word began to leak out. Social media is an unreliable partner for people trying to do something good. Or, even more optimistically, keep something quiet.

Roy Crawford had briefed Perkins about their plans for the afternoon concert and party. The Sheriff told his senior management team. A'ja Stokes reacted first.

"It is starting to hit Insta," she reported to Perkins. "Not a lot of details, but people are wondering what's going on."

Soon after, the lines were buzzing to city hall employees, Sheriff Department staff, and other emergency personnel. Their careful plan to have equipment in place by 10am was now shot. They needed to start moving the big city trucks, traffic barriers and other equipment now.

Perkins, Williams, Crawford and their senior staff all went to the Crisis Operations Center as soon as they could get there. By 4am the place was buzzing.

A bunch of disgruntled civic employees hauled themselves out of bed at various hours of the early morning once they started getting phone calls from their bosses. They left their wives, mistresses, and, in one intriguing case, both. They headed into the murky, steamy, humid, hot and breathless Florida night to fire up the city's fleet.

As more deputies arrived and began to patrol the city, it became obvious that some of the big trucks had already entered the city limits. Several were cruising around the downtown core, as if to scope out the terrain. Several others were parked on city streets. There were no incidents. Yet.

By 5am the Emergency Command Center was fully operational. The big electronic map of Port Manatee was displayed on the front wall. A clever computer technician was plotting the location of trucks downtown as reports came in from police cruisers and civic staff.

"So far it's still containable," reported one sergeant after he talked to his officers. The women and men in patrol cars were doing their own tabulations on the number and size of the trucks. "But, if it gets much larger, they are going to start getting the numbers in their favor."

That was enough to galvanize action. Crawford ordered all city vehicles to move into their preassigned locations. The slow trek began to reinforce key intersections.

Deputies began to set up traffic barriers hours earlier than originally planned. They readied spike belts in case a trucker was dumb enough to try to run a barrier. Tires for a semi are expensive.

The traffic management plan was to leave one lane open for cars to still travel into the city, if the police approved them. This would also provide a route for emergency vehicles, but it would effectively block all semi-trailer traffic. There would be blowback from trucks with legitimate deliveries, but for the next few hours Port Manatee was going on big-rig lock-down.

Four big garbage trucks rolled in to block access to city hall.

The streets became a quiet battle of attrition. As a truck tried to park at a major location, deputies would push back with warnings and even threats about towing and loss of the trucking license. Some drivers moved. A few said some rude things and locked their doors. A couple got on their cell phones.

Some air horns were blown, much to the discomfort of downtown residents who soon had their lights on, peering out of their high-rise windows into the gloomy, hazy night.

Perkins decided to do his own reconnaissance. He jumped in his official SUV with Lt. Stokes. They cruised downtown. There were several semis parked in places where there should not be a semi-trailer truck.

Perkins stopped behind one and put on his emergency flashers. He and Stokes walked up to the driver's door. The driver reluctantly cracked open his window. He looked bleary, like he'd been snoozing in the cab.

"Welcome to Port Manatee," said Perkins. "I'm Sheriff Perkins. This is Lt. Stokes. How ya doin'?"

"You the Shrff? Fer real, man?"

"Yes, I am. We always like to welcome our trucker friends to town."

"Huh. Hot damn. Never met me a real Shrff before."

"You from Arkansas?" asked Stokes.

"Hey, yeah. Shure 'nough."

"Anything we can help you with?" Perkins continued.

"Nah, man. Jess waitin' fer some friends to show up."

"Uh huh. Listen, we prefer it if you don't run your truck at night in the downtown. It sorta disturbs the residents," Perkins told the driver. "Mind movin' along?"

"Um. Well. See, I'm here for some…well, I don't rightly know whass goin' on, but somebody'll tell me. Some big to do 'bout screwing up some political assholes in city hall an' a big tax hike or somethin'. I dunno. Should be fun though. An' somebody's giving me a shitload of money for the week. Hey, man, good times." He paused to spit and then wiped his mouth with a dirty flannel sleeve. "Yuh know 'bout the big protest, when it all starts?"

"Yeah, I think maybe that's been cancelled," replied the sheriff casually. "But did yah hear 'bout the big concert and party for truckers? Texas Jack 'n his band's playin'. Starts after noon out at the county fairgrounds. I hear there's lots of cold beer, a free concert, maybe some line dancin'…"

He was deliberately dropping his g's and speaking more casually to try to gain rapport with the driver.

"No shit, man? For real?"

Perkins nodded. "Yup. Should be a blast. I'd get there early, yah know, get a really good parkin' spot. Be the first to meet the girls in the beer tent."

The driver brightened. "Hey, yeah. Sounds good. I wanna get some breakfast. Thanks, dude."

Perkins nodded, touched the brim of his hat, and returned with Stokes to his truck. Then he turned back to the truck. "Might wanna try Aunt Betty's over on Regent Street. They do a real nice breakfast." The driver waved his thanks.

"Pretty good performance," she admitted to him when they sat inside.

"Aw, shucks, ma'am..."

She snorted. Perkins started the vehicle and drove past the trucker they'd just talked to. His truck was lighting up, ready to pull out.

"Interesting that they don't know why they are here," he mused. "It's as if they just responded to some social media cattle call. But we now know they aren't really committed to some fanatical political sect or something." He shook his head. "And we found out that somebody's paying them, or at least covering expenses. We need to trace the money once this is all over." Stokes nodded and made a note on her cell phone.

"I think the message about the free concert just might get out there," Perkins continued as he wheeled his vehicle back toward the Emergency Center. "Kim had a smart idea. We just have to peacefully push and motivate the truckers over there."

The barricades were up now on the perimeter main entrances to the city.

They saw a dozen semis parked, and three more arriving. Well, if it was just fifteen or twenty trucks and not the several hundred they'd been alerted to, that was manageable, thought Perkins.

It wasn't good, but it should be manageable.

CHAPTER 85

JIM CRANDALL ROLLED out of bed after the second snooze alarm sounded. He groaned. He and the J-Men had met last night for a little impromptu early celebration of the success of their civic blockade. It was possible a few adult beverages had been consumed.

Crandall rubbed his face with his hands. They felt dry and rough. He coughed deeply a couple of times. Spitting up the phlegm drove him into the bathroom. He hacked and coughed a few more times. Was the stuff supposed to be that sickly yellow?

He peed. For a long time. It was a sickly yellow as well. He stared, then flushed. Geez, maybe it was time to ease up on the beer and maryjane just a bit.

He coughed one more time before grabbing his razor. The sound of the razor scraping his neck and face seemed to be very loud this morning. He wiped the razor, turned on the hot tap in the shower stall and stood there for a long minute before hitting the cold. Crap. He jumped back from the faucet and readjusted the H and the C. He used to be able to stand the temperature extremes. The hot loosened him up, the cold rejuvenated a tired, hung-over body. Not today.

Getting old and out of shape really sucks.

He went into his meagre side of the closet. Beulah had become kind of distant the last couple of weeks. He hadn't talked to her yet about his brilliant plan to get her taxes lowered. He wanted it to be a big surprise.

He fumbled through the few hangers on his side. For some obscure reason, she hadn't been too enamored with doing his laundry anymore. He sniffed at a couple of T-shirts. The red one with a cock-eyed eagle on its front seemed the least malodorous.

He shook his head to try to clear it, grabbed the last of the coffee in the pot and stood in the worn kitchen. Beulah must already be out in the fields, he figured. Well, this would be a memorable day for her once his plan worked.

Lots of trucks were pouring in. Last night the J-Men had met with a couple of guys who claimed they were the leaders of a bunch of the big rigs. Who knew? From Michigan and Louisiana. Anyway, they could certainly hold their beer.

Everybody had agreed to start flooding into the city center at 11am. That would let them take over city hall about noon, which would mean great media coverage. The plan, Crandall recalled vaguely, was to parade the big convoys into the city from Jacob's field where a bunch of the trucks had overnighted, assuming Jethro hadn't screwed-up that simple assignment.

And Jim Crandall would be right there, leading the J-Men and leading the invasion. It would be memorable.

He would have liked another cup of joe, but Beulah hadn't left enough. He shrugged, annoyed. Have to grab one on the way. Maybe a donut or two.

He looked at the clock. Holy crap! How could it be 9:15 already? His phone rang. "Yeah?"

"Jim! It's Jed! We gotta get rolling, man! Like right now! The Sheriff is trying to shut down the city!"

"What?"

"Where the hell you been? We're getting reports from a bunch of the boys. There are traffic blockades going up on the major routes into town! That fuckin' sheriff is trying to shut us out!"

"They can't do that! Public highways. We're allowed on 'em."

"Yeah, well, you tell him that! Just get your ass down here right now! We're at the Ugly Porker. But we've gotta roll!" Boone slammed his OFF button. Crandall was left holding his phone, stunned.

He rushed out of the kitchen and threw himself into the front seat of his truck. It took a couple of tries to crank over but it finally did. He sped out of the driveway in a cloud of dust and fear. He never saw Beulah waving at him from the north field.

CHAPTER 86

"JUST A FRIENDLY reminder, folks. Downtown Port Manatee is currently under a health and safety warning. Apparently a gas line got nicked during some construction, so the police and fire people want to avoid traffic going down there until things get cleared up. So please stay away from there. We'll let you know here on Country 103 on your FM dial when it's safe to go down there again. By the way, have you heard about the pop-up concert this afternoon at the Palmetto Fairgrounds? Yeah! It's just been announced, and it looks like a blast. Texas Jack and the Armadillos will be playing. And it's free for all of our trucker friends! Yes, you heard me. A free concert with this wonderful country star for all you 18-wheelers. I'd be heading out there right now if I were you. Get a good spot. We're expecting all sorts of big rigs to join us. 'course, if you drive a little truck, well, c'mon out as well! I'll be right back here on Country 103 after Texas Jack's latest hit: "My dog loves me more'n my girlfriend."

Duke Simmons hit the off switch on his microphone as the music cranked up. He'd never heard of a pop-up concert being done by Texas Jack. No warning. Some crappy local band as the warm-up. For some reason the city seemed to be pushing this hard. But why wasn't his radio station out there claiming sponsorship and introducing the acts and getting all the credit for this concert? What was wrong with the management of his station? Where was the Promotion Manager, what's her name?

The studio door pushed open and the Manager appeared. "You're doing great, Duke, just keep mentioning the free concert. Lots of food trucks. Cold beer. Hot music. Free to get in for all semi drivers. Well, for everybody." He nodded and turned to leave.

"Hey, Bill. Why aren't we out there claiming this show? Who's actually producing it? I never got any advance notice. Can we get Texas Jack on the air?"

"Yeah, sure let's get you out there as soon as your shift is done. Take the big station cruiser. Be good publicity for your show."

With that he pushed open the heavy soundproof door and left. He left a very confused mid-morning announcer.

Shaking his head, Duke waited for the last chords to finish before opening his mic. "Hey, friends, just wanna let you know that I'll be out at this big free concert this afternoon at the Fairgrounds. It's gonna be a blast, so if you drive a truck, c'mon out and bring your pals. Should be fun to see all the big rigs that are visiting Port Manatee. Love those trucker guys and gals. Gimme a big whoop if you're in your truck right now!"

Air horns sounded from the eighty or more trucks that were in a loose assembly on the side of County Road 19. A few dozen more were gathering at the truck center just off Interstate 75. Another sixty were on the main highway. Many more big rigs were arriving.

Everybody was twitchy. Most of them were a little hung-over.

The gathering at the barbecue joint was another sixty or seventy trucks. Those drivers would be heading downtown to lead the invasion. Crandall was desperately trying to hold the invasion together but was losing control of the mob.

Banjo muttered to himself as he sat in his cab. He was getting restless and hungry. His semi-trailer was named "Sheila." I mean, really, Banjo continued as he finished the last of his tepid coffee, who cared that much about taxes in this shit-hole town? This whole thing wasn't real well organized. Who would care if he skipped it? He'd still get the $3,800 he'd been promised for expenses. That concert did sound like fun. Texas Jack was a great favorite among truckers.

Gosh, it was hot already and it wasn't even 11 o'clock. Some cold beer would go down very nicely. Maybe just do a little swing through the downtown, scare the crap outta them city hall goombas, and then head for the fairgrounds.

Yeah. Sounds like a plan. "Lefty, Lefty, come in," he called on the CB.

"What's up, Banjo boy?"

"Tired of waiting. Thinkin' maybe that free concert with Texas Jack sounds fun."

"Yeah, heard 'bout that. Who's in charge of this here thing? Ain't really well put together. I jus' want my money and then

I'm headin' back out." He paused. "That concert does sound like a kick. Lemme talk to a couple of the boys."

Banjo clicked off his CB, cranked up the FM radio and sang along with another Texas Jack hit song: *"My girlfriend met my wife and I'm so sorry. I'm not there but they're both real horny. I want them both but this lyric's so corny. Time to find me a new girlfriend named Courtney."*

It was a catchy tune, but the lyrics weren't gone to win a Grammy.

Chapter 87

JIM CRANDALL WAS desperately trying to salvage his truck-in. Jed and Jeb were having a fight, Jethro was drinking beer and Jack O'Hara was running around waving his Confederate sword. Nobody was in charge. The drivers were demanding their expense money. Horns were blowing and drivers were cursing. It was turning into a chaotic mess.

Reports from truckers circling the highway around the city were that the Sheriff's office and city hall maintenance workers had effectively blocked the main access routes to downtown.

Crandall was hung-over, angry and not thinking really well. He tried again to exert control.

"We'll just bust 'em down!" he shouted. "Those big rigs'll clean out those cop cars on the first try!"

Silence greeted his proposal. There were seven men and two women standing in a loose half-circle at The Ugly Porker. They were apparently the leaders of a bunch of out-of-state drivers.

"Yeah, maybe. Not sure that's what we signed up for. You said we'd drive into downtown, take it over, shut down the main streets for a day or two, have a little party with our people, get paid, then bail out and get back to work," Lanny O'Brien said to Crandall. "Looks like you missed the opportunity to get into town."

"No, no. We'll send a couple of trucks busting down the barriers and the rest will follow. It'll work."

O'Brien spat into the dirt. "Not sure I see you in your big rig leading that, Crandall. I jus' see you in a little wimp-ass old Dodge Ram." He spat again as his pals laughed. "Runnin' a police blockade is a whole different can of shit from sitting in a truck on a downtown street." He hawked a giant booger and spat. Everyone quickly hopped back one pace. "Not me goin' down that road."

Another trucker shrugged her shoulders. "Lanny's right. You start charging through a police barricade, somebody's gonna get hurt or shot or somethin'. Ain't gonna be me or my boys."

Jed Boone had stopped fighting with Jeb and looked on at the botched plan with quiet satisfaction. He'd come to really dislike Crandall and his ego after he'd dreamed up this downtown invasion.

One of the women turned to look at Boone. "I think we'll just take our expense money now and mosey along."

Boone swallowed hard. He was hoping to avoid big cash payouts or electronic transfers from the on-line funding that had come it. It was now an impressive total. Almost 2.6 million. Surely he'd be entitled to substantial compensation for his own expenses and hard work being the paymaster.

"Uh, well, that might be a bit of a problem. You see..."

It got real quiet. The crowd of truckers moved to surround Boone, Crandall and the other J-Men. Their faces were fixed and their eyes were hard. "You'd better not be suggestin' that the cash ain't here, brother. Cause that would upset everybody. Don't think I'd wanna be the one to tell 'em that they ain't getting their money."

Crandall looked into the eyes of the group that had suddenly grown. The mood had changed abruptly. It was obvious that the J-Men had lost control of the event. It was starting to blow up in spectacular fashion.

"Well, mister?" The group pressed in a little closer. Jethro was trying to muscle his way beside Jed, but other drivers had sauntered over to the cabinet meeting. The rumor of no cash was spreading quickly. The chain tightened around the J-Men.

Jed was no dummy. He was especially no hero. "Hey, hey, friends! No problem. No sirree. I'll go and get the expense money. I'll need to go to the bank for more cash, of course. It'll take a little time."

"Sure. We'll just have Louie and Betty and Big John go with you. Just for your protection, of course."

O'Brien pointed at three of the biggest, toughest drivers in the group. "Why don't we all meet up at the concert this afternoon? That was right neighborly of somebody to 'range a free concert fer us." He looked around at the drivers. Everybody nodded. "OK, the Fairgrounds at 2pm." He stared hard at Jed. "You'd better have all the expense money we got promised. Otherwise..."

He let the unspoken threat trail off. Crandall and the J-Men understood.

Jed, Jethro and the three-member protective detail left for the banks. The other truckers drifted back to their cabs, talking. The consensus quickly became 'screw this shit, let's go party.'

Word went out on cell phones and CBs. Nobody had any objections. A few minutes later the roar of big diesels starting up echoed across the roads and highways.

Perkins and his officers heard the engines rev from the trucks on the highway. Instinctively they all loosened their weapons, checked their equipment and moved into position at the front of the barricades.

A couple of the biggest trucks rolled up to the first barrier. One of the drivers waved out the window. Uncertain, Perkins looked around and then slowly came forward.

"Been a blast, Sheriff. We're all heading for that concert thing at the Fairgrounds. C'mon over, join us." With that he tooted his horn a couple of times and put the truck in gear. He led a parade down the highway toward the fairgrounds.

Perkins sagged in relief. A couple of his officers rushed up. "We've been checking with the other outposts. They are standing down! The truckers are turning around!"

There were headshakes of relief. Perkins phoned Roy Crawford at the Command Center. "I think they are dispersing," he said. "That crazy free concert idea seems to appeal to them. I'm not sure we understand what just happened, but I think the city is safe."

"That's what we're getting as well," Crawford said. "My people are reporting no accidents or injuries. No confrontations. City hall is secure. I'm going to start having my people stand down after an hour, just to be sure, but then they can return to base."

"Understood, Roy." The two both paused as they savored the moment. "I think I owe you a beer."

Crawford laughed. "I was just going to say that I owed you a couple of beers."

"Well, a pair always beats one of a kind!"

Crawford laughed again. It was nice to be able to laugh after the pressure and problems of the past few days. "I'll talk to you later." They both hung up.

The city workers began to dismantle the road barriers an hour later.

"Let's get more officers down to the Fairgrounds to help direct traffic," Perkins suggested. "It looks like a big crowd gathering." An officer nodded and went to his mobile radio to arrange traffic and crowd control.

As Perkins stood beside the entrance to the highway, a big green semi-trailer came surging over the rise. The driver saw Perkins and slammed his brakes. He rolled down his window.

"Hey, Shrff. Yuh was right. Aunt Betty does a real nice breakfast."

CHAPTER 88

THE LOCAL BEER distributor thought this was the best day of his life, including his second wedding in Vegas. He'd contacted the regional brewery in Tampa the night before and they sent a reefer down, loaded with beer. He'd arranged for a dozen attractive young ladies he used for promotions to serve the beer. They wore cut-off jean shorts or little skirts, T-shirts with the corporate beer logos splashed on them, and perky little caps with their ponytails sticking out the back. They all looked cute as hell.

The drivers were impressed. They were also enthusiastic about sharing their CB handles and cell phone numbers. The young ladies were very selective.

The beer guy had gotten every plastic tub or bin he could rustle up, bought most every bag of ice in the county, and had packed all the tubs with beer and ice and cold water. It was still the best way to serve beer to a crowd.

The truckers started to roll in about 1:00pm. There wasn't anybody on stage yet, so a bunch of trucks cranked up Country 103FM. Duke Simmons had just arrived and soon figured out what was going on. As soon as the fair's PA system was set up he jumped on stage and started MCing the entire thing.

The food trucks barreled in. Thai. Hot mini-donuts. Burgers. Pizza. Middle Eastern. Tacos. Carolina barbecue. Grilled cheese sandwiches. Shawarma. Didn't matter, a crowd was quickly lined up in front of all of them.

The deputies onsite called for more support. They emphasized it was a happy crowd but there were a lot of people. They just wanted to be sure of keeping the peace. The Inspector sent out ten more units. He called the National Guard, thanked them, and told them to stand down.

A big truck with sound equipment arrived. The roadies moved quickly to roll the big amps and mics out of their cases and set up the stage for Texas Jack and his band. The truck drivers milled around peacefully, having a cold one, still trying to get the phone numbers of the girls in the bar, and laughing at the idiots who had tried to organize this protest march.

"Pretty good protest so far," chortled a driver from South Carolina to his new friend from Alabama. They clinked cans.

There was a brief fight over Florida's and Georgia's chances in the upcoming college football season. The deputies quickly sorted it out. No charges were laid. The officers understood where football ranks in southern culture. Besides, the two deputies had a long-standing disagreement over LSU and 'Bama.

In the middle of the afternoon Jed Boone and Jethro rolled in, accompanied by their three very large new friends. The leaders of the various bands of truckers got together. They efficiently got the drivers to line up and recorded who got their honorariums paid. It only took an hour. Everybody was very happy, except for Jed, who saw the bank account from all the Go-Fund-Me money drop to near-zero. 679 trucks at $3800 each swallowed the cash that had been donated. There would be no residue to recognize his own hard work, Jed thought bitterly.

No one sobbed on his behalf or offered to share their money.

Duke Simmons got the place hopping. The opening act showed up about 4 o'clock. They started to get their equipment on stage and warmed up. The band members looked out at the crowd. Two of them nearly fainted. They'd never played to more than thirty people before.

Perkins rolled in. He got reports from his officers. Everything was good. The toilets were working fine, the beer was still cold, the food trucks were doing land-office business, and the DJ on stage was banging out the country hits.

After his updates, Perkins returned to his SUV and leaned against the side. He realized suddenly how exhausted he was. The pressure of the last few days and the adrenaline high that comes before a dangerous confrontation were now crashing down. He looked around. It was going to be a beautiful evening. On an impulse he phoned Samantha.

"Hey. Why don't you and Kim, maybe Samira if she's not doing anything, get Roy and come out to the Fairgrounds? This crazy concert idea for the truckers is turning into a party."

Samantha offered a quick yes. She called Kim and then Samira. They both agreed it sounded like fun. Rosie was bouncing with excitement. Roy was ordered to pick them up at 5pm. Perkins promised a police escort.

When Roy's vehicle arrived at the Fairgrounds, the officer directed them to a place at the back of the crowd where Perkins had parked his SUV. It had become the unofficial VIP area. The Mayor arrived a few minutes later. So did Willie Williams, who looked drained. He conferred with Perkins, grinned, and then reported to HQ where he was and that he was going off-duty. He opened the tailgate of his SUV and sat down heavily. The truck creaked as the rear end got squashed.

Roy Crawford went off to buy an armload of beer. Perkins always kept a change of clothes in his trunk, so he was in civvies now. He'd reported to headquarters and then told them he was off the clock. He was looking forward to a beer or two.

Roy circulated the beer. The first ones went down very smoothly. Willie did his in two big swallows and looked around for a second. Perkins slammed one into his hand. The captain deserved it. Perkins went over to a young officer and told him he would be driving the captain home later that night. He then offered another beer to Willie. It wasn't refused.

Duke Simmons introduced the warm-up band about 6pm. ThE RoAdKiLl. Their music pretty much matched their name, but nobody cared. They played for 30 minutes. Somebody from the city gave them a check for $500. Everybody was happy.

Several hundred cars and vans carrying local residents had been pouring into the fairgrounds as word spread about the concert. Truckers mingled happily with the locals. Torches were lit as dusk set in. The warm, flickering lights enhanced what had become a community celebration.

During the intermission, Perkins and Crawford saluted each other. "Saved the city," was their consensus. They got a bit exuberant. The ladies looked on in amusement.

Samira leaned into Perkins. "Your detective is making a very good recovery," she told him. "He's working his butt off on the rehab." She smiled. "And his partner is dating one of my nurses. Michelle. He'd better be nice to her!"

Perkins grinned back at her.

Rosie was offered tidbits from many hands. There were lots of other dogs for her to play with. She was bounding all over the fairgrounds.

Another round of beers. A visit to the Thai food truck for Pad Thai and spring rolls. Their timing was good, as all the trucks were desperately phoning for more supplies.

The beer tent was more fortunate. The reefer truck still had ample inventory. The beer distributor had given up counting the cases sold. He was having trouble finding enough room in the trunk of his car to stash the cash.

The girls were getting very big tips.

"Anyway," said Perkins, "at least we're out enjoying the night and not trying to haul trucks away from city hall as the network cameras roll. Thank God this ended the way it has."

Crawford nodded agreement. "This concert idea of Kim's was really brilliant."

Kim opened her mouth to speak. Samantha glared at her and shook her head. Kim paused, then shrugged in frustration. Samira observed the two curiously.

"It gave the truckers a fun way out," the city manager continued. "It defused the whole situation." He leaned over and kissed Kim. "Everybody is happy with the ending. The Mayor is thrilled."

The Mayor smiled and nodded agreement as she popped a fresh beer.

Duke Simmons came back to center stage. His ego blossomed every time he was at the mic. "Now, ladies and gentlemen, truckers all, Country 103FM is proud to present this exclusive concert just for you—welcome Texas Jack and The Armadillos!!"

Roy, Kim and Mayor Sonja Rodriguez all twitched at the radio station claiming credit for the concert. This was a city-sponsored event. They looked at each other. There was a collective shrug of the shoulders. At this point, who cared?

A shaggy-haired man in his 30s advanced to the front of the stage. He wore dirty Levis, a red checked shirt, alligator boots and a battered cowboy hat. His guitar was worth a hundred times more than his wardrobe.

The Armadillos struck up the first chords, and Texas Jack's distinctive, deep baritone rang out. The crowd quieted immediately, except in the beer tent. That was excusable.

The crowd surged toward the stage. The parked trucks had created a perimeter surrounding the stage, the crowd area, the beer tent and the food trucks. The crowd was in a happy mood and was soon shuffling and swaying to the music. A few intrepid truckers spotted the beautiful women at the back of the crowd. It didn't take them long to dash over and ask Perkins and Crawford if they could ask the ladies if they would like to dance.

They had both barely nodded when the young men asked the five women. The mayor, her chief of staff, Samira, Kim and Samantha grinned and sashayed into the crowd. A crude dance floor had formed, and the women and the truckers were soon surrounded by a big crowd clapping and cheering them on. Other drivers were lined up for their turn. The women's dance cards would be full until next April. Many couples soon joined them in the circle. Many different dance steps were displayed on the grass; none of them would get the person invited onto "Dancing with the Stars."

Texas Jack kept belting out his hits and the crowd kept applauding the band and hollering for more. The manager for Texas Jack, who had opposed this free concert—well, he opposed anything free involving his prized performer—looked at the crowd and the iPhones recording the event and figured he could spin this on TV entertainment programs for the next six months as the biggest free concert graciously put on by a country artist in many years.

He just had to figure out what the hell the 'good cause' was.

The spike in record sales and goodwill would be worth millions. He smiled avariciously and told one of his flunkies to get him another cold beer. Very cold.

Perkins and Crawford watched their ladies dance with a dozen different men. The men lucky enough to get a dance were very polite. The two armed deputies that Perkins had assigned to watch over the ladies would have had nothing to do with that, of course.

The Sheriff is nobody's fool.

Texas Jack and the Armadillos finally wrapped up their concert. The crowd demanded three encores. The ladies returned to Crawford, Perkins and the remaining city hall staff. They were all breathless, flushed and grinning. "Haven't had so much fun in years!" exclaimed Her Honor as she bent over to catch her breath.

Duke went on stage to announce that the city was letting all trucks remain at the fairground for free that night. Washrooms would remain open. The drivers cheered and headed back to the beer tent and the party was on.

The Sheriff and Roy Crawford nodded at each other. They had made that decision earlier, because nobody wanted any problems on the highways.

Duke kept Country 103 playing on the PA system. The dance floor was still getting a lot of use. So were the washrooms.

Perkins had his arm around Samantha. Rosie was lying down, exhausted by the hundreds of new friends she'd made.

"I think we escaped a lot of trouble today," Perkins said quietly. There were nods of agreement.

The torches that had been lit earlier were dying out.

There were no J-Men at the party. Once the expense payments were completed, Jed and Jethro had stolen a couple of cold beers and disappeared into the night.

This was no celebration of the plan to close the downtown and hold city hall to ransom, thought Jim Crandall bitterly as he sat in his darkened pick-up at the back of the fairgrounds. He drank another beer. The entire event was an abject failure.

Jedediah would never be invited back on COYOTE News, since he had predicted the entire city would be shut down by concerned truckers from all over the USA. Jock and Jacob would just disappear into their own holes; they wouldn't be seen again. Jeb understood that this was the end of this odd little group. The J-Men. He shrugged. It had all gotten weird in the last little while. He would miss The Ugly Porker though.

Jim Crandall finally left the concert and drove around for a while. He was in shock. He still didn't understand what had happened to his truck-in and the lock-down of the city. It was such a great plan. And it would have gotten him back in Beulah's good books. He thought about that. Maybe it was time to give her some more attention and support. He didn't really have a home without her.

As that sunk in, he swallowed the last of his beer. It was warm. Ugh. He tossed the can into the bushes. He drove the back roads until he got to Beulah's farm. He stopped near the front porch to park in his usual spot. Then he glimpsed a pile of things on the porch. He got out to investigate. Well shit. It looked like his clothes and personal stuff had been dumped on the top step.

He looked up at the house. No lights. He walked up and tried his key. No luck. He knew what that meant. It pretty much summed up his day.

He stood there for a moment. Well, it had been fun with Beulah. Mainly. Mostly. Some of the time.

He kicked the edge of the porch and exhaled loudly. He turned again to look at the locked front door.

He gathered the pile of dirty clothes and tossed them in the bed of his pick-up. Beulah still hadn't washed his things, he thought. It didn't take long to load his stuff.

He gave a little salute to the house. Maybe Beulah saw it; probably not. Whatever.

He got back in his truck and popped another brewski from the cooler on the passenger side floor. There were only two left from the dozen he'd put on ice. He shook his head. He put the truck in gear and pulled out, narrowly missing a gatepost. It had turned into a really, really shitty day. At least nothing else could go wrong.

He turned right and drove onto County Road 34. He accelerated.

Behind him, flashing red and blue lights suddenly lit up his rear-view mirror.

THE END

ABOUT THE AUTHOR

GORD HUME IS the creator of the popular "Samantha and the Sheriff" adventures. This is the fifth book in the series, which has generated an enthusiastic readership in North America and beyond.

Gord is also the author of seven non-fiction books on building better cities and improving communities. The books have been highly popular amongst municipal leaders in more than 22 countries around the world. Gord has been a sought-after keynote speaker at major conferences in the United States, Canada, Europe, Asia and New Zealand. He was elected to London City Council four times.

He has enjoyed an award-winning career in broadcasting; founded a newspaper; and been a leader in many civic, charitable and community foundations and organizations.

Gord loves exploring the culture, cuisine and history of people and nations around the world. He has visited nearly forty countries during his life-long passion for new adventures and experiences.

Gord now shares his time between London, Ontario and St. Pete Beach, Florida, where he continues a busy schedule of writing and doing media commentary on current affairs.

www.gordhume.com

Enjoy all the "Samantha and the Sheriff" adventures:

Sapphire Blue

Alligator Alley

Singapore Bling

Martinis & Manicures

Torches & Trouble

Cossacks & Caviar

www.ingramcontent.com/pod-product-compliance
Lightning Source LLC
Chambersburg PA
CBHW070625170726
48291CB00003B/883